Praise for *Open Me*

"Locascio is a lovely, imagistic writer, and she's especially exquisite on the female orgasm, evoking a purple smoke that becomes a motif . . . *Open Me* spends nearly as much descriptive time on mucus, crotch odors, and the grime that accumulates in the creases of an unshowered body as it does on the violent beauty of sex—a choice perhaps even more daring that the novel's nuanced exploration of a teenage girl's sexual imagination." —*New York Times Book Review*

"Locascio manages in this novel to critique white supremacy and false tolerance while also celebrating a young woman's sexuality and her right to it—a difficult, and often joyous feat that marks her as a remarkable author to keep your eyes on." —*NPR*

"If you're looking for a sexy and smart summer read, look no further. In this erotic coming-of-age story, Lisa Locascio explores the female body, politics, and desire." —*The Millions*

"This steamy and intellectual debut novel is an ode to the female body." —*Refinery 29*, "The Sexiest Books You'll Ever Have the Pleasure of Reading"

"Summer is for sexiness, so yield to this coming-of-age novel about a teen whose erotic awakening in Copenhagen circles around two men: an older local and a refugee from the Balkan War." —*Elle*

"Locascio practically invents a new language, conjuring pure feelings and colors, for their sex . . . This provocative, intimate, and metamorphosing character study vividly captures a young woman's life-earned education." —*Booklist*

"Imbued with sex and politics, Locascio's debut novel casts the traditional bildungsroman into a darker, more feminine light . . . Locascio centers the female body exquisitely. A debut exploring how we open up to others—and, more importantly, ourselves." —*Kirkus Reviews*

"*Open Me* will remind you, viscerally, of the heady joys (and terrors) of being 18 and discovering the boundlessness of your pleasure." —*Refinery 29*, "The Best New Books for August"

"A surprising, bodily coming-of-age story at the intersection of one young American woman's sexual awakening and the tense political environment in which she finds herself." —*Literary Hub*

"Locascio's story of a young American abroad is unflinching in its portrayal of sex, desire, racism, and the excitement and confusion of youth. Infused with erotics and politics, this is a novel that will haunt you." —Viet Thanh Nguyen, author of *The Sympathizer*

"Through the care of her tremendous observations and the beauty of her prose, Lisa Locascio writes a kind of love letter to the female body and all its power and visceral complexity. This is a story of many important layers, but one of the many reasons it remains distinct in my mind is because of its honesty about our complicated, yearning physical selves. A remarkable, fearless debut."
—Aimee Bender, author of *The Color Master*

"Captivating and darkly clever, Locasio's debut melds self-discovery and self-abnegation with raw, muscular grace. By turns beguiling, guileless, and penetratingly felt, this book seethes with eroticism, both physical and emotional—you won't dare to pry yourself away from it."
—Alexandra Kleeman, author of *You Too Can Have a Body Like Mine*

"An evocative and compelling remapping of Bluebeard's Castle for our times. In *Open Me*, Locascio offers a daring, unapologetic, and vital exploration of female desire."
—Emily Fridlund, author of *History of Wolves*

"Not since Henry James' Daisy Miller have I been so beguiled by an American abroad. Lisa Locascio's Roxana Olsen may only be eighteen but she is already a desperate sexual adventurer. Part captivity narrative, part political awakening, *Open Me* will open you, reminding us that nothing really happens until it happens in the body."
—Darcey Steinke, author of *Suicide Blonde*

"A lush, evocative novel you won't be able to put down. *Open Me* is a masterful debut." —T.C. Boyle, author of *The Harder They Come*

open me

A Novel

LISA LOCASCIO

Grove Press
New York

Published simultaneously in Canada
Printed in the United States of America

First Grove Atlantic hardcover edition: August 2018
First Grove Atlantic paperback edition: June 2019

Library of Congress Cataloging-in-Publication data is available for this title.

ISBN 978-0-8021-2964-2
eISBN 978-0-8021-6570-1

Grove Press
an imprint of Grove Atlantic
154 West 14th Street
New York, NY 10011

Distributed by Publishers Group West

groveatlantic.com

19 20 21 22   10 9 8 7 6 5 4 3 2 1

TO THEIS

The soul! Its glyph is *sak nik*, "white flower."

—Mayan glyph teacher to Mayan children, *Breaking the Maya Code*

COPENHAGEN

1

LUFTHAVN. I rode an escalator in a tall fair cloud that became the line for passport check. Mine was brand-new, stiff in its plastic cover. Inside a glass box sat a carelessly beautiful woman with light glossy hair. She flipped through the passport's empty pages, stamping the very last, and turned her severe blue gaze on me.

"Welcome to Denmark," she said. Like a spell.

Beside the baggage carousel stood a couple with matching blond haircuts, the man's arms folded across the woman's shoulders. She leaned back into him, rocking on her heels, and he bent and kissed her forehead through its feathery fringe. Their hands twisted together over her flat chest as she whispered into his parted lips. I swung my bag from the conveyer belt against their legs and passed through two sets of doors into a white glare.

I thought I knew exactly the kind of person who would be waiting for me. A real ponytail-and-sweatshirt type, a casual but enthusiastic athlete whose mouth always hung slightly open in a laziness people mistook for a smile. Kari, her name would be. Or Patty. Nicole.

A man stepped into my path and did a funny thing to my name.

"Roxana Olsen?" *Rhox-ahna Oh-la-sen.* "I am from International Abroad Experiences."

I took in his knit hat, gray button-down, black pants. His eyes the blue of a frozen morning under brows like smudges of ash. He was so pale it was hard to see him in the bright light. He took my hand as if to shake it but didn't close the grip. My fingers swam in his, little fish. "Sown Holmgaard."

"Sown?"

"Well, you might pronounce it, er"—he switched to an American accent, folksy and earnest as a TV dad—"Søren."

"Oh. Like, S-O-R-E-N?"

"S-*EU*-R-E-N, yes," he said. "The *o* has a slash through it."

"Søren," I tried.

"Yes." He looked down. I was still holding his hand. I let go.

Søren led me from the baggage claim into another, higher room, where we stood silently until a train glided in. When it stopped, he lifted my bag. I followed him aboard to a bench upholstered in riotous gold and teal. At the other end of the car a woman scream-laughed, "Stop-uh! Stop-uh!"

I caught my reflection in the window. Shiny face, oily hair with ideas of its own, my whole head overcompensating for nine hours of dry canned air. My thighs spread across the seat like squashed dough.

The train came up from underground into a rush of green bushes. We passed windows of gleaming plaited pastry, sloping tiled roofs, a bright yellow sign with a black Scottie dog carrying a basket in its mouth. Fingers of gray light fell across the sky. The train turned and the rim of blue water on the horizon disappeared. Quadrangles of grass bordered the tracks. The buildings grew denser, penetrated by a freeway populated with white trucks and small black cars.

"You are tired." Søren smiled, and I noticed his crooked front teeth. He took off his hat, revealing a shaved head, receding hairline visible in his stubble. "You are at university?"

"No. But I will be. In the fall."

He narrowed his eyes for a moment and then relaxed them. "You mean autumn," he said, like there was a difference.

I looked out the window. A damp, overcast day, not much like June. People appeared, riding bicycles. In my peripheral vision, Søren rubbed the top of his head. "I am also a student. A graduate student in literature."

"Cool," I said. "I like to read."

"It is hardly just reading at this stage." He laughed, stretching his arms above his head and resettling them at his sides. "I am writing my thesis."

I squinted at him. "Don't you read books to do that?"

"Of course I do. Again and again." He bit his wet bottom lip. "We are the next stop."

The train went back underground, lights blinking on as we entered a tunnel. Slowed.

"That's cool, that you study literature," I said.

He looked at me, hopeful, silver eyed.

I followed Søren down the platform and up a staircase to a wide intersection where vehicles flew past newsstands, grand buildings, sidewalk cafés with awnings over wicker chairs. The horizon was dotted with obelisks and spires, the air moistened and scented with grilled meat and spilled coffee. The low fluttering monotone of a strange language. Everyone said jet lag made you tired, but I felt I had passed through exhaustion into a hallucinatory state.

A flashing herd of woman cyclists raced by two and three abreast, bright scarves at their necks. Søren pulled the back of my shirt, forcing me up onto the curb.

He took my shoulders and turned me to face him, eyes wide. "Never stand in the path for the bicycles."

"Sorry. I've never seen one before."

He looked at me like I had pissed on his shoe.

At the curb a giant bright red insect folded its wings out and back over its mirrored antennae. I blinked and we boarded a bus, Søren feeding coins into a small machine. As we pushed down the aisle, I withdrew my overstuffed wallet, dangling receipts and key chains. Would he accept dollars? I tapped his shoulder.

He shook his head. "No, Roxana, you are paid for. In your tuition." He turned my duffel bag on end and leaned it against his right side. He was wearing his hat again. I hadn't even seen him put it back on.

All the passengers looked straight ahead, as if there were a rule against turning. At the fourth stop, a woman with a double stroller bearing twins boarded. Dark glimmered at the edges of my vision. I was so tired. I closed my eyes. There was a strange sound. The woman wheeling her stroller back and forth. What was she doing? I opened my eyes.

She spoke incomprehensibly at me from under her frizzy hair. Søren was busy on his phone. The woman repeated herself. A man on my right gestured with his chin. A pair of blonde teenage girls seated across the aisle directed me with pink fingernails. What did they want me to do? Why was everyone so angry?

"I'm sorry?" I said softly, not expecting to be understood.

"Oh, English?" The woman with the stroller said. "Move. You are in the place for prams."

"But there's nowhere . . ." I made a vague movement of my arm.

Søren looked up from his phone, put his hand on my shoulder, and pulled me back, wedging my ass into his crotch to free up six inches of floor as he spoke to the woman in their language. She slid her behemoth carriage into the new space and set about tucking blankets around her twins.

Søren's heart beat against my spine. I stared at the babies' blue shoes, counting one hundred throbs of his pulse as the warmth of his body seeped into my back. What did he smell like? What did I smell like? My toes bumped hard against the stroller and the babies turned their liquid black eyes on me. We stayed that way for two more stops, my smile blinking on and off, the bus throwing me against Søren again and again.

Finally he pulled at my sleeve and we disembarked. The wavelike facade of a vast building curled toward a spill of cobblestones, a thick green slope of park, a low stone wall. We approached its dark front door. Søren reached for me and I looked down, afraid that I would blush, but his hand continued past my body and pressed a beige button labeled ADMUSSEN. A buzz shook the door frame. Søren hoisted my duffel over his shoulder and in we went.

I followed him into a vast gray antechamber, vacant save for a row of locked mailboxes built into the far wall and a short staircase leading to another white door. Blue light fell from a portal in the distant ceiling. The door opened to reveal a woman's fox-like face surrounded by a ruff of wiry hair atop her child's body. She chirped a sound between "hey" and "hi." Søren returned a chirp of his own, and with white claws she beckoned us into a hallway narrowed with stuff. A wooden rack held a confusion of shoes. I tripped on a bunched runner, its pattern long since stamped out. Shadows drifted in the murk at the end of the hall.

She sought my gaze and held it. "I am Berta Admussen, American Roxana." She could have been forty or seventy, this foxwoman, in her costume of cream quilted pullover and pencil skirt. White lashes haloed uncannily light blue eyes. She had a triangular nose and a wet pink mouth.

I extended my hand and she gave me a card: her name and a string of numbers engraved on heavy stock. *Birthe*, the name was spelled.

She and Søren issued undulant tones at each other and then she turned to me, prying a silver key from a large ring. The old-fashioned kind, with a figure-eight cutout at the top and a big tooth at the bottom.

"The door is behind you."

I felt Søren's hand, hot and smooth on my dampening palm. The foxwoman stood very still, watching us. Was he really holding my hand? No, he was feeling for the key. He wanted to get me into the room so he could go home. I gave it to him. A long low moan that neither Søren nor the foxwoman seemed to hear echoed down the hall.

The room had the same high ceiling as the hallway, a window, a pale wood desk and chair, a small television mounted in a high corner, an armoire on carved legs, and two girlishly geriatric twin beds. Chintz curtains, cabbage rose bedspreads and wallpaper, a tall white pitcher on a stand. For light, I had a too-bright overhead fixture or a tiny wire lamp on a bedside table too small to accommodate a book.

"Two beds," I said.

"Often couples stay," the foxwoman said, as if this was an explanation. "If you will have overnight guests I prefer to be informed." She produced her sharp little incisors in a smile. "The television does not work. Later, I will show the amenities. I do not want to bore Søren."

Søren stepped away from me, smiling to cover the movement. "I will go now."

"Wait!" I squeaked too loudly. Wasn't this supposed to be a study abroad program? "Where does everyone else live?"

"The others are in residence in Amager, near the university," he said, as if I would know what this meant. *Umma-urr.* Was that a place? "You are a late addition." He and the foxwoman laughed and the geometry of the room tilted, as if someone had picked up the diorama in which we stood. I was worried I would throw up or fall down or both. Whatever force had paused the scary fatigue that had built every moment of my sleepless flight completely deserted me now. I closed my dry eyes, took two breaths in, let them out. When I opened them again, he was gone.

The foxwoman lingered for a moment, no longer smiling, and then she, too, disappeared.

I dragged my duffel into the bedroom, ready to spend an hour or two ordering my things. But within fifteen minutes my assembled belongings were put away in drawers or hung in the mushroomy closet. I opened the window. My view was an interior courtyard hemmed by redbrick walls. The sky was white. The scent of trees and wet pavement cooled my face.

I went out into the dark hall with my toiletry bag, passing closed door after closed door. With its fancy sconces, crown molding, and tall, shuttered windows, the apartment bore traces of having once been much nicer than it was now. The grand parlor had become a laundry bullpen, sheets and towels stacked on dusty end tables. I ran the back of my hand against a tower of terry cloth so rough it reopened a torn cuticle. Sucking blood from my finger, I walked into the next dim room.

In the gloom a massive dog considered me with light blue eyes. A husky or maybe a malamute, with a wide friendly face and gray-and-white fur, twice as big as any I had ever seen. When he was seated on his hindquarters, the dog's nose came to the bottom of my rib cage. He considered me for a moment and threw up his head, howling. I took a step back.

The dog calmly walked around me and blocked the door with his body, cocking his head to one side. He howled again, eyes glistening.

The foxwoman materialized at the far end of the hall in a strange little hat that hid her pointy ears, holding something coiled. A bridle, a whip? When she reached me, I saw that it was a leash.

"Hello." She gave me her fangs, nodding briskly. "You have met Wvhobah."

"Is that a Danish name?"

"English. I am surprised you do not know. For the poet. Wvhobah Frost."

"Oh." I sent my mind back to AP English class. "Robert."

Dazzled by so many recitations of his name, the dog turned in a small circle and gave another howl, gazing at his mistress.

The foxwoman grimaced. "Perhaps you seek the toilet?" She flipped a switch, revealing a sparsely decorated kitchen, and gestured to an orange bowl of green apples on a round table. "Please eat one if you're ever hungry. But please do not eat all of them." She fanged me again. A joke.

We stood in silence until I noticed a white phone on the wall and remembered Mama and Dad.

"May I make a call?" I asked the foxwoman.

She nodded. "Your program has told me that you would wish this. Instructions for how to reach the US"—*Ooh Us*—"are beside the receiver."

I waited for the foxwoman to leave the room. When she instead leaned against the wall, looking at me levelly, I picked up the phone and dialed my house. It rang three times, a different sound—a mechanical tone, not the synthesized burr I was used to—before the answering machine picked up, a robotic woman's voice reciting the number and ordering the caller to leave a message after the tone. My parents had never bothered to record a personalized greeting.

"Hey Mama. Hey Dad," I said without thinking, and then remembered. "Or whichever one of you gets this, I guess. I'm here." I caught myself before I said where. "Flight was fine. Everything's okay. Miss you." I waited, thinking one of them might pick up. That was the usual pattern—Mama or Dad rushing into the kitchen to grab the phone before the caller finished talking. The machine was full of messages interrupted by their distracted, out-of-breath hellos, records of the way everything in life seemed to surprise them.

No one hurried to answer me. I hung up. When I looked at her the foxwoman was beaming, as if I had pleased her. I shivered. Why was everyone in this country so strange?

We continued down the hall and stopped in front of the last of seven identical white doors. "The toilet for guests," she said gravely. I followed her inside. It was two rooms, first a small antechamber containing just the toilet sandwiched between, on the right, the door to the hall, and on the left, a door into a second, more spacious room, where a wide fogged-glass window separated a shower stall from a sink beside a tall row of empty shelves. The foxwoman showed me how to lock the shower room from the inside with a small hook and eye at the top of the door frame. This way, the toilet and shower could be used simultaneously by total strangers—the bather's privacy guarded while the toilet remained accessible.

"You know, with all the guests, it must be this way," she said. I nodded. Was there even one other guest?

Robert moaned again. "He is complaining," the foxwoman said. "I must take him." She and her dog had the same white-blue eyes, identically strange in the shadowy hall.

At the far end of the hall she opened a door and stepped into a rectangle of light.

"See you," I whispered.

I went into the bathroom, locked the exterior door, peed, and walked into the inner chamber without bothering to unlock the outer door and latch the inner. I didn't like the idea of some stranger using the toilet just feet from me while I was in the shower room. I wanted the whole space to myself. I was worn out on public spaces after a day spent in the perpetual exposure of traveling. Besides, I hadn't seen or heard anyone in the apartment other than the foxwoman and her beast. Solitude seemed an available luxury.

In the mirror my hair was full of static. Pimples had erupted under my chin. My breasts, shapeless in my soft old bra, sat under my shirt like a second, higher stomach. "Ugh," I said, to hear a sound.

As if in response, the outer door rattled, its hook clanging loudly in its socket. I froze and stared at the floor, an unremarkable stretch of white tile, and silently counted to sixty, trying to weight each number with a full second. Eventually the stranger gave up and creaked back down the hallway. With leaping steps I turned off the bathroom lights and ran back to my room, leaning back against the door after I closed it behind me.

The walls swam. I wanted the sky to change from pale to dark, for permission to put on my nightie and go to sleep. But outside it was bright as noon.

I went to one of the beds and tried to pull down the covers. It was so tightly made that cramming between the sheets was like putting on pantyhose. On the tiny bedside table a disk wrapped in gold foil lay on a tiny lace doily. Printed in black ink on the foil, surrounded by a braided ring, was the word LAKRIDS. Beneath, a tiny translation: (CANDY).

I unwrapped it, revealing a shiny thin black coil, and bit. Salty licorice. Sour bark coated the inside of my mouth. I wanted to rinse with water, to brush my teeth again, but I wouldn't go back out. What or who else might be waiting in the hall? I tried to picture who else might stay in such a place, but all I could imagine was a giant skulking raccoon, a monster-size version of the one that had taken over our garbage cans in the alley behind my house the year before to have babies.

Yesterday I had seen another raccoon, on the tarmac at O'Hare as I waited for takeoff. Or was it today, the same day? I stared out at the planes arrayed at the gates, jet bridges like parasite tentacles penetrating their cylindrical bodies, my seatmate, a displeased-seeming man in a khaki sport coat, sighing heavily beside me. The sky did something obscene and orange as a prelude to sunset. Then there was a tiny movement in the corner of my eye, a person or vehicle I thought, but when I turned it was a fat little striped animal with a fluffy tail hustling near the open bay where they loaded the in-flight meals. It must have been terrified, surrounded by the oily smell of heavy fuel in that place of great sound and heat.

Then we pushed back, taxied, lifted into the sky. Flew through an opaque, elongated night.

I chewed, swallowed, wiped my tongue around the inside of my mouth, and closed my eyes. I didn't know anything about Denmark yet. That the raccoon, which they call a washing-bear, does not even exist there.

When I was little, Mama did all the laundry. Our clothes churned together in the big red washer and dryer in the mudroom, a small, narrow space directly below my bedroom with a floor of bright red tile that held the machines, a long folding table, bins and baskets for sorting clothes, and a matching red metal drying rack stowed behind the door. In the corner stood a tall white industrial plastic shelving unit on which Mama arrayed her jewel-toned detergents—grand bottles of the liquid kind, clear jars of capsules like candy from the future—and potions for soiled clothes: creamy purple and blue softeners, mild soaps for delicate fabrics, pails of powder. The purple plastic radio on the top shelf was always tuned to the news. In the long rectangular window above the machines, a view of the alley and our garage hung like a photograph.

She did the wash on Sunday mornings, starting early, when I was still in bed. I woke to the machine's soothing thrum, the water rushing through the pipes in the walls and ceiling. After breakfast, I liked to go into the mudroom and watch through the washer's large porthole as our clothes were beaten into waves of soapy water. I would press my palm against the shuddering pane to feel the warmth through the thick concave glass.

After the last load was done, Mama wiped down the machine with a silk handkerchief dabbed with lavender oil. She sprayed the inside of the dryer with a solution of vinegar and water, left it open for an hour to air out, and then ran it again with only five dryer sheets inside. In the summer, she set up the drying rack outside, and by afternoon the delicates—Mama's and my own nicer dresses, Dad's work shirts and ties, and everyone's underwear—came back inside scented with sun and wind. In the winter, she unfolded the rack in the mudroom itself. Even when it was cold outside and the space doubled as a container for the shucking of coats and boots, it was spotless. On Sunday mornings, it filled with sunlight. The clothes that dried inside absorbed scents of lavender and vinegar and soap.

I always thought Mama loved doing laundry. Why wouldn't she, with her special ability to resurrect clothes? But one afternoon around my thirteenth birthday, she carried a red plastic basket of laundered, neatly folded clothes into my bedroom and put it down on my bed.

"Clean!" she called.

"Thanks, Mama," I said without looking up from my book. The main character had just found her toy poodle in a puddle of blood. I knew she would soon have to either die or kill the murderer.

"Roxana, put the book down."

I closed it around my index finger. She made me wait, removing her pink bandanna, carefully refolding it on my bed, and retying it over her hair. Mama had shown me how to do this many times, but bandannas always slipped off my head.

"I need you to do your own laundry from now on, all right? You know how. You've seen me do it a million times. All right?" She blinked, which meant that the only wise answer was yes.

Mama had always been insistent on self-sufficiency. She had issued warnings, in various bad moods over the years, of an impending reckoning that would result in me doing my own laundry, even learning to iron and sew. Such events could be avoided, I had believed, if I was a good enough girl. If I kept from making her mad, which I tried so hard to do.

"Yes."

"Remember. I won't tell you again, and I won't do it for you if you forget."

I gave her a weak smile, trying not to cry. Mama wiped her hands against each other a few times and left. I threw my book across the room, hoping for a resounding boom, but my pitch fell short and it fluttered to the carpet.

I had no idea how to do laundry. I had figured it was something I would learn when I went to college. I could identify the basic ingredients: clothes, detergent, dryer sheets. But what about the color-safe bleach, the fabric softener? The machine seemed to want them, with its many pockets and labeled ports, but I didn't know where anything went. And yet somehow Mama expected me to know. Had implied with that methodical retying of her bandanna that my not knowing would anger, humiliate, and sadden her, all at once.

The answers to these questions were delivered to me over the course of six weeks during which I destroyed all my favorite clothes. The machine's brutal convulsions ripped out every seam of the velvet jacket I privately thought made me look like the picture of Eleanor of Aquitaine in my social studies textbook. My blue corduroys were reduced to doll size. My favorite soft gray T-shirt emerged from the dryer with bleach stains emanating from the neckline. Only a handful of already ill-fitting clothes remained unscathed, like some kind of cruel joke. When I could, I wore the ruined clothes around the house, hoping Mama would notice and help me. But she didn't. And I was too afraid to ask.

That was the year when girls at school started to care about clothes. Before, they had mostly targeted my personality, my small voice, the clumsiness that made me last pick for every team. Now what I wore mattered too. Over spring break, I begged Mama for a pair of the heavy-soled leather sandals that the dominant clique had decided were their trademark. When she finally gave in I wore them proudly the first day back from vacation, convinced the popular girls would reconsider their cruelty and desist. Instead, none of them ever wore their leather sandals again after that day. It took me a solid month to understand that they weren't making fun of me, exactly; they were mocking each other for owning the same shoes as I did.

Why didn't they like me? I didn't have a ready answer. For as long as I could remember I had had one friend, my best friend, Sylvie, the sole exception to the distaste for me that united the others. But they liked Sylvie—who held them at a cool distance, neither accepting nor rejecting their friendship—quite a lot. They seemed to adore her as much as they delighted in ostracizing me.

Of course, she was beautiful and smart, but I considered myself, not as wholly lacking these qualities, only possessing them in subtler—privately, in moments of high feeling, more refined—shades.

One Tuesday after a long weekend in April about a month after the sandal incident, they all appeared at school wearing dark-wash boot-cut jeans and fatigue-green T-shirts with the word SUPPLY stamped across the front in militant white capitals. Had they all gone shopping together? The iconic outfit had even materialized in Sylvie's closet. When I asked her how she found out about the store in the first place, she gave me a pitying look. "I read about it in the paper, Roxana," she said, as if the *Tribune* was a place a sixth grader might reasonably seek fashion advice. Another thing I didn't know.

Even after the sandals I was hopeful that if I could look like the other girls they might see that I was like them. So often I heard them discussing something I liked too—a band, a television show, a book—and the illogic of my exclusion settled on me like a thundering headache. They wouldn't talk to me for long enough to find out. I had to show them. If they could only see that I was part of their world, maybe I could enjoy some of its privileges: pool parties at the country club where all their parents belonged, ice-cream dates with the cute sandy-haired boys who wore basketball jerseys under open flannel button-downs, tiny butterfly hair clips they were always attaching to each other's lithe braids.

I was determined to get something from Supply but Mama wouldn't take me. We only went shopping twice a year and only ever at discount department stores staffed by exhausted women in gray vests and at meticulously clean secondhand shops run by recovering addicts.

"It's not so much that I'm chasing deals, although of course that's part of it," Mama told me once as we drove to the rich suburb that held one of these thrift stores. "It's more than that. It's a way of telling them they can't just do whatever they like with my money and my time. I'm in control."

Them: stores, companies, anyone who might wish to influence Mama to act against her best interest. She was proud of her resistance, took on a philosophical tone when discussing it, which she did every time we went shopping. Her proud statement of individuality always struck me as an elaborate way to say that no, we couldn't go to the mall.

I finally convinced Sylvie to take me to Supply the weekend before seventh grade ended.

"I don't understand," Sylvie kept saying as her mom drove us through Creek Grove to the town center where the store had just opened between a hair salon and EarthLodge, a place I loved that sold high-powered magnets, astronaut ice cream, and pens that wrote underwater. "It's just a store."

I couldn't bear for Sylvie to know how badly I wanted the other girls to like me. She acted like she didn't care what they thought of her. Maybe she didn't. But she had never experienced anything other than their admiration.

"I'm curious!" I said, stretching my face into what I hoped looked like relaxed interest. "To see it!"

Sylvie gave me a dubious look. "'Kay."

I hummed and whistled the whole way to the store, thirty-six dollars in my wallet, the entirety of my savings. Despite the risk of Sylvie finding out the broader mission behind our trip, I was excited. The Supply outfit was cool, and I was convinced I'd find something magical there. A navy jacket with epaulets like I'd always wanted or white shorts that would fit perfectly. Maybe both. If all the other girls could find something that looked so good on them, I could too.

But when we got there, I saw it was just another store, with recessed fluorescent lights and an army of skinny blonde salesgirls who wanted to know, again and again, if we needed help with anything. Everything was too small and too expensive. Thirty-six dollars could buy nothing worthwhile, only a cheap plastic headband, a flimsy gray scarf, and three pink bobby pins clipped to a scrap of plastic labeled SUPPLY, which was what I bought. I was so disappointed. But I refused to give up on the idea that the store was magic—the idea that I could make the others see me. I wanted something to show for my efforts. Even the Supply shopping bag, a drawstring jute sack, was coveted at school. The popular girls carried their books in it. Sylvie's mom's face fell when she saw it in my hand.

"Oh sweetie, I would have loved to buy you something. You should have told me," she said, as if Mama would ever have allowed it.

It was no secret that Sylvie's family was richer than mine. Her mother was corporate counsel for the biggest pharmaceutical companies in Chicago, and her father owned factories in Morocco; Mama was a nurse, Dad a medical equipment salesman. We were just different, and the difference didn't bother me. I loved going to Sylvie's big house and fancy birthday parties. But Mama was suspicious of their easy generosity and always told me not to let Sylvie's family spend too much on me—"too much" meaning basically anything at all. I could read these feelings on her face every time Sylvie's parents invited me to go on vacations I wasn't allowed to join, every time Sylvie gave me a brand-new pair of boots or dressy winter coat or some other extravagant gift.

Behind her mother in the mirror Sylvie held a silky moss-green blouse to her shoulders. How pretty the color was against her hair and skin. It was a button-down, the kind I couldn't wear because my breasts made the buttons gape. Fury at Sylvie flooded me. Her good taste, her small chest, her generous mom, and most of all her sense of restraint, picking out just one top when she knew full well her mom would buy her an entire closetful. "Nice," I smiled.

She grinned. "Show me what you got!"

Leaving the bobby pins in the bag, I pulled out the headband and scarf and wrestled the tortoiseshell plastic onto my head. The ends pinched hard and the band hovered a half inch above my hair. I hadn't tried it on before buying it. "How does it look?"

Sylvie shrugged, obviously trying not to laugh, and turned back to her reflection. "It's different," she said.

By the end of the car ride home the band had already given me a headache. The following week, the bobby pins disappeared into my hair, never to be seen again. The scarf didn't last much longer. After trying and failing to incorporate it into my outfits in every way I could imagine—tying and twisting it around my neck in various knotty patterns; using it as a belt on a shapeless dress—the scarf evaporated in the washing machine, so cheaply made that under the pressure of soap and water it simply disappeared.

"Roxana?"

White stucco met white wall in a blank corner. Rain drummed on the roof. The windows leaked cool blue light. Where was I?

"Roxana?" More knocking. "Roxana?"

I freed myself from the sheets and stumbled to the door. "Coming!"

Søren stood in the dark hallway, holding a small white bag and a paper cup with a plastic lid, beads of water on his black woolly hat and blue-gray slicker. Rain had stained his white sneakers gray.

He pressed the cup into my hands. It was wonderfully warm. "You must eat. And stay awake for as long as possible. Otherwise the jet lag will be very bad."

We stood looking at each other. He took off his hat, rubbed his shaved head, and put it on again.

"Is it the next day?" I asked.

"No." He shifted his weight from foot to foot. "It is the same day."

"The day I got here? Saturday?"

He nodded once. "I did not want to let you rest too long. You will have a hard time on the trip to Roskilde tomorrow if you don't sleep tonight. Drink this. It will wake you up a bit. May I come in?" Without waiting for an answer he slipped into the room and sat down on the twin bed I hadn't slept in, handing me the paper bag. Inside was a thin sandwich of grainy brown bread filled with taupe paste and thin slices of cucumber.

"Are you a vegetarian?" Søren asked.

I took a bite. It tasted like nothing I'd ever had, creamy and meaty with an undertaste of wet dog, full in my mouth like peanut butter. "No, why?"

Søren smiled. "It is leverpostej. Pork liver pâté."

"Cool," I said.

"Very good!" He clapped. "A surprising American. Most spit it out."

"Thank you, Søren. You didn't have to do that."

"I wanted to wake you and give you dinner, to make sure you did not have your night in the middle of the day. It is important to establish an eating schedule when you travel. To adjust to the new time zone." He pulled his hat down over his ears, a sliver of his torso glimmering briefly underneath his jacket when he raised his arms, and he nodded at the empty paper bag. "This is real Danish food. Every child grows up on leverpostej." He grinned.

Like peanut butter, I thought again. "Do you eat it straight from the container with a spoon when you get home from school?"

He looked aghast at the idea. "That would be terribly unsanitary."

I glanced at my hands. They were blurry. "Maybe I should go back to sleep," I said.

"We will go for a walk," Søren pronounced. "A beer."

I was suddenly alert. "Give me a minute."

He opened the door and stepped back into the hall. I grabbed my jacket, calling over my shoulder. "Søren? What time is it?"

"A few minutes after eight o'clock in the evening."

"It's so bright outside!" I pushed back the curtains. Light coated the evenly spaced gray stones of the street, the smooth walls of the other buildings, the pearl sky.

Søren's dark clothes and pale skin came into focus in the hall, sharp as a photograph. He smiled. "In the north, summer days are very long."

2

THE WALLS WERE COVERED IN LAYERS OF OVERLAPPING STICKERS. Hundreds of candle nubs burned in nests of melted wax among the bottles behind the bar. Punk music played quietly from a paint-splattered radio. We were the only customers. The bartender, an aproned man with a great quiff of brown hair, spoke softly as he drew beer into two glasses from a green tap. After Søren paid, the man leaned carefully against a wood beam that split the wall behind the bar in two. He looked a workingman's saint, silhouetted in fire and booze.

Our table was covered in decals: DELICIOUS FLORIDA ORANGES. A DAY AT THE FAIR. WELTSCHMERZ. Søren's bare head gleamed in the low light. Sylvie always complained that bald men were unattractive. I smiled, liking the idea that she could be wrong.

He gave me a little nod. "You have brothers? Sisters?"

"No. It's just me and my mom and dad. Or, well, I guess it was just me and my mom and dad. Two weeks ago they told me they were getting divorced." I emitted a manic bark, a sort of laugh.

There was no concern in his face. "I see. And what will you study in university?"

"Maybe literature. But you can't really do anything with an English degree but be a high school teacher, so I actually was thinking about business. You know, to work at a company or something? But since my parents announced they were splitting up, I thought maybe I could be a therapist? To help people?"

Out loud, the ideas that had gained a veneer of resolve in my head sounded half-formed and desperate.

Søren peered at me over the top of his beer. "I think it is very different in the United States." What was? When he pulled the glass away from his face, his upper lip was covered in foam. "You were surprised by your parents' decision to divorce, yes? But it is probably for the best. They will be happier."

Why did everyone say that, as if their happiness was so easy to figure out? I had lived with them all my life and never been able to figure out what they wanted. And he didn't even know them. "Splitting up won't solve anything. It can only make things harder. It's ridiculous. And selfish."

He cocked his head. "Why is it selfish to end a relationship? Could it not be an act of generosity, to the other person and to yourself?"

But what about to me? I thought but did not say. Since the announcement of the divorce, everything had been all about them.

"Mine have split up a long time ago, almost twenty years ago, when I was ten." Søren went on. "But they are still friends, still see each other."

"The divorce didn't make them hate each other?"

"They never married." Søren rubbed his hands together. "You are eighteen, yes? Is this your first time at a bar?"

"Yes," I admitted. "But it's not my first time drinking." I gulped my beer with what I hoped was gusto, feeling happy activity in my neck and hands.

Sylvie and I had started drinking together in eighth grade, when she found a bottle of red wine marked VAMPIRE in the miniature bar her parents had set up to the right of their kitchen sink. We sneaked it up to her room, still fairyland-themed then, and drank it in ponderous gulps from the water glass on her nightstand, afraid we'd reveal ourselves if we went back down for another cup. After that we filched from Mr. and Mrs. Elmaleh as often as possible, sampling whatever looked or sounded most exotic: pomegranate liqueur, a fancy rose-infused gin, a faceted bottle of cognac in its own silk bag. I liked drinking. Not for the drunkenness but for the feeling of conspiratorial intent, the way it dropped a velvet curtain around Sylvie and me.

The picture window at the front of the bar showed a tiny street. People passed on bicycles and foot, talking on phones or to friends who walked beside them. Men and women carried briefcases or wore backpacks or bags slung from their shoulders. They sipped from bottles of water and sent text messages and laughed. The light had only grown brighter, bluer.

Søren went for another round and I was suddenly sure he wouldn't return, that he would abandon me at the bar. I walked in a small circle around our table, swaying on one heel, so that if he didn't come back it would appear that I too had been about to depart. How would I get home?

He returned with more beer. My relief dropped me back into my seat.

"Tuborg. The other famous beer of Denmark," he said. It was more sour than the first, thinner.

Strings rose from the radio behind the bar. Søren yelled in Danish and the bartender removed himself from his perch among the candles to increase the volume. A man's rich voice filled the room. Thundering bass and timpani. Søren closed his eyes and my cathedral feeling whirred, filling me.

It was my special secret, the way my body prickled and beamed. On the handful of Saturdays when Mama and Dad had taken me downtown to museums or to the orchestra. In my grandma's living room when she played Beethoven piano sonatas on her old record player just before it was time for us to go home. During the multipart harmonies the school choir sang in the winter and spring concerts. I wasn't a member but I loved to listen.

Sometimes it even happened in the privacy of my bedroom when a favorite song came on the radio. It took me over, took me out, made sense of all the upping and downing of my days, the way formless hours could fall wide as splayed knees. It was a gathering together, the generation of a geometric narrative, a vast structure that suggested I had a place within it, was bigger, more important, more fated than I feared. The first time I ever had the cathedral feeling had been when I was five on a trip to my dad's college, a beautiful campus in the middle of nowhere set with grottoes and grand auditoriums, dominated by a church that seemed older than old. It soared above me gray and majestic and I went transparent, became a part of everything.

When I told Sylvie about the cathedral feeling one night in her bedroom, a space that seemed hung with the feeling's fetters like ribbons, she laughed at me. "Oh, Roxana, you always want to be magical." And again I was a bag of feelings with no start and no end, a tunnel through which sensation moved.

The silence was huge when the song ended. "Do you know it?" Søren asked. "Sam Cooke."

"I don't," I said.

"When I was a little boy, my mother often sent me to a little store to buy cigarettes. The man at the store kept a small turntable behind the counter, on which he played many records, records my parents played all the time. But he also played one that I had never heard before. A beautiful voice singing about love and freedom."

Søren finished his second beer and balanced his chin on his fist, looking at something I couldn't see. I wanted to know him—the other Søren who appeared when his eyes went distant.

"He was a good man. A hard worker. He did not think anyone owed him anything. He was very grateful to Denmark for accepting him as a refugee and proud of the fact he had taken almost no assistance from the government. He didn't just come here to live off the state as many do. Anyway, that is how I became interested in African American culture, which led me to African American literature, and that is how I somehow became that dreadful thing, a graduate student studying literature. All because of a Palestinian playing Sam Cooke." He laughed.

"Søren." I heard my voice, high and uncertain on his name. "What do you mean about people wanting to live off the state?"

He looked into his beer. "It is a bad situation, with so many immigrants here now. There are many cultural conflicts, not easily solved."

"Oh," I said.

His eyes blazed at me. "You are a woman. Do you want a man to tell you to cover your lovely hair?"

My lovely hair. "No, of course not," I said, shifting in my seat.

He beamed at me and I felt like such a good girl.

"Is that what your thesis is about? African American literature?"

"Yes." He leaned back in his chair and made a pyramid of fingers under his chin, looking up as his spoke. "I am exploring the ways in which Viola Ash's fabulist fiction—I designate it fabulist rather than under the more common and general grouping of science fiction precisely because of works such as *Spirit Home,* which maintain Ash's interest in the layered possible realities but deviate from the conventions of sci-fi—the way this preoccupation with the unreal intersects with her portrayal of racial identity."

"Cool," I said. I realized I was drunk and decided to be secretly, covertly drunk. Drunk in mind only, not demeanor. "When does the sun go down?"

"Ten thirty, eleven o'clock? It is not even July." *Yoo-lee.* "The days will soon become even longer."

My abdomen was suddenly full to bursting. "I have to pee," I announced and immediately blushed. What a little kid thing to say. Søren pointed to a small hallway and I stumbled to the bathroom, a tiny shaft just large enough for a toilet and a sink. The mirror held a strange brightness that smoothed my features.

It had always been hard to tell if I was pretty. Mama and Dad and Sylvie said I was. But if you were pretty, weren't other people supposed to see it? Wouldn't the popular girls, and the boys over whom they held sway, have responded to my beauty? I always just looked ordinary to myself. Hair the color of brown rice that couldn't decide if it was curly or straight, light eyes, rosy cheeks that freckled in summer. Nothing about me drew the eye like Sylvie's sharp features and smooth black hair, and everything I wanted to wear looked funny on my body. Breasts that had been big from their first appearance on my chest, soft tummy, wide hips, a butt whose crack peeked above every pair of pants. Medium height, medium mouth, pale neck. I thought my hands were nice, when I hadn't chewed my nails too much.

That night my hair was French braided away from my face in two plaits that ended just below my shoulder blades. The clothes I had quickly thrown on—a blue jacket, tight black jeans, my softest green T-shirt—felt handmade for me. I peed for what felt like an hour, staring at my face from the toilet. My glowing skin. Why had I ever thought that I was ugly?

When I returned, a new beer waited sweating on my half of the table. My foot turned under me and I fell into my seat.

"I should take you home," Søren said. "You are very tired."

"I'm great." I took a long sip. "I think I got my second wind."

"Your what?"

"My second wind."

"I do not know this phrase."

"It's like—you have newfound energy after being worn out."

"Ah! I see," Søren said. "And this is related to the phrase 'three sheets to the wind'?"

I laughed. "Different winds." I was finally drunk enough to ask. "Do you have a girlfriend?"

He flinched. "I do not. My girlfriend—my ex-girlfriend— she has just left me. But it is all right." For a moment his face was anguished, and I felt I was seeing him again, the Søren inside. I wanted to comfort him. But then he ironed out his features, folding his hands neatly on the table. "She moved to Norway. She is a nurse, and she has a job there. She is a very good nurse. She will be happy."

This struck me as impossibly sad. "You couldn't move to Norway?"

"No. It is complicated." He gave me a tight smile. "I did not want to move to Norway."

We stared at the stickers on the table: WE ARE THE PEOPLE OUR PARENTS WARNED US ABOUT. THE ARC DE TRIOMPHE. Paris, where I was supposed to be.

When I was six my father gave me a shining red rubber ball printed with white stars and sent me into the alley behind our house to play. That was where she found me. Sylvie in her Pocahontas dress. We played until warmth seeped from the dark folds of shadow, from her hands on my sweatshirt and the princess crown askew on her head. And she asked me to be her best friend and I said yes. Then she asked me to go with her to Paris, and the world was a word in her mouth, and I said yes.

She had books of photographs of the City of Light, souvenirs from the trips her parents had taken there before she was born, favorite movies. But to me Paris was Sylvie's bedroom, with its miniature Eiffel Towers and paintings of black cats and swan-girls stretching in falls of sunlight; her dresser, desk, and side tables painted with green hills and gray castles and white beaches; her pink velvet window seat; the lavender sachets in her drawers; the light passing through her sheer blue curtains. I understood Paris as the sharp pang of wanting something I didn't even know existed before her.

Sylvie. Always inside me like another, better self. Beneath everyday desires and victories and defeats, behind school and parents and teachers, we passed into the realm of shared diaries and the humid intimacy of our beds on nights we slept together. My best friend. My only friend.

"Do you have a boyfriend, Roxana?"

I snorted. "Nope."

We drank. The radio played classical music now, so quietly I wondered if I was imagining it.

"You are a serious person, focused on your studies."

"That's nice of you to say. But I don't think that's why. It just hasn't happened for me, unlike for basically everybody else I know. Plenty of people going to way better colleges than me seem to have no trouble getting laid, if that was what you were implying."

Søren stroked his face. "I was not."

"Well, they do."

He leaned across the table. "Roxana, you are quite loud. Just so you know."

My face burned. When I spoke again it was from behind my glass, in a near whisper. "Sorry. I just meant to say that people definitely do have sex. A lot! But not me. Not me."

Søren looked pained. "Well, that is your choice, of course. I wasn't so much talking about sex as relationships, matters of the heart. You should not—I mean, you should not feel that you need do anything that you do not wish to do. I—well, I sound like an idiot. But all I mean is that that is fine. Everything is fine."

Isn't sex a matter of the heart? I wanted to ask him. But I had started talking and I couldn't stop. I wanted to tell someone. I would probably never see him again after the program began the next day, anyway.

"No it's not," I said, feeling the alcohol. "It's hard. It's hard when your best friend is very beautiful and everyone, even boys, even boys you might like, tells you that. Even your mother and father tell you. And it's hard because boys never talk, except for when they have to talk to you in school, the rest of the time they just huddle together and you never know if they're laughing at you. And then, then when you finally get to be alone with one you like, a boy you really like, it gets all screwed up. Of course." I took a miniature sip, looking into Søren's face. "Can you explain it to me? Does it get easier? At all?"

On the table his hands worked. "You are quite angry."

"I'm not." I poured beer down my throat and thrust the glass back down on the table, sloshing liquid over the sides. Søren's chair skidded back like the spilled beer was fire. Calm down, I almost said. I should take my own advice. Inside I felt sloppy. I wanted another beer, but he probably wouldn't buy it for me. I squinted at his pale shape feeling angry and worn out—sick and tired, I realized. Suddenly I knew exactly what that meant. I wanted something from Søren and he wouldn't give it to me. No one would.

I would tell the story so that I knew for sure that it was pointless. Liking him.

"Two years ago I went to Homecoming with a boy I really liked, Hunter Landson. Homecoming is a school dance where—"

Søren nodded thoughtfully. "I know from movies."

Hunter. He is always to me as I first saw him, a slinking honey-eyed boy in a blue plaid hoodie, dark hair lank as dog fur on his thin neck. He crossed the threshold of our honors chemistry classroom, that yellow-lit hall of flame and hypotheses, holding his hands in his kangaroo pocket as if it were a lady's muff. When he was led to my table and told to sit, he took off his backpack, and I saw his hands, lithe and slim fingered, gloved in rosy skin.

"Hi." He tapped the notebook I'd had custom-made at the drugstore, with a picture of my cat, Mushi, as the cover. His cuticles were neat and smooth, unchewed. "That your kitty? I have one too." He leaned in close, hair in his eyes. When he spoke, spray coated my nose. "Her name's Peanut Butter."

How long had I been wanting? Forever. In Hunter, those swirling emotions at my dark center coalesced into a person. A purpose. Hunter saw me.

Our conversations were meted out by his tic of jerking his head back to flick the hair out of his eyes, a violent motion. Our hands touched each time we lit our Bunsen burner. It took only a few days for me to conjure him in my bedroom after I turned out the lights. Rolled under my torso, my arm became a part of his body. Now leg, now arm, now cock, or what I could imagine of it. My fingers his attenuated ones. It felt as if I had been doing this since before memory.

One day in class Hunter's T-shirt caught as he took off his hoodie, revealing a trapezoid of lean flesh bisected by a line of rich auburn hair—his treasure trail—and a purplish nipple, winking and puckered in the perpetual lab chill. His arms were covered in scabs, mostly thin scratches, but here and there a deep gouge or scrape hashed over with brittle crust.

He caught my eye. Flicked his hair. Saw me see the scabs, the question in my face.

"I volunteer at the animal shelter and the cats really tear me up when we play. You're sharp, Roxana. I can't hide anything from you."

I sucked my bottom lip into my mouth and tore a wing of dead skin from my lip with my incisor, peppering my tongue with blood. Under our table I wedged my fist into my crotch.

We lit the flame, raised the beaker.

In the last week of September I wrote the question on a piece of computer paper with a tiny brush dipped in lemon juice and slid it across the invisible boundary we observed on the desk.

"Hold it up to the Bunsen," I told him. "A message will appear."

He lifted the paper, applied the flame.

Will you go to Homecoming with me?

"Aw," he said. "Of course."

He reached over and touched my shoulder, one grip, one squeeze, and I felt so fine I thought my clothes might fall from my body and expose me.

Sylvie was jealous. She said she wasn't, but she was.

On the night of the dance, Hunter appeared on my doorstep, red sneakers peeking out from beneath his dress pants. He brought me a flower, a big silvery lily, not a little girl's wrist corsage but the kind that had to be pinned to the bodice of my dress. I could smell the mints from the rectangular case perpetually silhouetted in his left front pocket.

Hunter shielded my breast with his palm, easing the pin through the dense beaded fabric of my dress. When it was done he stepped back to consider his work. Took my hand in both of his.

"Perfect," he said.

He held my hand all night. When he had to let go—to pick up a fork, or go to the bathroom, or gesture as he spoke—he gave me a little tap, as if to say: "I'll be right back." He opened every door for me and laughed at all my jokes. We slow danced.

And I grew bolder, sure I was going to have a boyfriend. I let my happiness hang out of my dress like a third breast.

We did not kiss at the dance, although every moment I thought we might. When they dimmed the lights. On the dance floor. While we stood in the hall and he got quiet and I got quiet. But it didn't happen then, or when the lights came up, or as we filtered out to the chilly subterranean parking lot and climbed into his mother's sedan. A pearl rosary dangled from the rearview mirror. He turned the key in the ignition and high soaring synths filled the car.

Hunter laid his hand on mine where it sat in my lap, and pressed his mouth to my ear. "I want to be alone with you. Tonight."

All I could do was frantically nod. We rode the glimmering Eisenhower out of the city. The tall buildings on either side had always seemed forbidding, massive ships threatening to embark, but with Hunter they became friendly sentries squared against the orange-purple sky. We entered Creek Grove and I realized Hunter was taking us to the grade school where we had both attended kindergarten through fourth grade. That we hadn't known each other then seemed amazing to me. I had been near him, so close for so long, and not even felt it.

Hunter parked, came around to my side of the car, and opened my door. "My lady," he said, and I forced my breathing slow.

We walked to the old playground, hot night wind spreading my skirt behind me. We swung on the swings, falling and floating, that fantastic arc. Eventually Hunter suggested we go sit on the bench under the trees behind the school.

In elementary school that bench was where I hid from the other girls. Their favorite game was the one where they interrogated me to prove I wasn't as smart as everyone thought I was. If I answered right, I was doomed. "She thinks she's smart, too," they sneered. Back then I thought the bench had powers of invisibility and protection and fated magic—a node of energy—and maybe I hadn't been wrong, because now I was going to sit on it with a boy. This boy, with marked arms and hair as soft as the evening air. I was going to touch it. Move it through my fingers.

On the bench Hunter pulled a tiny bottle of vodka out of his jacket.

"Is that from an airplane?" I asked.

"A minibar. I raided one with my cousin last summer. I've been saving it. Brought you one too." Hunter retrieved a twin bottle from his other pocket and handed it to me. I had a brief moment of feeling superior—his idea of a dangerous good time was two mouthfuls of tepid vodka, while I had been mixing cocktails with Sylvie since middle school—but then I realized how sweet it was that he had thought of me. We made little wordless toasts, nodding at each other. When our bottles were empty, I wasn't drunk, just cold. Hunter took off his jacket. I thrilled to wrap myself in it.

For a while our silence was companionable. Hunter dragged his feet through the dirt under the bench. Then the quiet grew loose and unnerving. The moon was yellow and too bright in my eyes. I wondered when the kissing would start.

"What are you thinking about?" I asked.

Hunter started laughing again and couldn't stop. There was some sound under the laughter, something like "you." Maybe a word, maybe not. I had never seen him like this. In class he was still and calm. Now his gurgling escalated. None of this seemed to include me.

"Hunter, I can't understand you," I said finally.

He shut up so quickly it scared me. The wind pushed his hair into his eyes. He jerked it away and kissed me hard. My first. I realized then he had been drinking all night. All those trips to the bathroom. But I didn't care. His tongue was finally in my mouth. I had wanted to feel it there for so long.

We broke and stared at each other. His eyes were wild as he pushed the straps off my shoulders. I unbuttoned his shirt and pressed my palm to the center of his chest, disbelieving my bravery. We kissed again, his heart having a fit under my palm. He spread his jacket over the little patch of land behind the sandbox that no one could see from the street.

It was easy to take off our clothes, to be next to each other in our underwear. I wasn't scared at all. Had I ever been? Our bodies stretched through the soupy night.

Hunter undid his pants and took off my underwear. Pretty silver butterfly-motif lace, my nicest pair. I had worn them special. The sky was so big. I lay down, air highlighting me between my legs.

He got on top. Rubbed himself against me, parting my pubic hair. That blunt edge. Oh.

I wanted to have sex. I had said yes. It was only complicated for a minute. Then it wasn't, and there was a rushing sense of another, inside and outside. Betwixt. Severe.

The wind licked my shoulders and neck. I felt a way I had not known before, the way a person cannot make herself feel, a place she cannot go alone. I opened my mouth and made a little sound and I could not believe I had spoken. In the instant, all I wanted was to know that nothing had changed.

Hunter answered with a yelp, as if he were hurt. A single inelegant jerk of his body.

I wanted to say something but couldn't think.

He rolled away. Pulled out. Knelt to do up his pants.

I lay feeling not what I had felt. I didn't know how much time I needed to get there, or where there was, even. I had only an idea, from myself. A warm golden room, an oval.

"Come back," I said, forcing a smile into my voice. "I didn't—"

He squinted. "You didn't what?"

I kept smiling at him.

Hunter's face darkened. He stared at the ground. "My parents made me promise I'd be back at one. We should get going."

I pulled the collar of his jacket up around my neck, imagining he was kissing me there. I wanted him to touch me again: my shoulders and neck and between my legs. But that was done. My discarded dress's cheap silver stars puddled around me. I stood to step back into it, revealing my ruined lily, crushed beneath some limb, and felt an odd dripping. His semen tracing down my thighs.

Hunter handed me my underwear without looking at me.

He was too drunk to drive and seemed to have forgotten about his car. We walked to my house in silence. The moonlight had taken on a wintry cast. When we got to my yard I asked quickly so I wouldn't lose my nerve. "Would you come inside and say hi to my mom?"

I could see her silhouette in the front room through the curtains. She was reading. Not waiting up, just still up. It was not late.

Hunter laughed, kind of, pointing to the dirt on his jacket, and smiled at me as if we had come to a mutual understanding. He gave my hand a last little tap and turned away. I went inside alone, feeling jagged.

Nothing like this had ever happened to me before. I wasn't planning to tell Mama, but when I saw her sedately arranged in her pajamas with a book in her hands, I just started talking. If he wouldn't talk to me about it, she would. Someone had to pay attention to me. For the dance my parents had granted me an evening without a curfew, meaningless now. Everyone, including me, had assumed something was going to happen. But it hadn't. Why? I wanted someone to tell me. It would have to be her.

She became more and more erect as I spoke, until finally she was standing, pacing. "Please tell me you used protection," Mama said when I stopped talking.

I had forgotten protection even existed. She went into the bathroom and locked the door. I sat listening to her yell.

Mama came back, her purse already slung over her shoulder. "Get in the car, Roxana."

We drove past dark houses. For a few minutes I thought Mama was taking me somewhere to get rid of me, that she was done with me for good. Instead she pulled into the parking lot of the twenty-four-hour drugstore and steered me through the fluorescent aisles to the pharmacy counter, where a very young woman in a white coat sold us the morning-after pill. It was two pills, actually, identical and pale. I couldn't tell them apart from the ibuprofen tablet Mama gave me to take too.

"This way we don't have to worry," Mama said, tucking me into bed. We, I thought. Like it was my parents' body, not mine. Like it was their choice. Maybe I wanted something to worry about. Something real. "But next time you're sure as hell going to use protection. I'm going to make you an appointment to get on birth control this week. Do you have any questions?" Her nurse's poker face: straightforward, willing to deliver necessary information. As if she wanted me to request a tutorial, an informational pamphlet. A demonstration on a banana.

I shook my head. No one would want to touch me again, I was sure. For years, certainly, maybe for the rest of my life.

The pills made me sick enough that Mama let me miss school on Monday. Later, there would be a repeat of this sickness, turned down in volume, when I began my birth control prescription and started swallowing a small peach-colored tablet dry every night before bed, and I wouldn't be allowed to miss school at all, despite the nausea and exhaustion the drug brought on as my body adjusted. But on the Monday after Homecoming I was allowed to stay in bed all day, drinking ginger ale and waiting for Hunter to call. When the phone finally rang after school, it was just Sylvie. There would only be Sylvie, now, as before.

"Oh my God, Rox," she said. "I'll kill him with my bare hands."

That made me smile.

"Still, though," she went on. "I'm not exactly surprised. I totally saw this coming."

I waited for her to tell me why, grateful to be welcomed back into our world.

"Roxana." Søren reached across the table.

I drained my beer. "Sorry I talked for so long."

He shook his head. "That boy was an asshole, yes? Did he apologize?"

I laughed. "No."

The next Monday I found out that Hunter had asked Mr. Dungeness for a new lab partner. For the rest of the year the teacher himself worked with me, fumbling niceties behind his

smudged glasses, obviously embarrassed by the evidence of a
social drama of which he wanted no part.

"Sylvie said he was probably really embarrassed. That men
have a hard time with things like that. Their pride gets hurt.
And that Hunter was obviously immature, that she had noticed
that from the beginning."

Søren stood, collecting our empty glasses. "It's getting late.
Shall we have a last drink?"

I nodded and followed on wobbly legs. The bartender ex-
changed our empty pints for two tiny glasses, which he filled
with a clear liquid from an unlabeled brown bottle.

"Schnapps," Søren said, like the name of someone he loved.
"We call it a little sharp one. For after dinner, the end of the
night. Now."

He picked up one of the tiny glasses. I lifted the other.

"To better days," Søren said, and drained his glass. The
liquor burned its way down my throat, leaving me coughing.
Søren and the bartender laughed, exclaiming to each other, and
we left the bar. Outside, the air was cool and the setting sun
dressed the storefronts in fading light.

I was still gasping. "What did you say to him?"

Søren smiled. "That you are better than us. Not so used
to the poison."

I felt seasick. He was a fast walker. I had to concentrate
to keep up.

We passed a group of blonde women with beautiful shoulders. Søren did not turn, peering instead at me with concern.
I ducked my head to hide my smile as we descended into the
subway.

I must have fallen asleep on the train. The next thing I
remember was a feeling like surfacing from great depth, Søren

nudging me with his elbow. The light hurt my eyes. I followed him off the train and up onto the darkened street. The buildings were blocky mountains rising into the purple sky, deep purple, more blue than red. Shot through with stars. Silver thread wrapped around everything. Søren took my arm. The warmth of his body. Under my feet the sidewalk rolled like in a cartoon. I sat so that I wouldn't fall. He said my name and laughter caught in my throat. He hoisted me under my armpits and pushed me up the stairs. "Wait," I said. "Wait." But we were already in the foxwoman's hallway. She appeared in the shadows in a robe of quilted milk. Robert came out of the darkness and pushed his giant nose into my crotch. I laughed until I couldn't breathe. The foreigners sounded like birds. Søren took me into my room and sat me on my bed. How kind of him, I thought. His arms moved, reaching for me, I thought.

Instead Søren took the little digital alarm clock, set it, and put it down on the bedside table. "Goodnight, Roxana," he said.

I went to hug him, but changed my mind and lunged for a kiss instead. My wet, open mouth landed on his neck. He pulled away.

"Don't worry," I said. "Don't worry."

He disappeared. I stretched out on the little bed and closed my eyes. I saw the place where Hunter's fine hair touched his soft neck. Søren's eyes. "Of course he acted like that, Roxana," I heard Sylvie say. "It was too much too soon. I almost feel sorry for him."

On and on we rode in the golden dawn, the trees thick and green over us. Into their purple shadow, out into fuzzed light. Again. Cirrus on the horizon, running clementine to outer space blue.

To turn we leaned into the bend. Thought of leaning. Dreamed the cicada whirring of wheels. We didn't glide. We flew.

I stopped my panting to listen for Sylvie's. My chest pistoned and the edges of my vision flashed. But even after I heaved, fire in my lungs, I couldn't hear her.

We rounded the thumb-like green rise blotted with impatiens. A stout brick edifice appeared, sturdy on its broad plot. Our high school. I let go of my handlebars and straddled my seat, seeking my old face in the windows on the top floor.

Sylvie spun past, her pink sneakers braced against the pedals, her kite's tail the long black braids she had tied with green ribbon.

"Loser!" She called behind her.

The day became opaque, the sky evening to blue, disappearing the gold. Bared sun beat the back of my neck.

I closed my eyes. Loser. Come on. Loser. Do it, loser. When I opened them, she was gone.

I dismounted and began the walk down the hill.

Once Sylvie's bike had been a tiny pink thing with white wheels, its handlebars sprouting sparkling silver streamers. Now it was an Italian model slim and shiny as silverware, for which her parents had paid three thousand dollars. An entirely different species from the scuffed black three speed I had inherited from Dad.

Sylvie jutted a hip in my direction, her mouth curving a closed smile. "Feel better?"

"No. I haven't heard anything since the interview."

"'Cause you killed it."

"I had trouble getting the video to work."

She sighed, thumbs flying on her phone. "Even after we practiced?"

"I don't think it was my fault."

"You're right." Sylvie laughed. "It must have been International Abroad Experiences, which does like a hundred of these a day. Not my best friend who is a little forgetful. Hmm. I wonder." She drawled the last syllable of the word.

I yanked my shirt down over my hips. It immediately hiked itself back up.

The street was absolutely quiet, the school and fields staged and empty as a diorama.

The night before, the night after graduation, we were in her bedroom, still in our white dresses, hair sprayed hard to hold against the wind, shimmery rivulets of eye makeup striping my face. Had anyone remembered to take a picture before I started crying about the divorce?

Sylvie pressed an ice cube wrapped in a paper towel to my eyes, smoothed my hair back under a headband, gave me cold water from a blue mug. Held my hot hands in her cool dry ones. She sat behind me and locked her arms just under my breasts. My ass filled the concave basin of her lap. She always smelled of lemons. Honey shampoo.

"I don't think you understand," I heard her whisper. "None of this shit matters at all. We did it. We made our dream happen. We are going to Paris." My nipples tensed when her breath touched my ear. The mosquito net moved limply above us. I felt sad for it, a useful thing restrained from its true purpose. The windows in Sylvie's room didn't even open. Your dream, I thought and then felt bad, as I always did, for not better appreciating how generous she was to share it with me.

When I turned my head, Sylvie was asleep, mumbling something that might have been French. I switched off her bedside lamp and nuzzled between the cushy rises of her breasts, provoking little snores. Her heart beat low and steady beneath my ear.

My Danish hangover was a steady pain at the back of my head and a jumping stomachache. I was grateful that Søren didn't speak. We were going somewhere to meet the other members of the program, a route that took us by pale buildings with many windows and peaked roofs and arches and painted molding, gilt-lettered names hung over their entrances. Restaurants and bars advertising steaks and drink specials, shops full of books I couldn't read. An AFRO HAIR AND BODY SHOP displayed two enlarged photographs of a smiling blonde woman before and after the application of two feet of platinum weave. A set of massive gray buildings floated over the water. Filing cabinets for human beings.

"The university," Søren said, turning to me. "Does your head hurt?"

"No." My head immediately throbbed, punishment for lying. "Yes."

He looked contrite. "I'm sorry, Roxana. It was a bad idea to go to the bar."

"No!" My voice was too loud. "I had a good time."

I thought of the kinds of things I should be asking him, to make our relationship real. "Søren, where are you from?"

He smiled indulgently, as if I had forgotten. "Denmark."

"Yes, but where?"

"Hummingen. A town on an island called Lolland."

I couldn't even begin to pronounce the words. "Is that far from here?"

"Three hours south on the train."

"How can you take a train to an island?"

He looked at me steadily. "Bridges, Roxana."

"Oh." What an idiot he must think I was.

We entered a high-ceilinged purple room, a circle of couches at its center. A row of computers stood on tables against the far wall.

"Wait here," Søren said. "I will find the others."

I didn't want to meet anyone. "Can I check my e-mail on one of the computers?"

"Of course," he said, leaving.

I kept accidentally tapping the extra letters on the Danish keyboard, œ, å, ø. There were six new e-mails, five spam, one from Dad.

Hey Sweetie,

I am sure you are busy. Mama and I loved your message! So glad to know you are doing so well. We miss you! Hope Paris is exciting! Bon voyage!

Love,
Dad

That they had received the voice mail together—*loved* it together?—but not bothered to call me back made me comfortable perpetuating the fiction that I was in Paris with Sylvie.

Dear Mama and Dad,

All is well. Today Sylvie and I meet the other people in my program. I love and miss you guys! I will write more later.

Love,
Roxana

Nothing from Sylvie. Smoothly, slowly, the bones in my hands gliding over each other, I opened a new e-mail window and started typing.

Hi Sylvie!

No.

Dear Sylvie,

Not that, either.

My dear Sylvie,

Too weird.

Hey Sylvie,

What was there to say? Sylvie had already surrounded herself with newer, more exciting people. She didn't even care enough to write.

The day after graduation, I had received a voice mail.

"Hello, this is Jennifer Lindsey with International Abroad Experiences calling for Roxana Olsen. Unfortunately, we are not able to include you in the Parisian Experience program, as it is fully enrolled. The acceptance letter you were sent and the processing of your tuition payment were administrative errors. We apologize deeply for these. Luckily, we have had an unusually low number of applicants to our Hoogah Danmark program this year, so we've been able to transfer you over. As a sign of our appreciation for your flexibility, we've booked you a first-class seat on a direct flight from Chicago to Copenhagen, same day as your original departure. Your ticket to Paris and tuition has been refunded." She paused, and then added, as if I had won something: "That's right, this is on us!"

I deleted the message. Dialed her.

"Jennifer Lindsey." There was laughter in her voice.

"Jennifer, this is Roxana Olsen. I received your message. I have a question. I sent in my registration for the Parisian Experience at the same time as my best friend, Sylvie Elmaleh. Has she been bumped, too?"

I immediately regretted the childish phrase. My best friend.

"Well, now, 'bumped' isn't the language I would use. And we generally have a rule against releasing client information, but I will make an exception." Jennifer Lindsey's fingernails clicked against a keyboard. "Sylvia is still enrolled."

"I can't believe this." I said to prolong the period in which this was true. "I'm supposed to leave in six days! Does this have to do with my interview? Sylvie said it was just a formality—"

"I'm not at liberty to discuss that. Now, I really need to know if you are interested in our offer of enrollment in Hyggelige Danmark. The program is the same length as the Parisian Experience, eight weeks. You begin in Copenhagen, capital of Denmark, which, as I'm sure you've heard, is the happiest country on Earth! You will spend a week exploring the city's many cultural treasures, eating open-faced sandwiches, and walking along the docks of Nyhavn." She was reading from a brochure. "Then, after you've visited Christiania, the city-within-the-city, and Roskilde, home to the Domkirke and Viking Ship Museum—"

Hyoolee. Neehown. Ross Killed and Dom Kirk, mutinous brothers at sea. The names made my head hurt. I cut her off. "I'll have to call you back."

I lay on my bed, imagining I could see myself from above: the shape of my body, or the comforter cover above the dust ruffle. But it wasn't real. I couldn't see anything.

For a while I cried, ragged sobs that hurt. Then my tears dried up and my voice went away. I felt my face with my hands, my oily skin, my raised pores, my fuzzy eyebrows. I tried to curl up and go to sleep, but every position was uncomfortable. I leaped from the bed and paced the room, tracing different shapes, S, X, circle, spiral. I pinched the soft skin of my upper arms without my fingernails, then with. Hard. Harder.

I looked at the pictures of Sylvie, of my parents, of Paris. Who were those people? What was that place? If I had ever known, I didn't anymore.

When I came back to myself it was dusk. Purple outside.

Dad sat next to me in a shirt and tie, staring at his phone. "What's going on? When I got home you were fast asleep. Are you sick?" Keeping one thumb on his screen, he leaned over and kissed me on the forehead. Did he know?

My shoulders hurt. I peeled up my sleeve and saw yellow blots where I had pinched myself.

"Dad." My voice caught on the word. I closed my eyes, took a deep breath. "Dad." It came out a sob.

"I'm sorry, sweetie." Dad leaned forward, eyes still on his phone. "We didn't know the news of the divorce would upset you so much."

The divorce! "I'm not sick," I said.

Dad's phone beeped. He returned his attention to it. "Are you sure?"

I slipped my legs out from under the comforter. "I'm going to the bathroom."

"Try not to worry. Paris is going to be great."

"Thanks, Dad."

They told me they were separating a week before graduation, on the porch with Mushi, where I had been reading old copies of *National Geographic* Mama kept in a wicker basket next to the love seat. A tribe of Mexican Indians who could run faster than anyone else in the world were dying out—eating too much fast food and getting hit by cars. Narwhals jousted in the frozen ocean, but no one knew why. Catholics in Los Angeles had begun inventing their own saints. A saint of death, a saint of violence, a saint of pain. In the alley, kids screamed, "No! You're killing me, you're killing me!"

The heat rose and thickened around two. I went inside and ate. I went back out to the porch and took a nap under a photo spread on rare birds. When I woke, the sky had dimmed to a silvered blue, afternoon turning into evening, and my parents stood before me, holding hands.

It was too early for them to be home and they were weirdly dressed up, Mama in a lavender pantsuit I had never seen, Dad in the stiff blue pinstripe suit he had worn to Pawpaw's funeral. The worst thing was Mama's hair. She always wore it pulled straight back into a bun at the base of her neck, but it was slung over her left shoulder that day, limply touching her collarbone.

"Sit down, Roxana," Mama said.

"I am sitting down." Wicker cracked under me as Mama nodded at Dad.

"Roxie," he said. "Your mother and I—"

"What, did you guys get all dressed up to tell me you're getting divorced or something?"

It was an old joke. They were always fighting and making up. But that day their faces flashed and I felt the love seat move under me, like a boat.

They were just back from a lawyer's office. "This doesn't mean I don't still love and respect Mama," Dad said. He would be living in a nearby apartment while I was in France. No final decisions would be made until the fall, they promised. Not until it was time for me to leave again.

"We're just very different people," Mama said.

Shortly after my twelfth birthday, I had realized that my thighs doubled in size when pressed against a chair, and for weeks I refused to sit in a position that flattened them. At school, I suspended my legs an inch above the seat in frantic twenty-second bursts, trying to quiet my panting. Then one day I just forgot about it, a reprieve that lasted six years, until that very moment. I tried to raise my thighs but couldn't. I was already shaking. Powerful neons ripped through me. Mama had a collection of scarves in these bright colors. Acid green, cyber yellow, electric blue that burned my eyes. The love seat wasn't a boat anymore but an airplane. I had lifted off into the sky.

I left Dad in what had once been his and Mama's room and locked the door to my bedroom. From my window I saw that only his car was in the garage. Mama wasn't home yet. Good.

I typed "Denmark" into a search engine. The word "Dansk."
Where had I seen it before? A map appeared: a little mitten jutting
out into the ocean above Germany. A series of islands between
Scotland and Sweden. It looked cold, just an oven mitt in the sea,
kind of like Michigan, where I had spent several childhood vacations. The house we rented there had a dock and a yellow canoe,
and there were boats in Denmark too. Sailboats, gray-blue water,
castles, a statue of a mermaid, flat food. Pictures of Danes showed
tall blonds in skinny pants, their light hair pulled back to expose
sharp cheekbones.

Denmark was a nation of five and a half million people, the
oldest monarchy in Europe, and, indeed, had been declared the
happiest country on the planet. I watched an American talk show
host walk through a sleek modern apartment, sunlight streaming
through its wide windows. "Mostly everyone lives like this," a
woman in a fluffy orange sweater said in perfect English. I read
about pork meatballs, boiled potatoes smothered in brown sauce,
spherical pancakes, rye bread spread with pork liver, all to be
washed down with beer or schnapps. My family never ate pork.

Elderly Danish people danced in funny outfits on the dark
sand of cold beaches.

A famous painting appeared: two women in long dresses
walking along the seashore at twilight, their backs to the viewer.
Friends.

I imagined Sylvie walking down a Paris street alone, smiling.

I typed in "hyoolee." No results.

I went down to the kitchen and made a paste of cocoa powder,
sugar, and a little water in the bottom of a tall glass. Then I filled
it with milk and mixed. If I kept my thoughts and perceptions

in the sensory world, I wouldn't be able to feel sad. I would only pay attention to what I could see, hear, taste. Touch. The cold glass in my hand and the rich cocoa on my tongue. I stared out the window, listening to the sounds of summer as they came through the screen, trying to focus on the sweetness of the drink, the smooth milk. I could tune out the ambient bug song and just hear the cicadas screeching smoothly above the lawn mowers and cars, the kids playing, the sizzle of meat on a grill. It was like learning to separate instruments on a recording: at first, I was only aware of my ability to segregate sound, of the silence behind all the noise, and for a moment I thought that was what I was hearing. But then my ears adjusted again, and I realized there was no true silence, just the high cicada vibration, a hum so shrill it was the silver lining of quiet.

Sylvie's mom answered the phone.

"Please," I said. "I just need to talk to Sylvie for a second."

She sighed. "Does it have to be right now? We're doing yoga."

I could see her in her white leggings and big T-shirt. Probably a French one, from her huge collection, advertising an exhibit at the Pompidou or a gallery show. Sometimes I thought she wore them just to annoy me.

"Sorry, Mrs. Elmaleh, but yes."

Then Sylvie's voice was there in my ear. "Hello?"

"Don't take too long, Rox! Let Sylvie get back to her inner peace!" Sylvie's mom shouted, before I could say anything. I hated that she had adopted Sylvie's nickname for me.

I closed my eyes and tried to get it out quickly. "Sylvie! Sylvie I'm not going to France!"

She laughed again. The spa music in the background got louder. "I totally promise I will call you back, Rox!"

"Sylvie, listen. The woman from International Abroad Experiences called me and said there had been a mistake. There isn't a place for me on the trip."

"Sure. Sure, I believe you." The music changed to something more frenetic.

"It's not a joke. I have to go to Denmark instead. Or stay here. But I can't go to Paris with the program. I have no say in it. I'm not kidding." I hadn't wanted to cry.

Sylvie hissed at her mom. The music stopped abruptly. "What?"

"They said I can't go. They changed my ticket."

"What do you mean?"

"They fucked it up, Sylvie. I'm supposed to go to a program in Denmark instead. I don't want to go." A tiny hope flickered in my chest. "I think I'll probably just end up staying home."

I waited for Sylvie to say that she would stay with me.

"Rox," she said. "This sucks."

"They would give you back the money if you stayed. We could save it for college. Get better jobs here this summer. It could be fun, in a different way."

Sylvie laughed. "I am not staying in Creek Grove and working some shitty summer job instead of going to Paris."

I skipped to my second tiny hope. "I was also thinking maybe I could just go to France with you anyway. Maybe I could stay with your aunt and watch her kids?"

There was a long silence before Sylvie said, "Her apartment is really small. Really, really small. I don't know where they'd put you." She coughed. "Plus, if you had to reschedule your ticket right now it would probably be really expensive and use up a lot of the money. So, you know."

"Know what?"

"God, I can't believe you're not coming."

Maybe she closed one eye and put her thumb over my face; maybe she used a big pink eraser to smudge me out of her future memories. Whatever she did in Paris, she was alone now, at cafés, in clubs.

"So, what's in Denmark?"

"White people and potatoes."

Sylvie didn't laugh. My face was so hot. I blinked once, twice.

The spa music started up again in earnest. Tinkly bells and soothing synths. Sylvie's mom had turned the yoga back on.

"Rox, I should probably go," Sylvie said. "Okay? I'll call you later."

I stayed up until two that night, but she didn't.

The next day I woke to Mama in the doorway of my room. Her gold hoops caught the sunshine peeking through my blinds. She came and sat on my bed.

"Roxana." Her face was soft. She kissed my forehead and found my hands. "Sleepyhead. Time to get up."

"Is it?"

"It is now. You're awake."

Mama steered me over to the mirror and stood behind me. How many times had I searched photographs of us together for resemblance? My face was round where hers was long and angular. My eyebrows were straight feathery lines over my eyes; she shaved hers off and drew new ones on, thick and sharp.

Her hair was neat and small in its bun; mine got in everything. Mama and Dad sometimes found it in their food.

"Remember," Mama said. "College is your real goal. Paris is just a reward. College is your future. Paris is just a vacation."

A vacation, after all the trouble Sylvie and I had gone to find an educational program our parents agreed to. After all the jobs we'd worked at to pay for it. I avoided her eyes in the mirror. "Yes."

"Don't get it mixed up." She closed her arms around my shoulders and pressed me in a hug so hard it almost hurt. "I have to leave for work. Clean up your room, please."

Her face hung behind me in the mirror, a mirage.

Sylvie didn't pick up when I called. Mama and Dad had a late meeting with their lawyer. "Order a pizza," Dad suggested on the phone, but I didn't want to spend any of my money.

I walked to the dresser and ran my hand along the lid of my jewelry box, watching in the mirror. I twisted a curl of my hair around my index finger.

Mushi clawed at the doorknob to be let in, but I ignored him. I dialed Jennifer Lindsey's number.

Yes, I told her. I would go to Denmark.

3

I STOOD AT THE UNIVERSITY COMPUTER LAB IN COPEN-
HAGEN, MOUTH COCKED. Opened a new window.

Dear Sylvie,

Fuck off

"Roxana?"

At the sound of Søren's voice, I closed everything. I felt
dizzier than I had the night before. Dizzier than when I had
woken that morning to the black drumbeat of sunlight through
the chintz curtain and the screaming alarm clock. I did not
want to start the program today. I turned, trying to make my
expression presentable.

Søren was alone. He took off his hat and rubbed his scalp,
a gesture I was beginning to recognize as a tic. "I am sorry to
tell you, but we have missed the group's departure for Roskilde."

A reprieve. I could have kissed him.

"It is my fault. My error." Søren squeezed his hat. "There
are trains leaving every hour. We can catch them, but we must
hurry."

He turned and began walking quickly toward the door. Let's not, I don't want to go, I almost told him, but then I heard Mama reprimanding me for not appreciating the opportunity to visit a new place. I followed Søren outside and back down into the subway. We boarded the train like strangers and rode three stops in silence before disembarking and crossing a square dotted by thick cement pillars that marked the distance from Copenhagen to Stockholm. Rome. Paris.

Then we were underground again, on another train, the commuter rail to Roskilde. Sets of four seats faced each other across small tables beside long windows on either side of a wide aisle. Søren sat curled over a book with a blank red cover, head bent almost to his chest, his lips moving. Mama would have reached between the chair and his body to poke the small of his back, make him sit up straight. The train passed through fields occasionally interrupted by towns of ranch-style houses. A tall woman in a neat burgundy suit with a gray scarf tied around her neck appeared in the aisle behind a concessions cart, her brown leather pumps soft on the carpeted floor. She stopped beside our table and repeated a litany in Danish. Søren didn't look up.

I pulled my debit card from my wallet and said, "Coffee, please."

She lifted a ceramic carafe from her cart and poured a long stream of coffee into a paper cup.

"Maelk?" She waved a small blue container at me.

"Yes, please." I tried out a word I had heard Søren use many times. "Tak?"

"You are very welcome," she answered in English. I handed her my debit card, hoping it would work. She slid it through her machine, handed it back, and put my coffee down on the table, along with two small blue containers and a shrink-wrapped cookie.

"Tak!" When she wheeled away I realized that I had been holding my breath.

Roskilde was a winding street of white storefronts, their windows all hung with printed TILBUD banners. Søren charged ahead and I raced to keep up, dodging racks and tables of ceramics, women's clothing, textiles. In one display a miniature family of astrological figurines stared. A centaur, a bull, a ram, a goat. TILBUD! TILBUD! TILBUD!

Søren led me up a low hill toward a redbrick church with two towers topped with pointed spires. To one side stood a domed building of the same brick.

"This is the Roskilde Domkirke," he said. "The cathedral."

We continued past it and down the hill to a low white building with a flat roof whose high slanted windows looked out on a small bay. A long wooden ship stood on the grassy shore, covered with a blue tarp.

"Here we are." Søren frowned. "The Viking Ship Museum."

The last thing I wanted to see was a bunch of old boats. At the front desk Søren handed me a sticker, a black dragon's head printed in a white circle.

"Your ticket. Put it on your sweater and go on. I will find the group."

I drifted down a dark corridor, past lit signs that explained Viking history in three languages. Little pictures hung above the words, but the glass was smudged and scratched. I didn't see any people.

At the end of the row of panels was a tall coat rack draped with heavy pieces of cloth. A sign urged me to

DRESS LIKE A VIKING!

I took a purple smock from the rack and pulled it on over my sweater, draped myself in a blue cloak trimmed in fake red fur, and passed into a hall, warm for the first time that day. White sun poured over the skeletons of five ships, all shaped like big canoes. The biggest one was suspended above a dais filled with gray pebbles. Most of its hull had been lost to water and time. A few stray boards, the boat's last remnants, were suspended in a metal grid that represented the whole. The ancient wood was dark, glossy. How many waves had crashed against it?

I did what I was not supposed to do and ran my hand across the old wood, tensing for a reprimand that didn't come. It felt good. Smooth. Emboldened, I dragged my hand against its length, painting it with the oil from my skin. Bright pain ripped across my hand. A stripe of blood welled below the cushiony top of my palm. The old wood had cut me open. It hurt, but it felt good too.

I'm young, I thought to the ship. I haven't been around long. Teach me something. Show me how to feel.

"Roxana?" Søren appeared and I shoved my bleeding hand inside the fake fur cape. "I have been searching for you."

"Sorry," I said, cutting him off. "You told me to look around."

He sighed. "I thought you were lost."

"I'm not," I said.

He took off his hat and rubbed his scalp. "I have made a mess. The others left Amager much earlier today. The group has already been to the museum, and now they have gone again, on a day excursion of some kind. A boat trip and a picnic? Maybe a picnic on a boat. I am not sure. But they are gone."

A tiny pool of blood welled in my palm. I cupped my hand away from my body, trying not to stain the costume.

"It's okay," I said.

"We cannot catch up with them. You will not be able to join the group today."

"It's really okay."

Søren shook his head. "It is not. Roxana. It is my responsibility to broker a good cultural experience of Denmark for you. I am very sorry." He stared at the ground. He seemed so disappointed that I wanted to touch him, make him feel better. But I didn't want him to see my bloody hand.

"Look. I don't feel so good today." I said. "My head hurts. If you put me on a boat I would throw up all over everyone. This is the best thing that's happened to me today."

He looked up at me from under his brows. "But it is my job, and I failed at it."

"Are you going to get in trouble?"

He snickered. "No, the inmates are in charge of the asylum at the company. No one cares if things are done well."

"Only you, huh?" There was something sweet in the slump of his shoulders. I tried to catch his eye. "It's nice that you care so much. I think you're doing a good job."

He shook his head, rolling his eyes. "You have been here over twenty-four hours and all I've done is get you juiced and feed you leverpostej."

I was determined to cheer him up. "Then take me to do something very Danish. Something normal."

Søren touched his chin. "Well, it is almost lunchtime. You have a hangover. As do I. It is the weekend." He blinked. "Why are you wearing those clothes?"

"They belong to the museum," I explained and remembered my hand. "Søren, would you help me? They're heavy."

He undressed me gently, draping the Viking costume over his right arm. I inspected my hand while he arranged the clothes on their rack. Brought it to my mouth and sucked the blood. I swallowed, licked, and rubbed away the brown stain, avoiding the wound's curly white edges.

We were the only customers in a basement restaurant near the cathedral and our food had just arrived. My sandwich was a single slice of grainy rye bread, the same kind Søren had brought me the day before, topped this time with a thin fillet of fried white fish, a salad of tiny pink shrimp, slices of cucumber and tomato, and a dollop of creamy yellow sauce.

"Your smørrebrød is a stjerneskud. A shooting star. We eat them with a knife and fork," Søren said. "But Americans prefer to use their hands, I know."

I felt obscurely offended by this, but when I tried to give him a look I ended up just watching him cut a dainty rectangle of his pariserbøf, Parisian steak—a slab of ground beef fried against a piece of bread and topped with caramelized onions—and slip it delicately into his mouth.

"This is traditional Danish food?"

"Yes. But more importantly, we are behaving in a traditionally Danish fashion by chasing away our hangovers with more alcohol." He sipped his beer.

I winced. "I don't know. It's just making me feel worse."

"Then it is time for another beer. Let us make a preemptive strike." He mumbled Danish to the bartender, who went to the taps. I drained my glass. The cut in my hand was still tender at its lacy margins. The pain was gone.

We took the six o'clock back to Copenhagen. The sun had barely moved from its high place in the center of the sky. I was grateful when the train ducked into tunnels, draping us in dim artificial light. Across from me, Søren was lost in his thoughts, mouthing the same words over and over to himself. Something in Danish.

I twiddled my thumbs faster and faster, hoping he would recognize it as a sign of boredom. The motion grew more manic as I thought of things that spun round and round. Ferris wheels, dreidels, centrifuges. What was a centrifuge, anyway?

Søren let out a great cough-bark. I looked up. He was doubled over, laughing silently.

"What?"

He raised a hand, shaking his head, and finally wheezed as he caught his breath. "I'm sorry, Roxana. You had such a look of concentration on your face, and you were—I don't know the English. Trillede tommelfingre, we say."

I dropped my hands. "Twiddling my thumbs?"

"Yes! So fast, as if it was very important, just staring into space!" He cough-laughed again. It made me happy to see him smile.

"Where did you go?"

"Nowhere," he said humorlessly.

"I mean that you've been thinking about something since we left Roskilde."

"You are very perceptive, yes?" He rubbed his head. "I have been lost in my thoughts. In the bookstore in the train station I found a book of criticism recently published by a Danish scholar on the subject of African American literature. My subject. And it seems he makes the same argument I do, or at least have been planning to make, in my thesis. With different books and different terms, of course, but still, the same argument. So I have been worrying about that. If I want half a shot at a PhD, I have to make an innovative argument. To contribute something new to the discipline."

"That sounds hard."

He didn't seem to have heard me. "I have to completely change my approach. It was ridiculous for me to think that I could get anywhere with this argument. I found his handling of it weak, which means that mine must be much worse. Ah, fuck."

The weather in Søren's face changed and he lapsed back to worried silence. We didn't talk for the rest of the trip. I hoped the coffee cart would appear and lighten the mood, but it did not.

"I will take you back to Birthe's," Søren said as we arrived in Copenhagen. I saw myself alone in the foxwoman's weird room in the middle of the night, hearing Robert in the hall, waiting for the sun to go down.

We disembarked and crossed the busy station through a crowd of people dragging suitcases and eating pastries. Just as he had in Roskilde, Søren walked very quickly away from me without looking back. This time I didn't try to keep up. I let distance fall between us and followed him through the crowd. His shape felt unstable. I remembered his eyes, and the movements of his hands, but separated in the crowd I couldn't summon the feeling of his height, nor the weight of his body beside me, the spirit outline I could remember so clearly when I thought of

Mama or Sylvie or even Hunter. Why did I expect to be able to do that with someone I barely knew?

I found him blinking in the bright sunlight on a sliver of sidewalk. Across the street, a giant sign with photographs of sausages, flames, and smiling men in bow ties advertised a

SERBO-CROATIAN RESTAURANT!!!

We stood staring at it.

"Everywhere there are foreigners," Søren muttered. He cut his eyes at me. "Roxana, would you like to extend your Danish experience?"

It was like falling into the chorus of one of my favorite songs. Yes, yes, yes, a refrain. I nodded.

He led me to a white cart with a red awning in the center of the square. Printed on its windows, awning, and door was:

DAGMARS POLSEWAGN

"This is very Danish. A hot dog wagon."

"Chicago is famous for its hot dogs too."

"Really? How do you dress them?"

"Tomato slices, a pickle, relish, mustard, celery salt, chopped onion, and a sport pepper. On a poppy seed bun. I don't really like them."

"Please, what is a sport pepper?"

"A little hot pepper."

"Ketchup? Mayonnaise?"

"Mayonnaise? Yuck." Lifting my hair off my neck seemed to help my hangover. "Ketchup is against the Chicago hot dog rules."

"No ketchup for you. Do you want to try a French hot dog?"

"What is that?"

"You will like it, I think."

He ordered. With tongs, the old lady inside the cart lifted two thin hot dogs from a container of hot water onto the grill. She picked up a roll, squirted mustard into a hole at one end, lifted a dog from the grill, and pushed it into the hole, then repeated the whole process with ketchup and mayonnaise in the second roll. The hot dogs nestled in the bread cavity, tubes of meat inside a tube of bread. She wrapped the buns in paper sleeves.

Søren paid her with a few large coins and handed the mustard-only dog to me.

"A French hot dog, comme une baguette." His accent was good.

"You know," I said, "I was supposed to go to France, not Denmark."

He looked at me like I was crazy. "Who would rather go to Copenhagen than Paris? Why on Earth are you here?"

I shrugged. "A woman from the company called and said I was bumped to Hyoolee Denmark. What does that mean, anyway?"

"Hyggelige Danmark," he corrected. "It's bastardized Danish. Hygge is, how can I explain this, the national virtue? Coziness, cuddliness. A night in with friends in a comfortably arranged room. So the idea is that your experience of Denmark is going to be a lot of that."

"So far so good," I said hopefully. "I'm glad I ended up here."

His face darkened. He must be tired of me. Or thinking about his thesis again.

I took a bite of my hot dog. It was tepid in the middle. A sour pond of mustard gathered at the bottom of my bun. I swallowed the last wad of bread whole.

Søren finished his in three bites, looking distant. "And now, of course, I am thirsty. This way."

We crossed the square and another street, arriving at a busy cobblestone lane where there were no cars, only people. Two- and three-story buildings rose on either side of us, touristy gift shops, lit boxes selling gloves, cheap sweatpants, and I ♥ COPENHAGEN T-shirts. Their proprietors stood outside, smoking. The restaurants offered faded photographs of food: masses of supposedly Chinese congealed brownness, steakhouse marquees of charred slabs, vast trays of fries, all hung above windows into dim dining rooms. Every other place was colorful and well lit—every shop selling snow globes, T-shirts, leather jackets, amber carvings, tiny windmills—but the eateries were dark. I was glad we had gone to the Polsewagn.

We turned and a different class of restaurants appeared, with steel-accented interiors, bare surfaces, elegantly dressed light-haired customers considering glasses of red wine. I imagined us sipping foamy coffee drinks and fingering fine tablecloths in one of these clean bright places. But he stopped in front of a brick facade with the word BODEGA painted in chipped yellow letters and led me down a short staircase into a crowded bar.

The place was small, all its tables packed with old men drinking and filling glass ashtrays with cigarette butts. They wore heavy coats, even though it was June. In the low light and thick smoke, everything seemed overwhelmingly brown. A man at the bar tapped his pipe, packed a pinch of fresh tobacco, and raised his finger. The bartender, who could have been his twin, pushed a tall green bottle toward him. Their eyes caught, they nodded, and the bartender turned away.

The bartender handed Søren two bottles of Carlsberg, and said something to another patron in a trench coat and tweed hat who was sitting at the table nearest the bar. The man rose and moved to a bar stool. He and the bartender nodded at the table. I followed Søren and we sat down.

"That was nice of them," I said.

"It is only polite to make way for a larger party," Søren said. "We would do the same."

We clinked bottles and drank.

"Søren, you've bought so many things for me. Can I pay for these drinks to make up the difference?" I liked that. I could buy him a drink, no big deal, like I did it all the time.

He shook his head. "I said that I am reimbursed for the money I spend on you, but this is inaccurate. International Abroad Experiences gives me a fund from which to pay student expenses, a quite sizable fund, actually. The only requirement is that I submit an itemized receipt at the end of the summer, and by then what small amounts I may or may not have spent on beers with Roxana will be immaterial."

Like me. "But you have to make the money last, right?"

"The total amount the company gives me is quite high, around ten thousand US."

"That's so much!"

"I spend only a small portion. They give me such a large amount in case of an emergency. Lost passports, misplaced train and air tickets." He slurred derisively. "Children being children."

We drank. He suddenly seemed to be in a bad mood. Had I done something wrong?

"I'm sorry, Roxana," he said after a few long minutes. "I do not mean to be rude. But I believe I know what happened to your trip to France, and I am angry." He slipped his hat from his head. The soft black cap deflated in his hand as his head lit in the low light. I wanted to touch it. "You deserve to know."

I leaned across the table, feeling my breasts shift.

"I have worked for International Abroad Experiences for almost ten years. I started during my gap year. I was nineteen, and had just come to Copenhagen from Farsø. It had been my goal for so long, and then I was here. I was terrified.

"Hummingen, my hometown, is a very small place. Quiet. In the sixties and seventies, when people wanted to move away from the cities to start co-ops, it became quite popular. That's when my parents bought land there. All the old farmers were dying off, and the sixty-eight generation really thought they were going to remake society. Many families made their own clothes and grew their own crops. Everyone ate these horrible lentil stews, an idea of vegetarian food, but no one had any idea how to cook vegetables without meat. I played in the field alone most of the time. Now it is no place to live. Only pensioners and junkies. Any young person with half a brain leaves for the cities."

As he spoke I memorized his crowded bottom teeth, the inky dark behind. I wanted to ask questions, but I was afraid that if I interrupted I would never get Søren talking about his past again.

"I left too, of course. For Copenhagen. It was important to me that I not go right to college from gymnasium. I was far too young to begin a degree."

"How old were you when you began college?"

"Twenty-three."

If I finished college on time, I'd be out for a year by the time I was twenty-three. "What did you do until you started?"

"Went to concerts, read books in the library, took long walks all over the city. I made friends. Met girls." A smile lingered on his face. "But I needed a job. My mother had already given me all of the money she had saved during my childhood." He sipped his beer.

"How were you going to pay for college?"

"College is subsidized by taxes. Once you are admitted, there are few fees. You have already paid."

I swallowed my beer, swallowed again, and again, until I was just swallowing saliva. My first tuition bill had come in the mail right before I left home. $25,784 for tuition and room and board for the fall semester. On top of that Mama and Dad would have to pay two hundred dollars for "tuition refund insurance."

"So it begins!" Dad said, draining his lemonade. "So it begins. Oh, Christ." When I asked what tuition refund insurance was, he said, "It means we'll get our money back if you chicken out." He had refilled his glass, adding whiskey this time.

Søren was still talking. "I was desperate for work. It is very difficult to be hired in Copenhagen, and my only experience was working in a fast-food restaurant in Hummingen. It seemed a miracle when my father e-mailed that a friend of his had work for me. She had just founded a new company named International Abroad Experiences and was looking for tour guides. She hired me on the spot. She is an American, the one with whom you spoke, I believe. Jennifer Lindsey." He stood suddenly and inclined his head. "Bring your beer."

I followed him out to the recessed area in front of the bar. Søren took two cigarettes from his pack with his lips, lit them both, and passed one to me. I put it slowly to my mouth, trying to mask my eagerness to taste his spit. He inhaled contentedly. When I tried to do the same, the smoke came into me fast and toxic. I heaved.

Søren didn't seem to notice. "I learned shortly after I took the job that this woman was my father's lover, the person who led directly to the end of my parents' relationship. And I believe there was no bureaucratic issue with your trip. Jennifer's daughter Kelly decided that she wanted to go to Paris. So Jennifer canceled your enrollment and gave you this free trip as a sort of consolation prize. That is why you are here. Now that I know you and see what a wonderful person you are, I cannot stand the lie. I am sorry you did not go to Paris. I wish I could fix this."

"You think I'm a wonderful person?"

His face so earnest. "Yes, of course. A wonderful person. A beautiful woman."

My hand twitched around the cigarette. Sylvie and I had planned to try Gauloises in Paris. Instead, this was my first time smoking. I inhaled, his words unfolding in my chest—beautiful, he thought I was beautiful, what with my lovely hair and everything—and exhaled, giddy, feeling like a dragon. I was drunk again, somehow.

"I think your cigarette is finished."

I let the burning filter fall and ground it under the heel of my boot. Søren took another drag and blew the smoke out, considering.

"Okay," he said.

I opened my mouth to ask what he was agreeing to and he pulled me against his chest, pushing my face up to meet his, his tongue forging into my mouth. When it was over I was afraid to look at him.

He touched my face. "So now you will tell me if you want to kiss me back, or if I am an asshole who should take you home immediately."

I couldn't find words.

He grew serious. "Please forgive me if this has been a grave miscalculation, Roxana. I do not want to do anything that would make you uncomfortable."

I tilted my head back and kissed him. Søren held me at my waist.

"Well," Søren said, after. We looked away and back again. "I will buy you another drink."

"Sure." The word floated away from me, a balloon.

We walked back into the bar, not touching, our bodies moving in a charged sphere. When my beer was almost empty, Søren dropped his arm on my shoulders, loosely, casually.

"Søren," I said, settling into his arm. "We don't have to talk about it if you don't want to. But Jennifer Lindsey had an affair with your father?"

"She destroyed my parents' relationship. Or maybe not. When people are together for a long time, sometimes they simply tire of each other, not because they do not love each other. Love itself can be tiring."

It was a nicer way to think about what had happened between Mama and Dad. He stroked my neck. I bit my bottom lip to keep from moaning. How confusing to feel the pain of what I had lost alongside the pleasure of this new thing.

"But still. It must be hard to work for her, right? Is she still involved with your father?"

Søren laughed. "Certainly not. She has been through many men since him. He might have been her first Dane, but he was not the last." He thought about it. "Probably he was not even her first Dane."

I let my arm float close, closer to Søren's, until they touched and vibrated hotly.

"Enough about her." Søren tightened his grip on my shoulder. "How are you?"

"I need water. Can you ask the bartender?"

Søren called out and the man placed a short tumbler of water on the bar. I downed it in one gulp and pushed it back for a refill, but he was gone.

"Is something wrong?" Søren asked, as if alarmed that anything should displease me.

"Normally when I've had this much to drink, I try to drink about a gallon of water before I go to bed." I blushed on the last word. With the exception of my night with Hunter, all the drinking I had ever done had been with Sylvie. Drinking so much water had been her rule.

He smiled dangerously. "That will not happen here, I am afraid. We are on the metric system."

I kissed him. Shorter than before, a neat press of lips. He was so warm.

Søren kneaded his hat. "I want to ask you something."

"Shoot." I inverted the glass over my face. Shook it.

"You want water." He inhaled sharply. "At my apartment I have water. A tap, and many glasses."

My body flared. I couldn't look at his face. Søren balled his hat up in one hand and pressed it into the other, as if he were trying to make it disappear. I stared at the bar, trying to stop blushing.

"I am really trying to get fired, I suppose," he said.

"Let's go." I pushed back from the bar and turned to face him. I waited while he put his hat back on.

"I will take you back to Birthe's, after," he vowed, avoiding my eyes.

"Let's go," I said again, my wounded hand throbbing.

4

HIS APARTMENT WAS ONE LONG WHITE ROOM. A miniature refrigerator stood in one corner, a little tower of appliances stacked on top: a microwave beneath a hot plate beneath an electric kettle. The bathroom was a half space, the toilet crammed so tightly between the sink and the wall that I feared I wouldn't fit if I had to pee. I sat at a small blond wood table beside the refrigerator, drinking delicious cold water from a tall glass. In the far corner were a closet, a little stand, and a piece of furniture I tried not to look at or think about. A low white double bed.

When my glass was empty, Søren refilled it. After I had drunk one and half of another, he spoke.

"I apologize for complaining about Jennifer. It was inappropriate. Especially in front of a client." I tried not to be hurt that he called me a client. "It is easy for me to forget that my father also decided to have an affair with Jennifer. Who can say what causes anyone to do anything? Maybe my parents' relationship had run its course. Maybe the task of raising me had exhausted them, taken them out of love." Søren cracked his knuckles. "Relationships fall into a kind of loop. The loop itself is not a bad thing, it can be a loop of joy and excitement, but if you are not conscious of it, the loop comes to define everything you do together, your whole life with the other person, everything you produce, every failure you endure, every project you complete. Joy and excitement do not last forever. More often than not the loop sours. If you are lucky it sours to pleasant boredom. Pleasant boredom, I think, is the best you can hope for in the end."

"That sounds awful."

"I agree. Perhaps this is why I am single. But pleasant boredom is better than many things. Miserable boredom, for example. Or constant fighting, the kind that never really ends but is only turned up and or down in volume. Your days become a fog. A sort of haze hangs over the house. You speak polite as strangers, thanking each other for salt and towels, and even then, more likely than not, the facade rips away and the two of you are yelling, furious, ready to hurt each other in every way, and you can't even remember why. You walk swaddled in red cloth, your face shrouded in anger, feeling your way along the wall. But when you find the other person, when you touch them, the feel of their body and the sound of their voice is terrible to you, grating, gritty. Hideous, as if you have eaten garbage."

I touched his arm with my fingertips. "That's what it was like with your parents?"

He nodded. "And Mette. My ex-girlfriend."

It was remarkable—how jealous I could be of this person who yesterday I hadn't even known existed.

Søren cleared his throat. "I admire my parents for knowing well enough to split up. It would have been worse for them to stay together out of some sense of obligation."

"That's a very generous way for you to think."

His expression softened. "It is the way I must think. I love my parents."

"I love my parents too." They would never act the way yours did, I wanted to tell him. I saw Mama's and Dad's faces. Every happy moment of my life ran together into a great cloud of time, floating away from me. They had aged, I realized, had lost something they would not recover in raising me. Had given it freely to me.

"Roxana." I was crying. Søren came around to my side of the table, put his hand over my ear, and pressed my face into his stomach. He smelled of smoke and soap. "Why are you crying?"

I liked that he did not tell me not to cry. I sniffled into his shirt, laughing at myself. "I'm sad about my parents' divorce."

He lifted my chin so that he could see my eyes. "I understand. Believe me, I understand. You must take my word for it. Someday, when you think of this pain, it will be with tenderness for yourself. You will see how the pain became part of you, a part you would not change for anything." His voice rushed into my skin, my bones.

"I'm scared that love isn't real."

"I felt that way, once. I remember. The feeling is not that love is not real, but that it is impossible." His eyes were kind, his hand was warm and dry under my chin.

"Yes," I whispered.

"I am older than you," Søren said, stroking my face. "I offer you what I have learned. Love is real. But it can end. That is what makes it precious."

I wanted to argue with him, to tell him that true love lasted forever. But I had no evidence to support my claim. There was only one way to silence the ringing in my head. I kissed his shirt and the top of his jeans and his belt buckle and lifted his shirt and found his lower stomach, flat and furry, and kissed him there. He made a sound in the back of his throat. His hands on my shoulders, he hooked his fingers under my arms and pulled me to my feet. Arranged me so that my neck, shoulder, and collarbone made an uninterrupted expanse of skin. His tongue on my throat took my balance, made me limp. His mouth oscillated between my collarbones.

He came up for air, holding me a little away from him. I felt his eyes travel up and down my body.

"You have no idea, do you?" Søren asked.

"Excuse me?"

"A lovely and amazing woman comes to town from a faraway land, into the life of a sad and lonely man. Over their first beer together, she tells him about an evening when she wanted to make love, but the man, the boy, could not deliver. An evening when she was sixteen years old and undoubtedly lovelier than any woman whom that boy will ever meet for the rest of his life. Then the beautiful young woman gets so drunk that she lunges at the sad and lonely man and he has to take her home and go very quickly home himself so that"—he dragged his tongue down my throat—"nothing bad happens."

I gasped between my legs.

"And then, the next day, the lovely woman spends all day with the lonely man, as if there is nowhere else she would rather be." He lifted my chin to access the skin under my jaw and with his tongue painted stripes from the tip of my chin to the top of my shirt.

"I didn't know you felt that way," I said, squirming wonderfully at his touch.

"Really? You did not intend to seduce me? I do not believe you."

We tumbled onto the floor, him landing on top, one knee propped between mine. Every few minutes he pulled away and peered at me as if he couldn't believe I was there. I couldn't believe I was, either.

On one such break I gathered my courage and pressed my hand against his erection. "Roxana," Søren warned, jolting.

"Kiss me." I held his gaze. When I moved my hand his eyes went soft. I unzipped his fly as his mouth worked against my neck and felt him through his underwear. We continued like that until Søren rolled away panting and stretched out beside me.

"I am not sure this is a good idea."

His doubt stung. "Why not?"

"Do not misunderstand me, Roxana. Of course I want to make love to you. Quite badly." His hand floated over my body. He forced it back to his side. "But we have already gone far past the realm of appropriate conduct on my part."

I smiled. "I won't tell on you."

Søren rolled onto his side and took my face in his hands. "Roxana, it is not just this. I already feel strongly for you. If we do this, it will not be the same after. I will want to be with you."

My veins lit up with blood and burned and sang. There was a fluttering in my chest. "So be with me." He glared at me, trying to resist. I took his hand and kissed it. "Please. I want you to. I want to be with you."

"Very well." He helped me to my feet. We walked to the bed and faced its white expanse.

"I'm not a virgin," I reminded him.

Søren looked at me tenderly. "It will be our first time."

So many times I had imagined how it would happen, how I would get to be in this place, the close place, the sex place, the space of nudity and bodies together, rotating in whichever face, but all I had to go on were movies and television and books, dreams and the playground with Hunter. Nothing real. None of it shimmered. But now it was me. I was the shimmering thing.

"I want you to take off my clothes."

Søren undressed me as carefully as he had at the museum, folding each piece of my clothing into a rectangle on the floor. I was there and I was not. I was in my mind, where I had so long dreamed this, taking orders from the shape of my fantasies. He took the bottom hem of my shirt in his hands and I automatically raised my arms. He unbuttoned my jeans and I stood so he could pull them down, which he did delicately, his hands lingering on my thighs.

When I wore only my green underwear and purple bra, Søren turned his back to me and removed his own clothes. I felt whited out, on the verge of an ecstatic disappearance. His shoulders were narrow, his arms long; his chest was sprinkled with dark hair. Had the hair on his head been the same color? He wore tiny light blue briefs.

I felt shy when he turned back around. "You look nice."

"Thank you." Søren lay down on the bed and pulled me up so that we faced each other and kissed my hands. "You are so beautiful."

Every part of my body he touched made it true. He licked my neck, my back, my stomach, down across the tops of my thighs. My vision flashed white. I couldn't catch my breath. I flattened my palms against his hot skin. We found our way back to the same embrace as before, arms around each other, our cheeks hollow from kissing.

His hand alit on my bra clasp. "May I?"

I nodded and my breasts fell from my bra, heavy and warm. I turned my head to hide my face under my hair. Then his hands were on me, gentle, and I never wanted any other kind of touch ever again.

"You're flushed," he murmured. "Blushing. This is the word, yes? Blushing."

"How can you tell?" I put my hands on his head, felt its heat, the busy movement inside. "You can't see my face—"

"Your chest." He lifted his head and pressed a palm above my breasts. "Look." The skin was mottled, uneven in tone. "Women always blush there," he breathed into my ear, biting it. "Take off your underwear."

I yanked my underwear down and kicked them into a green curve on the floor.

He stood and hooked his thumbs into the waistband of his briefs, looking away as if it hurt to be seen. The first man who had ever stood naked in front of me. I had seen pictures, films, of course, but this was different. How weirdly busy his parts were in comparison to the neat simplicity of a woman's body. I reached to feel the underside of his purplish head, wanting to tongue the fine seam that bisected it from tip to hilt, and Sylvie's face appeared, obscuring Søren's body, split by the wide grin that came with her high laugh. I could almost smell her lemons and honey.

Søren leaned into me, pushing Sylvie away. He climbed back onto the bed and held me, bunching the covers between us.

"Shh, little Roxana," he said. "Shh. You make me shake."

"I like that," I said, and we laughed.

He took a deep breath and kissed my body again, this time not stopping at my waist but going straight down to my pubic hair, pressing his face into it, his hands on my hips. I lay back, burning with shocks of fear as he put his mouth on me.

This was it, then. This was why everything had happened.

He lapped at me and I stared at the white ceiling, beginning to understand. Pleasure could be mine, could go from being untouchable as an ancient ship to something real that happened between my legs, passing from the mouth of a person I barely knew into my body. If I'd only known it was possible to feel this way, that the feelings I could conjure alone on my own body could enter this higher, finer evolution, every moment of my life might have been easier. Every pain bearable, every disappointment manageable.

I bucked and roiled under his tongue and lips and face, falling through a collapsing series of rooms, one into another after another after another, into a shapeless, wonderful bottomlessness. Like a scene from a cartoon. Clocks and books and furniture floated around me as I went down, down, down and eventually landed softly on some dim, warm floor.

I twisted my thighs around his face. My body took over, tightening and releasing a deep muscle, trying to trap his tongue, to keep him there forever. I'm on fire, I thought. My bones are cooking to dust. All of me melting, breaking down. Faster, faster. The world changing with my every shuddering breath. I climbed the wall of pleasure and looked out from my flaming body, my eyes wet and low in my head. I was alone, riding my body. Purple, I thought, purple. I saw purple smoke and I came in his mouth.

Søren laid his head on my belly and hugged my hips. He looked up at me. I drew him up and pressed my tongue into his mouth, wanting to taste myself, but he pulled back and bussed me chastely.

"Skat," he said, a soft sound.

"What does that mean?"

"Darling." He looked at me with big eyes. "Darling."

"Kiss me," I said, but he had already wiped on the pillowcase. He pecked me on the side of the face and turned away. I drew my knees up to my chest, suddenly sad. Was it over?

Søren took a bright foil square from the drawer in his bedside table, and opened it with his teeth. He held the base of his penis in his left hand and rolled the condom on.

"I've never seen somebody do that before," I told him. "You're good at it."

He shook his head, grinning. "Please, Roxana. You make me feel guilty."

Søren climbed on top of me, his erection dangling between us, and pressed until it slipped below and into me. I tried to remember what it had felt like to have Hunter there, but I couldn't. All I could think was his name. Søren. That black fullness, that no-space breath.

He was nimble and athletic, precisely maneuvering my body into shape after new shape. I closed my eyes, leaving myself in his power. Him on top, his pelvis pressing against my own. That sliding, burying feeling. Then I sat briefly astride him, and he was in me deeper than before, our bodies meeting and locking at a hidden intersection. He licked and bit at my breasts. He lifted my hips and slipped out, bouncing against my thigh. We laughed and I came down again, guiding him back in. Then he was on top once more, trapping me. Behind me, his hands sliding up and down my slick body. He groped and thrust.

"Skat," he warned.

"What," I panted.

His eyes bulged like a dog's. "Skat."

"Yes." I reared back. "Now." He looked at me helplessly, his mouth half open. "I'm ready. I'm ready!"

He made a guttural noise and convulsed against me. A little strangled yelp. His shuddering, shaking breaths. Power, I thought, power, power. My power.

Eventually Søren stood, put his underwear and T-shirt back on, and climbed back into bed. I buried my face in the cleft of his armpit. He smelled of clean linen.

He closed his hand in my hair, raised a lock to his lips, and kissed it.

"How beautiful you are," he whispered.

Beauty, why Sylvie always got what she wanted. I had spent so much time studying her, trying to figure out why life looked so effortless for her, how everything seemed to come so easy. Now I was on the other side of the mirror. I felt different, but I didn't understand any more than I did before.

He fell asleep with his hand still in my hair. I let my thoughts run all over his small, clean apartment until I lost consciousness.

I woke in a wash of white. White sheets, white comforter, white walls, white light streaming in from a white window. A steaming white cup of coffee appeared. Søren stood beside the bed, fully dressed in a green sweater and jeans, his head covered by his black cap.

"God morgen," he said.

"Hi." I drank the coffee gratefully. Now was the time to be careful. To not assume anything. After what we had done together, anything could happen.

"Did you sleep well?"

"Yeah." He reached toward my face. Despite myself I leaned into his hand. The movement exposed my whole right flank to the room's chill.

I held up the two little quilts on his bed, like dolls slept there.

"Søren, what's going on with your duvet?"

"What do you mean?" He blinked. "Those are normal dynes."

"Doonas?" I tried out the word.

"Dynes," he repeated. "Is it different in America?"

"Yes. We use one big blanket. It's cozy."

"I prefer two. That way, there is plenty of blanket for each person."

"But what if it's just one person?"

Søren kissed me on the forehead. "Then you have two blankets all to yourself."

"What time is it?"

"Early. It was not so late when we fell asleep."

Being with him was strangely ordinary, as if we had gone our separate ways after the bar and were now meeting again in the morning. I had no headache or soreness, only a raw twinge between my legs that sparked when I shifted.

I pulled my dyne over my breasts. "I'm not hungover."

"I am glad I was able to get you all of the water you required," Søren said. It took me a moment to recognize this as a joke.

Dust motes slipped through a wide stripe of sunlight. The room was bare, with nothing on the walls. Even the kitchen seemed empty. The doors of the wardrobe in the far corner were open, revealing the empty interior. I noticed two suitcases stacked neatly beside the door.

"Are you going somewhere?"

He put his coffee cup down on the bedside table and took my hands, feeling the cut in my palm. He turned my hand over and examined it. "How did this happen?"

I took my hand away. "It's not a big deal. Where are you going?"

"I thought it presumptuous to mention this last night, but now you must know. I am leaving Copenhagen today."

"For how long?"

He gripped my hands, avoiding my eyes. "A few months, at least. I must complete my thesis, or else I will not receive my degree. My professors have already given me two extensions. I have had so much difficulty in writing. My uncle offered me the use of his apartment in Jutland, and I accepted."

"Where is that? Your hometown?"

Søren shook his head. "I am from the island of Lolland, to the south, as I told you. Jutland is to the north. And it is not an island. My uncle lives in a place called Farsø. He is hiking in Norway until Christmas, so his home is empty." Søren stared at his thigh. "You cannot imagine how ashamed I am to have failed in this way. It is my last chance to finish my thesis. I want you to know—"

We hardly knew each other, I reminded myself, and cut him off. "Where did the coffee come from?"

"What?"

"Everything's all packed up. There's no coffeemaker. So where did it come from?"

Søren let go of my hands. "I made it before you woke. Then I cleaned the French press, took it apart, and packed it. Now it is in that suitcase." He pointed.

He was good at making things disappear. He could erase me. And then he would vanish, too. There was a way these things tended to go. Even if you had never done them before. Having sex with someone you had known for two days was rarely the start of a long relationship. If that was even what I wanted. I couldn't think of what that would be, just now. But I was determined not to be a stereotypical girl and get my feelings all hurt. And if they did get hurt I wouldn't show him. I wanted to act the right way, strong, as if I didn't care.

"I won't keep you. Let me get dressed. What's going to happen to your furniture?"

"It came in the apartment. Roxana. You are angry."

I spied my bra against the far wall. How had it ended up over there? My clothes were still in the neat pile Søren had made, but my underwear was nowhere to be found. I fetched the bra and leaned over to put it back on, trying not to think about how I must look, waddling around like that, my thighs tacking from the night before.

"Roxana, wait."

I ignored him, getting down on my hands and knees to check under the bed for my underwear. It wasn't there. I crawled toward the bedside table.

Søren produced my underwear from the pocket of his jeans and waved them, a little flag. "If you are looking for this, I have it. Although I am happy to watch you continue looking."

"Were you going to take them?"

"They smelled like you."

I looked up at the ceiling, willing my tears back down into their ducts. "You know, I understand that we barely know each other, but you're a lot older than me, and I don't know anyone in this country—"

"I wanted something to remember you by if you said no."

I sat down on the bed, the sheets crushing against my damp bottom. "What do you mean, if I said no?"

"This may sound crazy." Søren pushed my underwear back into his pocket. He looked at me somberly. "It is a romantic idea."

The foxwoman wasn't home when we went to collect my things.

"This letter explains to Birthe that your plans have changed," Søren said, showing me a sealed envelope. "I texted her this morning that you would be leaving."

When had he written the letter? Before I woke up?

"As far as she knows, you are undertaking a special internship with the company, one that will take you further afield than the ordinary program stops," he went on. "All is in order."

How could he have known I would say yes?

"Forgive me for taking the liberty," Søren said, reading my mind. "I would have not been upset if you had said no. I just so hoped that you would say yes. I wanted so badly for you to. I have been just miserable, terribly sad, for such a long time." He raised his eyes. "I wanted you so badly."

I had come from across the ocean, the antidote to his sadness. Søren was like no one I had ever met. I made him happy. I wasn't the only one this time. He wanted me too. Wanted me more. Enough to do something about it.

Life had a shape and an order. Magic was real. Mine. I kissed his mouth.

Søren left the letter beside the bowl of green apples. Robert appeared and followed us to the door, moaning as we dragged my bags into the hallway. When I turned to pull the door shut, he was prostrate, resting his head on his crossed paws. He glared at me like I had hurt his feelings.

FARSØ

1

WE CREPT PAST THE CITY'S TURNED BACK, INTO VERDANT HILLS. On the table that separated us, Søren held my right hand in his. Our palms were almost the same color. The lines and crevices made a map.

His way of looking at me reminded me of Mushi's steady gaze. At home, in another time, another life. My body now electric, elastic. Reborn.

He smiled at me. "Are you excited to see Jutland?"

"So excited. Thank you for bringing me with you."

He laughed. "Do not be. It is very boring. And you do not have to thank me." His expression turned serious. "Roxana, it is very important to me that you tell me if you become uncomfortable or if you want to go back to Copenhagen at any time. I am happy that you are coming, but also concerned."

"Why?"

"We are at different places in our lives. There is a big distance between eighteen and twenty-eight."

"Not to me," I said, sad that he felt a difference between us.

He looked into my eyes. "I do not want you to do anything you do not want. It is all right if you do not like Farsø when we get there. You can go back to Copenhagen and rejoin the program at any point. I will help you."

"I don't want to go back to Copenhagen. I want to go to Farsø. I want to be with you."

I had said the same thing that morning in his apartment as we sat together on his bed, bathed in hot light from the window, my underwear still in his pocket.

He had closed his eyes in the sun. "Truly?" He asked, as if this were a miracle.

"Truly." I took the last sip of my coffee.

He lifted my hand and kissed it. "To have you there will make me so happy."

"Søren, I don't have much money. I was counting on using the meal plan."

He pulled me onto his lap, into the fierce belt of heat, and slipped a hand between my legs, tracing the rim of my ear with the tip of his tongue. "I want to tell you a secret."

I couldn't look at him. I turned my face to the blank wall. Moving day, I thought.

"I am done with International Abroad Experiences. Yesterday was my last day in Copenhagen. I am not leading an excursion this summer but will work remotely as the program's bursar." His hand undulated against my crotch. "Jennifer Lindsey owes me. I understand her secret now, how she works."

Søren's hand pushed into me. My thighs slipped against each other, abraded by his pants.

"Oh," I said, more a sound than a word.

"I want to treat you," he murmured against my neck. "Let me treat you."

I thought about telling him that I had money too, but decided against it. I wanted this gift. "Thank you," I whispered into his mouth.

He groaned deliciously. "As if I have a choice. Everything is different, now. If I had not met you, Roxana. Oh, I can't bear the thought." He gave a little cry, which I stopped with my mouth.

"Say you'll come with me," he pleaded, his eyes as dark as deep water.

Søren, his voice, his hands, his body, or the empty bedroom at the foxwoman's. Boat picnics with people I didn't know or the chance to go to a place where no one would be able to find me.

I laughed. "I already said I want to go. Let's go."

He filled my mouth with his tongue.

Now that we were on the train away from Copenhagen, the enormity of what I had done filled me in a slow, steady drip. What was scary was also exciting. Right? Seeking reassurance, I lifted his right hand, unfolded the fingers away from the palm, and held it against my lips.

Søren took his hand away and wiped it on his thigh. "Please, we're in public."

"Sorry." I hadn't even opened my mouth. What was there to wipe? I took his hand again, held it next to mine. He gave me a small smile.

I fell asleep against the cold window and when I woke the train was running over water. A distant rim of tall white windmills revolved in slow motion, their stems sprouting straight from the surface of the ocean. The liquid light reflected in Søren's eyes.

I made an exaggerated gesture of waking, stretching my arms and yawning theatrically. I wanted to ask how it was possible, a train on the sea. "Søren?"

"Skat." He turned to me, calm focus gathered in a knowing half smile. I could cross water, bridge or no bridge, to a place I knew nothing about, where no one knew I was going and no one knew me. With him anything could happen.

I looked down at the table, my question gone.

Søren checked his watch constantly for the last half hour of the train ride, swearing under his breath.

"Are you all right?" I asked.

He threw up his hands. "We are terribly late. Our tickets promised we would arrive at eighteen-oh-five."

"What time is it now?"

"Twelve after the hour. Seven minutes late already."

"You're impatient, aren't you?" I laughed.

Søren turned a blue glare on me. "When I purchase a train ticket I enter into an agreement with the company. A guarantee that I will receive a smooth travel experience in exchange for my money. The arrival time is part of this agreement. When the train is late, the company breaks its agreement with its customer."

"Oh. I guess I never thought of it that way. The one time I took a long-distance train, it was six hours late." I reached for him, but Søren's hands were out of sight, in his lap. He did not produce them for me. Had I said something wrong? "Is everything okay?"

He scowled and checked his watch again. "How does anyone plan his day where you come from, if trains run as they like?"

The train entered the station, passing a gray sign with FARSØ in white font, and came to a complete stop. "Eighteen eighteen. Unbelievable. I will carry the bags."

"I can carry mine."

"You cannot lift that." He dismissed me, shouldering my duffel.

Outside, the sky and everyone and everything under it was white and low to the ground: the curving cobblestone roads, the narrow buildings that lined them, and the Danes themselves, whose shapes somehow receded rather than grew as we approached. I followed Søren down a sloped sidewalk and around a corner. Signs I couldn't read and one-story houses with small square yards. Farsø.

When I was eight and first allowed to start walking home from school alone, Mama sat me down for a lecture about the importance of maintaining a good internal map. *Always know where you are. Don't lose your way. Watch, learn, and remember the way back to where you came from. Don't get dreamy.*

I walked in Søren's footsteps, trying to track the turns. Down to the big street, take a left, walk two blocks, turn right, cross the pedestrian mall, cut down an alley. I soon gave up. It was impossible to pick out a landmark among all the unfamiliar shapes on this new street. I would have to reverse all the directions to get back to the station, anyway.

But I wouldn't be going back on my own, I reminded myself. Wherever I needed to go, Søren would take me.

He spoke over his shoulder. "Roxana, could you not do that, please?"

"What?"

"Walk behind me."

"Why?"

He sighed. "Please just do as I ask." It was a different voice, formal and distant, the one he had used when we first met. Two days ago. I reminded myself that I knew nothing about him, that I had chosen to come here with a stranger. It was frightening but also somehow comforting, a reminder that this was an adventure.

"Sorry."

I rushed to walk beside him. He interlaced his fingers with mine and absently pecked the top of my head. "Are you excited to see the apartment?"

I nodded.

"It is much nicer than my flat in Copenhagen."

His bedroom in Copenhagen, the walls and bed and cheap blond wood armoire all washed in the thrill of our bodies together. Would I ever see it again?

There was no one else on the street. We passed the tallest building I had seen yet, three stories high. A white tower adorned with a steel flourish marked its front corner. Three of the buildings on the street were banks with ATM terminals lodged in their front windows. There were housewares stores like the ones I had seen in Roskilde and shops with racks of clothing on the sidewalk.

"Here we are." Søren squeezed my arm. I had completely lost track of the route. He opened a glass door and we climbed a narrow flight of stairs to a white landing. At the top were two white doors. Søren went to the one marked Ø.

"Apartment zero?"

"Oh, the *eu*," He made a little guttural sound. "Perhaps a joke from my uncle."

A joke? "How does the mailman know where to bring letters?" The panicky feeling I had been smoothing away rose in tense vibration. I'll need to send letters, I thought. I'll have to. As if ever in my life I had sent a letter.

"Letters are addressed to the side of the landing."

"As in left or right?"

"Something like that." Søren flipped through his ring for an ornate gold key with smooth rolling teeth and a perfectly circular top. The key to apartment Ø.

He led me into a room with pale wood floors and a high white ceiling. Two tall windows showed the gray street in which we had so recently stood. A pale blue couch wedged beneath the window in the far corner faced a small television on a dark wood stand. I trailed him into the small hallway that connected the front room to two more—on the left a narrow blue-tiled kitchen, on the right a tiny brown bathroom. There was a toilet and a sink, but no tub or shower stall.

"Is there another bathroom? Where's the shower?"

Søren pulled a white hose down from a mount on the wall that faced the door and stood between the toilet and the sink. "Hold it over your head, get wet. Turn it off, wash. Turn it on again to rinse."

"Doesn't the toilet get wet?"

"Obviously."

"And you turn it on and off to wash? Instead of just leaving it on like a normal shower?"

"Instead of just leaving it on as in an American shower," he corrected. "Yes."

He turned off the light and left the room. In the dark I squinted up at the white hose, imagining myself with perpetually greasy hair.

I found Søren in the bedroom, a white box with a low bed made with two gray duvets and two small pillows. A thin rectangular window stretched across the hall behind the bed, directly above the headboard. That was it. Nothing on the walls. The only other furniture in the room was a small wood dresser and a freestanding closet with a semitransparent front made of a material I could mark with my thumbnail. I had seen the closet before, in the apartment of one of Sylvie's older friends in the city.

"What do you think?" Søren's neck was flushed from the effort of hauling the bags, a vein showing on his forehead. He had changed into a shirt I hadn't seen before, a dark blue button-down with a wide collar.

I went to him and kissed him. He stroked my neck with his thumb and pushed his tongue into my mouth, taking me out of the room, out of my thoughts, out of time. I unbuttoned his shirt and pants. There, again, was his shrunken white chest, the pale pink nipples like coins. The light fluff of ash hair leading down into his white briefs.

I thought of Hunter's boxers, blue-and-purple plaid. My happiness then, a tiny flinty thing, multiplied now, stronger.

I felt Søren's erection. He was not a little boy. His heart beat right there, under my hand. I kept my hand against the head as I trailed kisses across his cheek to his ear. Søren reached into my bra and twisted my left nipple hard. My vision hazed over. I felt like I might cry. My chest bloomed magenta, fluid and hot. The pain; another kiss.

With him behind me it was almost like being alone. My arms and legs moved in my periphery. I couldn't see his face, could only hear his voice mispronouncing my name. He hooked an arm over my belly and walked me over my edge with his fingers. I fell into the thick meatiness of my orgasm, viscera, tissue. When it was his turn, Søren pushed me onto my stomach, pulled out, and came on my back. Warmth oozed down the sides of my torso, a shock. He leaped from the bed and returned with damp toilet paper.

"Oh, Roxana." He wiped me off. "Was it too much?"

I felt as if I had slept for hours, but it was still light outside. Søren snored under his gray duvet. I slipped out of bed and walked naked to the living room, a ghost. The translucent curtains drawn over the front window glowed blue and silver. Across the street, the closed faces of buildings. I parted the cloth, pressed my body to the deliciously warm glass, and shut my eyes. How fine to be a body against a smooth plane.

When I opened them again, a man stood watching me in the street below. Only one floor up, I could see him as clearly as if we stood in the same room. He was tall, with curly black hair and a beard that grew down against his neck, around which a green bandanna was tied. In his right hand he carried a red cap. The legs of his khaki coveralls were dirty with muck, the metal toes of his boots scuffed. His eyes were gray, his thoughtful expression some kind of smile.

Step away from the window, I thought, but I did not. I stared back until the man dropped his gaze and walked away.

I put on my sweatpants and Søren's discarded T-shirt to unpack while he slept. There were no hangers in the closet, so I folded my clothes into the top two drawers of the dresser. I stacked my books on an edge of the coffee table between the two couches, set my toiletries on the shelf in the bathroom, joined our toothbrushes in a glass on the edge of the sink, and arranged my notebook and pens on the table in the kitchen. I found the large heart-shaped rock Sylvie had given me at the bottom of my backpack and left it there.

Søren's uncle had left a quart of milk, a package of spreadable butter, and some cucumbers and tomatoes in the fridge. I took the tomatoes out and put them on the counter. In the cabinet above the counter were a few cans of sardines and a bag of dried yellow beans. A dark loaf of rye bread sat inside the wooden breadbox next to the sink. I was hungry, but not for any of these things. I thought about trying to make a meal of them, but I had no idea how. Besides, Søren would probably want to go out to eat when he woke up. Would the bars in Farsø would be like the ones he had taken me to in Copenhagen? I liked being a person who went out to bars.

I banged around the kitchen, closing cabinets and rear-ranging mugs, hoping Søren would rouse. When no sound came from the bedroom, I drew a tall glass of water from the porcelain sink and went into the front room. I watched out the window, wondering if the bearded man would return. The idea both frightened and excited me.

He did not. I turned on the TV.

There were only four channels. The first was a scrolling line of text on a black background. The next was a news broad-cast narrated by two men whose Danish sounded like anxious muttering to me. They cut to a diagram of complicated farm equipment and then to a clip of an old lady talking in front of a giant tire. The third channel aired a Danish sitcom. A man and woman in big sweaters had a comical fight, clinked beer bottles, and made up, earning appreciative canned laughter.

The last channel was showing an American movie with Danish subtitles, a science fiction epic about a family that travels to a faraway planet. Scientist parents and their three children, a seventeen-year-old daughter and fourteen-year-old boy and girl twins, all born on the spaceship. The parents homeschool—spaceshipschool—them and the twins are science geniuses. The elder girl plays musical instruments, paints, writes poetry, and dances for several hours a day, in a studio that transforms to meet her needs.

The sixth member of their family is an android designed by the parents. He is smart, funny, and very handsome. Exactly like a person in every way, except that he doesn't have any fingernails or toenails. He does everything the family cannot. He repairs the ship's exterior, anchored to the hull by his magnetized feet. He navigates the ship by speaking to the system in its special language. While the family sleeps, he tends the hydroponic farm. He is programmed to care deeply about the family. He knows this and in an early scene gives a speech about understanding that the sensations he feels are close to but not the same thing as love.

Unlike the rest of her family, the elder daughter has always struggled with her relationship with the artificial man. She finds his childlike curiosity creepy and turns away from the sight of his nail-less hands and feet. The android doesn't have a name. Everyone just calls him the android.

As their ship nears their destination, the twins develop special powers. The girl becomes telekinetic, the boy telepathic. Their parents disappear into the laboratory with the twins to test their powers. Left alone, the elder girl and the android discover a shared love of cinema and then of each other. But can it truly be love when the android is not a real person? In a moving scene, the android convinces her of the authenticity of his ardor.

"I feel as if I have been rebuilt with all-new parts," he tells her as they lie together on her bed, holding hands. "Some so tender and precious it is as if they have come from your body, my love. When I feel this way, I think that I am no more artificial than any lover in the long span of human history."

Immediately after this confession, they kiss. The elder daughter is happy. The android says that he is too. She falls asleep in his arms, and his body glows blue, lighting her face.

The next morning, the android loses control of the ship and it crashes onto a nearby planet. In the moments before impact, the android covers the elder daughter with his body, protecting them both. The twins' powers do not save them. Everyone dies except for the elder girl and the android. She watches him pull the bodies from the wreckage.

"I am very sad, a sensation I have never experienced before," he says, holding her as she cries. "I want to power down and never reboot, and I would, if not for you."

The planet is heavily forested and seemingly uninhabited. The android holds his mouth on the girl's in a long kiss, filtering the air for her until he determines that the atmosphere can sustain human respiration. They bury the family and leave the wreckage in search of help, crossing dense woods full of strange friendly animals but no people. The girl is inconsolable. The android gathers food and builds a shelter for her every night. He makes her smile by playing old films on the screen in his chest.

Sylvie and I had gone to see the movie the previous October. We each had a crush on the actor who played the android, a Swiss man with a perfect face and ropy limbs. The actress who played the elder daughter had never been in a movie before. They plucked her from some town in North Dakota for her big dark eyes and open face. This was the kind of thing, Sylvie and I agreed, that was always happening to other people, never to us.

I loved the movie from the first scene, but Sylvie hated it. She ticked off the film's flaws on her fingers as we walked into the long twilight, wet fall leaves squeaking underneath our feet. It was a waste of the actor's talent, the special effects were ridiculous and stupid, the plot made no sense, she complained. "At least he looked super hot," Sylvie said. "He has Egon Schiele hands. Did you notice that?"

. I nodded, but I had no idea what she was talking about.

"How are you supposed to feel sorry for people in a space-ship? And why did they introduce the kids with the special abilities if they were just going to kill them off?"

Sylvie loved to fight and hated to lose. Given an oppor-tunity, she was happy to argue me into exhaustion and claim victory by default. I wanted to protect the movie, so I kept my thoughts to myself, voicing minor critiques I didn't actually have: the actress who played the scientist mom was annoying; the spaceship was ugly.

"God, what a bore," Sylvie said as we got into her car.

Tinted orange by the streetlights, the raindrops on the windshield slid one by one into the wipers' trough. There was no rule that we had to love the same things.

"What are you watching?"

I jumped. Søren stood behind the couch. How had I not heard him come into the room? On the TV was one of the twins' experiments. The boy has read the girl's mind without permission. She traps him naked in a net and watches him struggle.

I picked up the remote and turned off the television. "Nothing."

Søren rubbed his face, yawning. "You must be hungry. And bored." He bent over the couch and gave me an upside-down kiss. "Already I have been a bad host."

Three days removed from home and everything felt like make-believe. I imagined the face of the bearded man in the street. He did not leer or gape. He saw me.

"Don't be silly," I told Søren. "I haven't been bored at all."

For dinner Søren made open-faced sardine, tomato, and cucumber sandwiches on rye bread. He produced a bottle of red wine and poured it into two short tumblers. We ate at the kitchen table, the never-ending day beaming through the windows, everything new and delicious. Afterward, we brushed our teeth, washed our faces, and went into the bedroom.

Beside the bed Søren stripped to his underwear. The sun's glow had taken on an otherworldly violet quality and in the weird light, Søren looked otherworldly too. I undressed, a new smell rising from my crotch. Søren peeled back the covers and I climbed in. He covered me with my duvet and got under his own, separating us with a margin of mattress.

"You don't have to sleep naked just for my benefit."

"I always sleep naked," I lied.

"Come here."

For a moment I thought we would have sex, and I was excited to do it twice in one day, to see what that was like. But when I scooted closer, he simply wrapped his arms around me and closed his eyes, cocooning me with his body.

I had always had trouble falling asleep. Yet I was gone that night before I could recognize my exhausted, confused happiness, so delicate it could crumble under my touch.

2

SØREN BUTTONED A GRAY SHIRT, STEPPED INTO A PAIR OF
DARK GREEN PANTS, AND THREADED A BROWN LEATHER
BELT THROUGH THE LOOPS, HIS HANDS BRIGHT AGAINST
THE DARK FABRIC. It was a cold morning; I didn't know what
time. I watched him for a long while before I said hi.

He bent and brushed his lips against my cheek. "Good
morning, little sleeping Roxana."

"Are you going somewhere?"

"The library." I looked for a nonexistent clock. White walls,
white light. "To work on my thesis. Why we came here. Remember?"

I sat up and the duvet fell away, exposing my breasts. "Will
you be back soon?"

Søren covered me. "In the evening, around six. A true
workday."

He pressed his lips to my forehead, another brief, dry kiss—
a peck, now I understood what that was—and left again, stopping in the doorway. "Are you upset?"

"No."

He sighed. "You are."

"I'm not! Of course I understand you have to go work. I
just thought we were going to spend the day together."

Søren put a hand to his head. "I am sorry, Roxana. I thought this might be a problem, and I apologize. Perhaps—"

He was going to say that I should go back to Copenhagen. "It's fine! Just tell me how to get to a restaurant or a coffee shop or something. I'll go exploring."

Søren winced. "I must tell you." He withdrew the large key ring from his pocket and dangled it from his left hand. "That will not be possible. There is only one key. And I need it."

"What do you mean?"

"The door downstairs is open, always," he said. "But the door to the apartment locks automatically, to secure it." He smiled at me. "To secure you. One must have a key to enter."

"Can you get another key made?"

"I will try. But for now there is only one."

It was Tuesday. Søren jiggled his knee, looking pained.

"I must keep my work schedule. I am behind. I have not been productive for several weeks, with life in Copenhagen being what it is." He put the keys back in his pocket, avoiding my eyes. "Things must be different here."

Then why had he brought me? I wanted to ask but didn't. "Okay," I said, not meaning it.

Søren sighed and sat back down on the bed. "I apologize, Roxana. It has been such an event, meeting you. I have felt happy, powerful even, for the first time in so long. For the first time ever, perhaps. It seems so natural to have you here with me. Almost as if it has always been this way."

"I think so too!" I said automatically, my mind working. Søren was complex I thought. He had many layers. I wouldn't immediately understand him. I had to be patient to have what I wanted, to be here with him. Everyone always said relationships were hard work.

"Unwittingly I have involved you in my oldest fantasy," he said in a low voice, looking at me sheepishly. "You see, since I was a small boy, I have had one dream of adult life. I saw myself working, although I hardly knew what that work could be. All it meant was that I must leave home, my most beloved place. But in my fantasy I did not leave my home empty. I had within it a lover who waited for me. A special woman occupied by her own affairs. Keeping the home fires bright, as they say in your country."

Oh. Under the quilt I relaxed my legs. Opened them.

"This dream has been with me so long I forgot it was mine alone. And now I have subjected you to it. I am sorry. I will not work today but find a way to make another key. Of course you should not be trapped here." He nodded firmly, as if accepting the right course of action despite his own desires.

I put my hand on his shoulder. "Go to work."

He lifted an eyebrow. The light from the window made his eyes translucent.

"I like your dream," I said. "I want to make it come true."

It felt simple, as if I held the fantasy itself in my hand, a blind cephalopod in need of my protection. This was a kind of bravery I could manage.

"You are certain?"

Before I could answer he covered my mouth with his and kissed me until my assent was a moan. Then he rose. "You are wonderful. Wonderful!" He sped out of the room and returned with a thick older-model laptop. "This is my computer, my first one," Søren explained, placing it beside me on the bed. "It is yours while you are here. So you can find the Internet."

I thanked him, eyeing the latch that held screen and keyboard closed.

"Shall I show you how to turn it on? No, of course not, you are much more intelligent than I." He hastened back to the door. "And so beautiful. I am so lucky! Until this evening!"

He beamed at me from the threshold. I blushed and blew a kiss, which he caught. Then the front door shut hard.

I lay quite still, trying to recapture the sleepiness I had felt in my first waking moments. Maybe I would feel better if I let the day get a little older, curled up under the covers and induced a nice dream. First I was cold, and all the covers couldn't warm me, not even when I layered Søren's duvet over my own and pulled both over my head. Underneath the light was pink and thick.

Then I became frantically hot. The tang of my sweat lodged in my nose. I had last shaved the day before graduation. I fingered the fuzzy hair that had grown in the ten days since and then held my hands under my nose. My sweat was vinegar sharp. Three sticky dried lines demarcated the creases between the rolls of my stomach. I scraped their whitish stuff up with my fingernails and rubbed it between my fingertips until it dissolved into oil.

Farther down was another smell, one I sensed rather than inhaled. The place between my legs. A force, an idea.

I had never settled on a name for it. Mama, ever a nurse, hated the use of "vagina" as a blanket term for the urethra, clitoris, and labia minora and majora. Nicknames like "pee-pee" and "private place" were even worse.

"Your vagina is inside you," she told me when I was very little. "You can't touch it without reaching inside, and you don't pee out of it, and the parts of you on the outside are not your vagina. They have their own names."

The sex ed books she gave me were written by doctors. One had an exhaustive chart of "common slang terms for primary and secondary sexual characteristics," which confused more than helped. Maybe they were antiquated; to this day I've never heard anyone refer to a woman's "honeypot" or a man's "peter." Their pages were filled with scientific drawings of genitalia interpolated with commonsense explanations of swelling breast buds and involuntary erections.

If these pictures embarrass you, one book suggested, *why not draw polka dots, zebra stripes, or other designs on them in colored pencil? Being a little silly will help you to feel more comfortable with these images, and with your own body.* But I couldn't draw on the illustrations. They looked like faces to me.

I liked the books, their dorky friendliness, but they didn't answer my questions about my own body. What about the excretions on the crotch of my underwear at the end of each day? The books did not explain the white goo that sometimes appeared there. They did not unlock the secrets of the yellowy mucus that occasionally clung in ropes between my body and underpants, nor did they teach me to divine the meaning of the rusty pre- or postperiod clumps streaked with veins of purplish tissue. How to determine whether a given intimate paste was a yeast-infected "yellow-gray" and "foul smelling" as the books warned? My body always smelled interesting to me; even when my stink was unpleasant, it was mine. How could they expect me to call any of these substances I generated discharge?

There was no hope of going back to sleep. I flung off the duvets, walked naked into the bathroom, carefully locking the door with its latch mechanism, like the one at the foxwoman's, and turned on the dangling showerhead, immediately spraying myself in the face with a torrent of freezing water. I screamed.

The shower took the better part of an hour. I turned it on, wet my hair, turned it off, frothed the shampoo against my skull, realized my hair wasn't really wet, turned it on again, added more shampoo, turned it off, poured a handful of minty liquid soap into my palm and rubbed it against my body, turned it on again, attempted to rinse. Repeated. The cold water made my skin so slick it was impossible to tell if I had rinsed away the soap. The water warmed only when I finally gave up on my hair.

"Wash between your legs," Mama used to say when she bathed me. Or sometimes: "Wash your bunny." That was what she and Dad settled on so he could bathe me without embarrassment—"bunny," a compromise Mama accepted because it was so cute. I liked it because I liked bunnies generally, but even when I was tiny I understood the difference between my bunny and actual bunnies. When it was his turn, Dad helped me shampoo and soap up my flat torso and then looked politely away.

"Okay, your bunny now," he'd mutter.

The last days rose around me, a cloud, as I washed my bunny for the first time in Søren's apartment. I stood engulfed in a new smell, that part of myself newly and rightly used, until it diffused under the water, hot at last.

Sylvie had found the long violet linen dress with the cap sleeves for me in a store called the Blue Bell. When I emerged from the dressing room in it, she gave me a glittering smile. "You look so fantastic, Rox. You look like a motherfucking fox and a half."

I twirled in front of the mirror, showing her the way the skirt inflated like a giant tulip, and even the shopkeeper came back to admire me.

I wore it that first day alone in Jutland, with all the jewelry I had brought with me. Rose-gold stud earrings, five neon Bakelite bangles, a metal ring that looked like a big cat climbing up my left middle finger. I smeared my lips with red gloss, tidied the room, made the bed, scooped up our dirty clothes from the floor. Domesticity!

The hamper was in the closet, under Søren's seven hanging shirts and a crunchy gray garment bag that held a three-piece gray suit. When I opened it, the bag released a breath, the last memory of a missing person, and I knew that a woman—Mette, Søren's ex?—had put it carefully away. I put my hand inside the jacket, feeling as if I were reaching into a body: the entire suit was lined in creamy salmon satin. It bore a hand-sewn label: SAVILE ROW.

I zipped the bag back up and lifted the hamper out of the closet, revealing a gray rectangle beneath. I tried to lift this, too, to see if there was anything under it, but it was surprisingly heavy, a metal lockbox with a complicated lock. The lid wouldn't budge.

I dropped my clothes in the hamper and went into the kitchen, where Søren had left a French press with ground coffee already in the bottom of the carafe. There was even a note in his hand, which was more extravagant than I had imagined. Tall loops and lingering lines. *Boil water in kettle and fill to top line.* No salutation, no signature.

All day I made myself busy. I swept the apartment, gathering a palmful of golden grit I threw out the open window. I cleaned the toilet, wiped down the sinks. I took the racks and drawers out of the refrigerator, scrubbed them in hot water, and reorganized all the food in the fridge. I straightened the scanty towels and sheets in the cabinet outside the bathroom.

All day I forced my thoughts from the gray box, from what was inside. This is where I'm living now, I thought. It felt like it would go on forever. That I could.

We quickly established our routine. I woke to the sounds of Søren's toilette and watched him finish dressing in underwear, socks, pants—the dark green jeans seemed to be his favorite— and a T-shirt beneath a button-down.

Some mornings we had coffee together, but mostly he went straight from the bedroom to the door. "Bye, skat," he called as he stepped out the door.

"Bye!" I waited for the sound of the door, sealing me inside. I was still waiting for a key of my own, but this seemed a distant concern. From the windows Farsø looked dull, almost static, while the inside of the apartment had become a world unto itself. My world. When he was gone, I brought my cup of coffee and glass of water back into the bedroom and climbed back into the warm bedclothes. Any pleasant time over coffee was a window that closed, creating the room of my hours alone, my real day, which began only after he left.

The first thing I did was head to the toilet to shit copiously. I couldn't remember a time in my life when I had been so regular. By the fourth day it had become a gleeful ritual. Waking and pouring coffee, yogurt, oatmeal down my throat, waiting for the ingredients to do their work. Filling up, emptying out, flushing it all down. Sitting there, I was lost again in the world of my body. Søren and I often made love in the night, one of us nudging the other to wakeful action and falling immediately back to sleep after. Some mornings I wasn't sure if I had dreamed it until I went to the toilet and my unwashed crotch and armpits and feet presented themselves. There was no one to rush me out of the bathroom. I could stay as long as I wanted.

The lunches I made for myself were haphazard and insubstantial. An apple, a single carrot. More yogurt, more oatmeal. Leverpostej, the pork liver pâté Søren bought every week at the slagterbutik, the slaughter boutique, the butcher shop. Slices of cucumber or tomato. Pieces of the ubiquitous rugbrød, the rye bread, toasted in the oven and spread with butter. Each ingredient sped my efficient bowels for an afternoon encore. I had never been any good at dieting, but here I was barely hungry. All I wanted was coffee and air and my thrilling secret life. I waited to become smaller.

I was an animal with elemental needs. After I ate and shat I went back into the bedroom to bring myself off in bed or on the floor, usually more than once. I had always masturbated, but never as much as I did in the apartment. Before I had been furtive, quick, doing it only when I had to, in the shower or in bed right before sleep. At home I rarely came, falling asleep with my hand still on my crotch and waking to my scented fingers.

Now my body was live. It could take me anywhere I wanted to go, and I wanted to go everywhere. The space between my legs became the center of everything, opened like a peeled grapefruit. I soaked my underwear so thoroughly that I had to change after or let it dry for hours against me, birthing another new smell.

I put my fingers inside my body and then in my mouth. I wiped my palm against my labia and rubbed it across my face. I imagined Søren doing it. Hunter. Other men whose names I had forgotten or never known in the first place, nerve magic sparking from head to toe, jumping up and down my spine. I became expert at conjuring it, walking myself right up to the moment when I was about to come, and then begging off by pulling my pubic hair or pinching my thighs. Or I let myself come but didn't stop, again, again. I did it until my legs shook and the room loosened, until I was dehydrated and bright shocks sparked at the corners of my vision. I came right on our sheets and wiped my face on the pillows.

3

WHEN I TURNED SØREN'S COMPUTER ON, INCOMPREHENSIBLE WHITE PRINT APPEARED ON A BLACK SCREEN, MS-DOS OR DANISH OR BOTH, CEDING EVENTUALLY TO THE DESKTOP. The keyboard was different, too. I had to pay close attention when I e-mailed my parents.

Hey Roxie, How's it hanging in Gay Paree? Love, Dad

Dear Dad,

Everything is going well. Today Sylvie and I went to see a really old church and tomorrow we will take an overnight trip to Versailles. I tried a new French food called quenelles, kind of a yummy paste-ball, which the guide said are a poached mixture of fish, bread crumbs, and eggs. It sounds kind of gross, but it was really good.

Miss you,
Roxana

I imagined Dad and Mama squinting at the e-mail, sounding out the strange word.

Søren had the Parisian Experience schedule memorized.
He walked me through the tours I was missing, the sights
I wasn't seeing. The Paris tour leader was a woman named
Signe, whom Søren admiringly called a terrific bitch. I liked
the image of Sylvie struggling along behind Signe on some
picturesque lane.

I thought I would feel bad about lying to my parents,
but I didn't. If I felt anything it was an echo of the impulse
to feel bad, a memory of the idea that lying was wrong. I was
just telling a different version of the truth, one that spurred
me into fantasies about how far my lies could carry me. I
saw myself pregnant, with a child even, Søren's uncle's apartment made cozy with colorful curtains. A pot on the induction
stove, a Pack 'n Play, an elegant wooden mobile from one of
the housewares shops. Søren read in an imaginary armchair
as a child with curly brown hair took his first steps, babbling
Danish babyspeak, and there I was at the laptop, still lying to
my parents about France.

Hi Mama and Dad,

Today we went to Reims to see the famous Gothic cathedral, where thirty-three French kings were crowned.
Wow, it was so beautiful! Sylvie thinks that Notre-Dame
is prettier, but I think it's Reims all the way.

By the time Søren got home from the library each night, between six and seven o'clock, I had transformed myself again.
I wiped down the surfaces, did my dishes, washed vegetables,
chopped them, put on a nice outfit. For dinner, Søren made
hearty dishes—delicious, simple food. My favorite was tomato

sauce with ground beef over pasta. On the table he kept the
sauce and the pasta in separate bowls. Leftovers went into the
fridge like that too, separately, in discrete containers, one of
pale starch, one of thick gravy. That was what Søren called
pasta sauce: gravy.

Søren cooked beef patties fried in butter. Bacon and eggs.
Frikadeller, the pork meatballs he called the national dish of
Denmark. Everything was served with potatoes, tiny ones he
brought home in clear plastic sacks or fist-size yellow ones from
the grocery store. One night he boiled pigs' hearts with prunes
in cream, a dish that looked like purple baseball mitts. My least
favorite was a kind of soup of boiled chicken and canned white
asparagus spooned into tartlet shells, whose texture reminded
me of drool. But I ate whatever Søren put in front of me. I felt
so adult standing there with him in the kitchen, drinking red
wine from a low glass.

"How was your day?" I asked, like some woman in a movie.

"All right," he pronounced grimly. "I did some work. Not
a waste, I guess."

"Good!" I arranged my features into what I imagined was
wifely transmuted pride. I experimented with pet names for him,
tried "darling," "honey," "my sweet," but none of them stuck.

Sometimes I tried to broach the topic of excursions, but
Søren didn't seem hear these inquiries. He just kept speaking,
returning always to his thesis argument and his terror that it
didn't make sense.

"My premise is that Ash and other African American writers working in the genre position otherness as a confrontation
between known and unknown that is designed to unsettle the
imperialist, colonialist, and racist implications of the traditional
othering relationship in which other is object and the narrative

is controlled by a hegemonically appointed subject. I have good support from Fanon, but it doesn't work entirely because he was a psychiatrist, not a theorist. Perhaps I can use Lacan, but I don't know if that's a good idea."

He smiled weakly. Relieved, I smiled back. His face fell.

"That was a joke! A terrible joke! Because Lacan was a psychoanalyst."

"Oh. Sorry."

He swore in Danish and put his face in his hands. "For fanden. What the hell am I going to do?"

I stepped closer, put my glass of wine on the counter, squeezed his shoulder so he would know it wasn't his fault.

Most nights he rallied after this nadir. Apologized, kissed me. Told me how happy it made him, knowing I was here in his uncle's apartment while he was out working. Raised his eyes to the ceiling, called, "Thank you, God I do not believe in, for sending this beautiful and patient woman to the saddest man in Denmark!" And he laughed and laughed and I did too.

One night he lifted his head, but instead of speaking to God he spoke to me.

"Roxana, you are my only joy. If this bastard text gets written, it will be thanks to you." He slipped his hand over mine. "So, given that you are its inspiration, can I ask you to read some of my work?"

His muse! "Sure, but I don't know if I can help—" His inspiration.

He was already withdrawing his laptop from his bag, lifting its screen. "Just read, please." He kissed the top of my head, wrapped his arms around my shoulders. "I have translated a bit into English for you. I need your help! Thank you thank you thank you! Tak tak tak!"

He kissed my ears, my cheeks, my forehead. Over and over again, like a little boy. I held very still, wanting it to last as long as possible.

The recently announced death of the author Violet Ash (born Violet Alva Marie Ash in Daly City, California, US, in 1940, died in La Grande, Oregon, US, in 2005) offers a grand opportunity to revisit her novel of 1980, *Spirit Home*. Despite the novel's moderated form, one cannot help but feel that the book is the arguably most emblematic fictional work of the African American author of science fiction. The novel is set in early 1980s US, in an era before identity politics had infiltrated intellectual discourse, before the insistence upon multiculturalism had reached Europe, and shortly after the television show *Roots* reached our screens and redefined the popular cultural narrative of African American experience significantly.

The document was ninety-five pages long. I looked up into Søren's face.

"What do you think so far?" He asked.

I barely understood it. "It makes me want to read her book."

He ran out of the room and returned with a paperback. The cover was long gone, leaving the yellowed title page to do its job.

I flipped to the first page, scanned it, and handed the book back to Søren. "Cool."

He didn't take it. "Aren't you going to read it?"

"Right now?" Didn't he know that was just what you did when people talked about a book they liked—say you wanted to read it, even if you didn't?

He smiled. "Is there something else you are doing with your days?"

I stared at him.

"Do not be a child about it. Perhaps it is for another time, for you." He took the book out of my hands.

I snatched it back. "I'm not a child."

He kissed me on the forehead and took it away again. "It is all right, Roxana. I was only joking. Do not read the book if you do not wish to."

"I do, though. I do." I was close to tears.

He dropped the book into his bag. Closed his laptop and took it away too.

"It is not your job," he said. "It is mine. Perhaps you can read more later. If you want. I am interested in your perspective." He stretched, cracking the tendons in his neck. "Oh, Roxana, if only I were you! I would understand these things much better."

"I haven't even started college yet."

"Yes, but you are an actual American. You have lived my subject." He tilted his head thoughtfully. "It is amazing to me that the immigrants in this country do not educate themselves about the African American experience. Perhaps if they read about the suffering caused by inflexible ideology, they would be more compassionate to the culture that has welcomed them here."

"What do you mean?" On the table my hand leaped nervously. I pressed my other on top to calm it.

"Immigrants come here and they want to tell us what to do. They act as if the state and its society are theirs to change and alter. As if it is not dangerous to do so. As if social welfare is not a fragile construct that can break under too much pressure. Pretending that religion is a force as real as the economy or the weather. Bringing the problems of their countries here. You know, Roxana, the system will not hold indefinitely. We cannot just take and take all the world's unwanted people. Our system is designed to help us."

"But if they are immigrants to Denmark, they are Danes," I said. "Like if you came to America to live, you'd be an American."

His face creased. "Which I would never do."

"Oh," I said, surprised that it hurt. He didn't notice.

"Denmark is the oldest monarchy in Europe. Our flag is one thousand years old. I know my own lineage back to the thirteenth century. Yes, there are immigrants, and yes, they can come and live here, but they are not Danes, and they must understand that. If they wish to be, they must work to earn the honor of citizenship. It is a privilege, not a right, and our system does not work if everyone does not believe in the same thing. We are supposed to be the happiest country on Earth. I am sure you have heard this. But how can such a happiness exist if there is discord and meaningless violence and a minority that insists on head rags for women and funny hats for men and Dark Age social policy?"

His voice steadily increased in volume until he was almost shouting, his hands rigid and flat on the table. Sometimes he got like this when we watched the news. One shot of a woman in a hijab or a municipal building repurposed as a mosque agitated him for hours. He peppered me with unanswerable rhetorical questions: Why did they insist on being to be so different? What were we to do if they "had their way," three words that grew more darkly threatening every time he repeated them?

It was the conversation we had begun at the bar. I felt ashamed for not arguing with him more forcefully then. His irrational anger at immigrants confused me. Søren was clearly a smart person. A loving person, at least to me, and I was different from him, wasn't I? I thought everyone—outside of overt racists, the kind of people I would be able to spot at a distance, the kind of people I was sure I had never met—knew that hatred and prejudice were wrong and tolerance and acceptance good. Those were the virtues that had been drilled into me for as long as I could remember. The first Thanksgiving and Anne Frank and the Underground Railroad and the melting pot and cotton plantations and Japanese-Americans in internment camps and the Trail of Tears and Auschwitz. After all that history, what else could a person think other than that it was obviously better to be good than bad to other people? It was simple. But Søren made it seem complicated and foreign, outside my realm of experience, and I was unsure how to disagree. Who was I to tell him what was good for Denmark?

In third grade my Earth science partner, Christina, was a sweet chubby girl from a big Greek family. In the spring we were given an owl pellet to dissect, and in the little clot of fluff and dust she found a vole skull that won us great praise. To celebrate, Christina invited me over that weekend to bake the Orthodox Easter bread tsoureki in her immaculate blue-and-white kitchen. When I arrived, premeasured ingredients were laid out on the counter in glass bowls, like on television, and oldies played softly from a wall-mounted yellow radio. Christina donned a clean red apron and handed me an identical one. I waited for her mother to appear, but Christina preheated the oven herself and proofed the yeast with warm water and sugar. I was impressed. At my house, I wasn't even allowed to turn on the stove.

We boiled Spanish onion skins and vinegar into a thick syrup that dyed a dozen eggs bloodred and kneaded flour into dough until our arms were white to our elbows. We wove the dough into plaits, pushing the red eggs into the interstices, and painted them with beaten yolk until they gleamed. "My mom says she feels like she's setting stones when she does this," Christina told me, which made sense, as her parents' union had joined two large Greek Orthodox jeweler families. Then Christina opened the oven, a terrifyingly hot black hole, and I slid the heavy baking sheets onto the spotless wire racks. Afterward, my unburned hands felt like miracles.

While we waited for the tsoureki, we played Go Fish with a deck of colorful, oversize cards and ate hard buttery cookies. I won again and again. Once the tsoureki was out of the oven, Christina set a second timer—the bread had to cool for an hour—and we switched to Uno. She won once, and then I won twice.

When the second bell rang, Christina took a tall thin bottle of nectarine nectar from the refrigerator, measured it into purple plastic cups, and cut great eggy slices onto two light blue plates. I didn't care for the taste of the bread, but everything else was wonderful, the kitchen, the glass bowls, punching the dough, coloring the eggs, playing cards, winning, sweet juice from an exotic bottle. A lifetime of afternoons spent baking in Christina's airy kitchen blossomed in my imagination. She would show me more Greek delicacies, I thought, build me up eventually to pastitsio and moussaka. But that never happened. In the languid breeze of classroom friendships Christina and I drifted to distant acquaintance almost immediately after that day. Still. When Søren got on one of his rants, I thought about that afternoon with Christina and her tsoureki, a visit to a place where things were different and more interesting, richer, exciting because of difference. Like my life now, I thought. Far from home, in a world where nothing belonged to me. Was that what Søren was afraid of—that what was familiar would become unrecognizable to him? Things like that came from inside, not outside.

Søren grew quiet. I looked up to see him gazing at me softly, his fury over. "Come here, little Roxana," he said, holding out his hands, and I climbed into his lap. He wrapped his arms around me and rocked gently. "I'm sorry I become such an awful man," he murmured. "You're the best thing in the world."

Time eddied and spent us, Søren's dry kisses good-bye in the morning and his cock sluicing in and out of me at night, onions and pork collecting in grease at the edge of the plate, the late morning headache I was never sure came from too much coffee or too little. I had always wanted to get to this part of a relationship—a relationship, that was what I had now, a real and prolonged series of encounters that stretched into a sturdy lanyard I could dangle around my neck or from the pull of a zipper—when the fear that what we had was only a glorious encounter would give way to the assurance of continued desire. I just wanted it to keep going, for everything to keep going.

One night in the second week we were eating, normally, and I was smiling at Søren, beaming, so glad to see him after our day apart, thinking about how lucky I was, when he calmly put down his fork and stared at me.

I beamed harder, sure loving words were headed my way.

"Jesus! Close your mouth!"

Søren laughed after he said it, as if I might realize my own boorishness and laugh too. Apparently I had poor table manners. Worst of all, he explained, was the sound of my chewing, my classless way of letting my mouth hang open while I did it. Correcting it seemed impossible. No matter how hard I tried to focus on moving my jaw sedately behind closed lips, I lost my concentration a few bites in.

"It is just disgusting," Søren said, shaking his head.

The scene repeated itself night after night. I forgot myself, apologized. Shut my mouth, tried to finish as quickly and quietly as possible. Tried not to show I was upset. Being upset made it worse. He threw up his hands.

"I do not mean to be cruel! But I can't eat, listening to that."

"Sorry, sorry," I muttered, trying not to cry. In those moments, I wanted to go home, anywhere familiar and safe. My house, before the divorce. The Paris I had imagined. But these places didn't exist anymore. And Søren's logic made sense. Of course the noise he described me making was gross, distractingly so. His imitation of it sounded vile, an openmouthed cud processing. Of course it wasn't so ridiculous for him to want me to eat quietly. Why couldn't I? After a week or so, Søren stopped chastising me, instead adopting the tactic of silently ceasing to eat and staring until I caught on.

Søren seemed as baffled that his irritation at my chewing upset me as he did at my inability to change it. For him it was a light that flickered on when I was doing it and when I stopped and the irritant was removed, the light turned off. Our dinners became quieter and quieter, the hum of the refrigerator and the nothing from outside filling the room. A chain of firecracker questions lit up my brain as I waited for the food to be gone. Where did the trash go when he took it out the front door? What other options were there at the grocery store? Why hadn't Søren introduced me to anyone? Was he ever going to take me outside?

I tried to pry around the edges of our life, stir them. The long evening hours stretched out in front of us and a spike of inexplicable terror would drive itself through my middle, a sensation like vertigo and drowning at the same time. I became afraid of time, a stealthy beast that roamed the apartment. Our third roommate. I was careful of it, fearfully avoidant and polite. I let it have whatever it wanted, tried not to pay attention.

The beast could be led out. Søren would snap out of it, be funny and kind again. He would talk about books and movies, pull me onto his lap and reverently smell my hair. He told me he had never met anyone like me. The feel of his body coiling my form became what was good to me, what I waited for. Because no matter what he said or did, at the end of those early nights Søren took me into the bedroom and made love to me. How I lived for the moment when he turned to me and pulled me by the hand back down the hallway to the white room where the windows throbbed with violet light. Sometimes he made me wait, sat me on his lap on the couch and felt me up from behind, pressed his open mouth to my neck and beat his tongue rhythmically into my skin, whispering, "Nej, nej, nej," while I squirmed and finally fought, assaulting him with kisses until he lay head-to-toe on top of me, our hands clasped over my head, his erection pressing urgently into my belly.

Fucking Søren, taking his pants down his slim hips, running my hands over his smooth bones up under his shirt, going at it so hard that we bruised each other. The way he came up behind me and rested his hands on my shoulders and chanted my name. Rubbed his stubbly head against my neck, setting all of me alight. The moment, in bed, when he lost control and bucked against me panting. My badges, my record.

I was proud of it all, so pleased with myself that I didn't notice my fear transform from a spike into an expansive garment that covered me neck to ankle, didn't see the beast grow elephant tall until it was too late. I couldn't see. I had been waiting so long for something to happen to me.

A week later, Søren announced a surprise and produced a small paper bag from his backpack. Inside was a tiny plastic baggie of dark greenish shards. I opened it. Sniffed.

"Pot?" The oily smell hung in the air between us.

"Hash, actually," Søren said, taking it from me. Hash. I had heard the word before, but I wasn't sure what it meant. It was somehow related to marijuana. I knew that. The shards looked like chipped chocolate or hard-packed dirt. In the heat of Søren's palm they made muddy smudges on the inside of the plastic bag.

"I felt nostalgic today and returned to those mongoloid twins the Madsen brothers. I used to buy from them as a teenager when we visited my uncle in the summers. Ah, memories!" He made an expansive gesture, as if he had told a charming childhood story.

"You shouldn't use the word 'mongoloid,'" I said.

Søren shook his head, the hash still proffered in his right palm. "English is hard enough without the American insistence on continually removing words from the vocabulary. I understand I am not to call people like this retards or morons or imbeciles. And now I cannot use the proper term for their condition?"

"Their condition?"

"They are born with it. In the chromosomes. Not enough or too many, I cannot remember. A bit of the—" He squinted and put on a dumb smile, curling his hand into a claw, and thumped against his chest, making a horrible guttural noise.

"Mentally disabled?"

I watched him try to hide his smirk. "As you say. This kind is generally sweet and well dispositioned. Below average intelligence and sometimes a bit fat, but they can work basic jobs. The eyes look Oriental."

"Are you talking about Down syndrome? People with Down syndrome don't do that." I gestured at his still-clawed hand.

"Certainly I cannot be expected to understand what this unfortunate accident of birth is called in every country." Søren's voice rose. "They have a fine life and I do not begrudge them it, the Madsens, selling hash out of their group home while the unsuspecting pedagogues happily provide them with an endless supply of little plastic bags for their 'craft projects.'" Pedagogue was a job everyone in Jutland seemed to hold, engaged at each level of the massive infrastructure of social welfare.

"They actually believe these two criminals make jewelry from beads, that that's what they're selling at such a fine clip." He laughed at the jolly thought of his mongoloid dealers.

"They live in a group home? Where do they get drugs?"

"Their mother's boyfriend is a Hells Angel. I have never seen fit to inquire past that fact."

"The motorcycle gang?"

"The Hells Angels are very contemporary, Roxana. In this country they are locked in a battle for drug territory with the Arab gangs." He laced his fingers behind his head, taking on a philosophical look. "I do not empathize with criminals, but given the choice, I will throw my lot with the Angels, I suppose."

Wasn't Søren a criminal too, buying drugs from disabled people living in a group home funded by the state? I wanted to ask, but his mood seemed to have lifted, and I didn't want to mess it up.

"Shall we?" He lifted the bag and held it over his open mouth, as if to swallow it whole.

"Sure," I said.

Søren's face fell. "I apologize, Roxana. I did not ask before I got the hash. I just wanted to give you some excitement."

I wanted to tell him that the days I had spent in the apartment were the most exciting of my entire life. Sometimes, walking between the rooms in the afternoon, I was overcome by wonder at where I was. At who I had become. And this feeling raised me, muting his moods and complaints about the sounds my mouth made when I ate, his lovemaking sealing me in my certainty: I was free but didn't need freedom. I could do as I liked, and I did. Our life together, we often joked, was my real International Abroad Experience. The only place I wanted to go was between his legs.

"Don't be stupid," I said.

He flinched. "Please do not call me names. I never call you names."

"I wasn't calling you a name. I was calling your idea stupid. Of course you haven't made me do anything. And of course I want to. I just never have before."

Søren straightened. "You need not to be embarrassed, Roxana. It was I who was embarrassed, thinking that I was corrupting you."

"You can't corrupt what wants to be corrupted," I said.

He liked that. Søren took a small chopping board to the table, withdrew a cigarette from his pocket, and passed it over the flame of a green plastic lighter, back and forth, until the paper blackened. He crumpled the tobacco into a pile, shaped it into a line the length of my pinkie, and sprinkled shards of hash over the line. Then, producing a cigarette paper from somewhere—had it been in the paper bag with the hash?—he flipped the cutting board over so the hash and tobacco fell neatly into the paper. Almost without looking he rolled this into a new cigarette. Twisted it together. Licked the seam.

Søren put a heavy purple ceramic ashtray on the coffee table and lit the joint with a match. I remembered another word for this kind of thing. Spliff.

"Watch." He took a long drag and exhaled a viscous blue stream. "Do you think you can do that, little Roxana?"

I held it to my mouth and tried to do as he had done. The smoke was thicker than a cigarette's. I coughed. Then I couldn't stop coughing.

Søren brought me a glass of water. "Let me help you."

He took another long drag, grabbed me by the shoulders, and gave me a long, openmouthed kiss, guiding the smoke into my mouth with his tongue. I froze, dazed, trying to hold it in. When I exhaled, the smoke seemed to leave me more slowly than before.

"A shotgun." Søren stretched the word luxuriously.

"Shotgun," I incanted.

I wanted him to shotgun me again, but he made me do it myself. This time the smoke stayed inside.

The edges of the room softened. How had I never noticed how comfortable the couch was before? Perfect, really, as if it had been made just for my body. When I looked at Søren, I had to hold my features carefully to keep from bursting into uncontrollable laughter. And yet I felt tender, too. I wanted to cover him in kisses. Nestle in the crook of his arm.

I climbed onto his lap and kissed his neck.

"Hello, little Roxana."

"Hi," I whispered, giggling.

"Do you feel all right?"

"Yes. Yes."

"Good." We fell silent.

"I feel really, really good," I said suddenly, and we laughed so hard I thought I'd pass out.

From then on hash became part of our nightly routine. Stoned, food was astonishingly good. After dinner Søren cleared away the dishes and stacked them in the sink to wash in the morning. We smoked more hash and Søren played music and I stretched back on the couch and let its waves crash over me. We watched dramas that Søren narrated for me.

"Now the vicar will be upset because the children have stolen the candlesticks. His sister is concerned because her crafts business is failing. That man is a former police officer with a passion for gourmet cooking. He is secretly in love with the woman who grooms the horses. That was on the last series."

The hash restored the relaxing time my problem chewing had punctured. Every night we spent a happy handful of hours on the couch, climbing all over each other, kissing and cuddling, staring at the television, drilling each other with questions about our lives before we met. Søren liked it when I asked him about my future, about what I should do in the ten years it would take me to catch up to where he was now. High, he was uncharacteristically optimistic.

"You will have everything you want," he told me. "I know you will. You are lovely and talented. You are a person of quality and discernment."

High, I believed that he was right. Nothing would go wrong for me. I would simply go and go and go. Up into the air like a balloon.

We grew sleepy, cuddled closer. I thought he was falling asleep. But Søren surprised me. As soon as I thought he was gone, he rose under me. His way of taking my body fit a fantasy. Mine. His. Ours. A young, unsure girl led astray by an unsavory older man. The fantasy drew us together, made the words he whispered in my ear real, gave his hands an edge as they moved outside and inside my body. In one moment I was beneath him, facedown in the couch cushions, feeling him grunt and push— in the next straddling him, my hands nearing his throat. The first time Søren laid his hand on my neck, my eyes rolled back in my head and I caught him inside me with my muscles and wouldn't let go. He pinned both of my hands above my head and made use of my helpless skin, biting my neck so hard that I had purple welts the next day. He bent me over in some corner, entered me standing as I braced against and let go of the wall. I wanted him to draw blood, for him to open me that way too.

We careened. I closed my eyes and saw a car crashing with us inside, smashing against each other. Dying. I let him turn me in his hands and learned to turn him, too. One night as I sat astride him on the couch, his hand lingered behind me. I became conscious of it. His hand was there for a reason. He tapped my asshole once, twice. Pressed with the pad. Pulled the finger back and dipped it in his mouth. I looked him in the eye and then his finger was in my ass, slow and difficult. I liked how hard it was. What it meant that he was there.

Every night we went a little farther. Two fingers. His bathrobe's terry cloth belt repurposed as a blindfold. I was his student, his charge, a responsibility he had chosen to abuse.

"Are you lost?" he asked. That was how I knew the game was starting.

"Yes," I told him. "Yes. I am lost."

I found the ritual incredibly sexy, an illustration of his dark scenario. Me as confidante, corrupted student, unwitting victim. Søren as Dracula, the Phantom of the Opera, Rochester, Heathcliff. All those forbidding men I sought out, again and again, rereading hungrily. Søren gave me the same frantic tremor as a vampire in Mama's bedroom once had.

When I was nine years old, Dad went out of town and Mama allowed me to sleep with her in their bedroom. We watched an old movie on the television at the end of their bed, and during it she fell asleep. I stayed awake to watch the next one, a Dracula film from before I was born. I thought the movie was boring and slow, not scary at all, but when I fell asleep I went to the vampire's realm, a garish pink and red place where all night he preyed on me. I could not wake. I could not sleep. I dreamed him and fled him. His blurry face just a gash below the black V of his widow's peak. Burning in my chest and throat and between my legs until I was only bone.

Somehow by morning I found my way back to Mama. It was the last time I was allowed that special little-girl pleasure of sharing her bed. Waking to her sweet smell, helping her briskly reorder the sheets. She looked at me like she knew.

At ten, I dreamed myself into the tower of a Swiss castle, trapped up high like Rapunzel but with no beautiful long hair to show for it, only a flimsy gown, drifting from implement to implement—spindle, churn, abacus, astrolabe—until I saw a boy in a far corner, a chivalric knight in armor and a bright green sash. Shining like a statue, coolly considering me.

Then everything went purple and I woke up upset, but I didn't know why.

After that, the dreams came once a year, like gifts, and always ended before anything could happen. I remember them clear as movies. Clearer for their sharp power, the queasy excitement that kept me ashamed long after I woke up. I wanted more to happen. I wanted to stay in the castle, to roam those rooms decorated as intricately as the illustrations in my book of fairy tales and finger the drapes, for the boys to do something. But I always woke right as it seemed the action was about to start. Frustrated, I read dream dictionaries, which mentioned something called lucid dreaming, a way of visiting the interstitial state between sleep and waking. Meddling with those shadowy meshes struck me as unwise. I had visited these meshes, where the vampire lived.

When I was eleven, a dream came in my own room, a vivid attack. A man with a scratchy red beard accosted me as I walked to school. Dragged me into an alley and ripped off my clothes, blue corduroy overalls with a pink T-shirt underneath. Yellow underwear with green polka dots. My new clear plastic backpack was dashed to the ground, spilling the pencil case and books arrayed so prettily inside. I was too little for a training bra, but he tore my long white undershirt in half and with his tongue drew a thick stripe of spit down the center of my chest.

I was naked. The man raped me. No colors swelled. I was conscious and terrified. My rapist had desperate, red-rimmed eyes and a morose matter-of-factness, as if his actions were pre-ordained. His face hovered, he breathed hard, he sobbed. He burned inside me, and in the dream I understood, without question, what this meant.

I was a little girl, a fifth grader. I had not yet begun to take showers. Mama still regulated my bath time, rinsed my hair, worked in the conditioner. She and Dad still tucked me in with a little ceremony of bedtime kisses and extinguishing lights. But that morning I woke a different person. The plastic gaze of my stuffed animals shamed me and I snapped at Dad when he told me to have a good day. I worried that it was a prophetic dream or that I wanted it. How and when it might happen. My own face in the mirror made me flush and wince in shame.

4

ON MY FIFTEENTH DAY IN JUTLAND, I WOKE TO SØREN KISSING ME ON THE FOREHEAD.

"Good morning, skat!" He squeezed me. "Good morning, little sleeping Roxana! I am going to take you on an adventure today."

I hadn't been outside in weeks. I put on my linen dress and my orange scarf, wanting to look nice. When I opened the door to leave the bedroom, a new, dry smell rushed in from the hallway, breaking the seal between night and day. The table was set with hard-boiled eggs in eggcups, rolls, jam, butter, and cheese. Søren showed me how to peel thin slices of the cheese with a T-shaped utensil strung with a wire.

"This is very nice," I said.

"It is my pleasure," Søren said, peeking up to give me one of the sunny smiles I remembered from the beginning.

It was our first real breakfast, the first nonstoned meal we had eaten together in many days. I watched him split a roll, butter it, spread jam over the butter, and drape a white sheet of cheese over the jam. The egg yolks were golden jelly, darker than any I had ever seen, and they tasted like sunshine. Only after we finished eating did I realize Søren hadn't said a word about my chewing.

"Ready to go, little dreaming Roxana?" Søren asked, packing items from the refrigerator into his bag. I took his arm.

Being outside felt like being high. I had missed the sun, its caress of heat. Everything looked friendly, the brick buildings, the pearly cobblestones, even the flat squares of pavement. I wanted to walk and walk. But Søren went to a little black car I had never seen before and opened the passenger door. Fuzzy upholstery and stale plastic. It smelled exactly like hot cars at home. He settled in the driver's seat and turned the key.

"I thought you didn't have a car." I said.

"It belongs to my girlfriend's mother," Søren said and then put his hand over his eyes. "Sorry. That was stupid." He slammed his head against the ceiling of the car.

"Please don't do that."

"I am an idiot." He head butted the ceiling again, hard, and then a third time. "The car belongs to Mette's mother," he said. "My ex-girlfriend's mother."

"It's okay," I said. "I knew it couldn't be your girlfriend's mother, because her car is a green Honda, and it's on the other side of the Atlantic."

Søren made a sound, half laugh half cough, and pulled away from the curb in silence. I shifted in my seat, stung. We lived together. Wasn't I his girlfriend? I wanted to ask, but I was afraid of what he would say, a feeling that was becoming familiar.

We came to a stop at a roundabout near a field, beside the smallest truck I had ever seen, beat-up and beige, toylike. A tall man in khaki coveralls walked out of the field and leaned over the side of the truck, digging in a canvas sack in the bed. He had black hair and a short beard. I recognized him, which was impossible.

"Do you know that man?" I asked Søren.

The man withdrew a large orange bucket and a power drill from the back of the truck. Wiped his hands on his coveralls, dug in his left pocket.

"Of course. Geden." Søren slipped into the muttering cadence of Danish. "Our local hermit."

"Gay-den?"

Søren shook his head. "Geden."

The middle of the word was a kind of swallowed trill. The soft Danish *d*.

"Gelen," I tried again. "Gethin."

"Closer." Søren smiled in the way that meant I should stop trying. "But that's not even his name. It's just what everyone calls him." He snickered. "It means 'goat.'"

The man looked up from his truck and caught me in his green eyes. I couldn't look away. Then Søren shifted into gear and we circled the roundabout, the man and his truck becoming specks against the field.

"He doesn't look like a goat."

"It is not how he looks," Søren said. "It is about how he acts. Greedy, cold. Only interested if you have something for him. He never talks to anyone, and if you speak to him he just stares at you as if you are not there. Honestly, I try not to think about him, because he can make me very angry, and I do not like being angry."

I nearly corrected him: Søren obviously loved being angry. But then I suddenly figured out where I had seen the man before. He had been in the street on my first night in Farsø, when I stood naked at the window. He was the one who had seen me.

My heart thundered. I tried to make my voice normal. "Did you work with him or something?"

Søren laughed. "No, I certainly do not work for the municipality, digging in the woods, as he does. But I think when someone is welcomed into my country after the failure of his own—when he enjoys all the benefits of Danish society, goes to our schools, is treated by our doctors, lives in our public housing—I think it is not ridiculous for me to want him to act a bit grateful and respectful of the culture that has been so kind to him."

"He's an immigrant?"

"An East Monkey."

"What?"

"An Easterner. From the Balkans. Bosnia. A refugee. A Muslim." Søren cast an annoyed glance at my lap. "Why are your hands shaking?"

I sat on them. "Why do you call him an East Monkey?"

"He's from the Balkans. The East. They're better at least than the Arabs, who make their women wear those rags and stand around smoking all day. And the Somalis, too, they're the worst, carrying everything they own in Ikea bags. Some of the Turkish and Palestinian women will go to school and become secretaries or work in shops, but no Somali will ever work. They just chew khat and sit around all day in public housing. No, I would say we like East Monkeys the best of all the foreigners that swarm here. But they are still a social problem. So ungrateful."

Shut up, I wanted to say, shut up. Don't show me how ugly you can be.

We stopped at a light. He turned to look at me.

"You hate them," I said.

Søren snorted. "That's ridiculous."

A high pitch was sounding in my head, like the tornado warning they used to drill us with in school. He is your boyfriend, I reminded myself. He is not a hateful person. He has experienced things you have not. Just tell him what you think. What you know.

"If they came here to get away from a war, they didn't have a choice, Søren. No one wants to leave home. And they still had to make their own way," I said. "Like anyone else."

The car picked up speed. Outside: empty fields, the occasional barn, groups of two and three grazing horses. Søren sat furiously rigid in his seat.

"I don't think you're racist, but you sound really racist when you talk like that," I said. I wanted to roll down my window and climb out.

Søren snorted. "If one sounds racist, one is racist, Roxana. Action is what makes a person, and talk is a kind of violence."

I was stunned that he was admitting it. But then he kept going.

"I am not a racist. You do not understand. My feelings have nothing to do with race. An East Monkey like Geden is not even a different race. You can see that as well as I. This is cultural. People pretend multiculturalism is a wonderful force, as if we all live in a clothing commercial, but it has the power to destroy the state, to dismantle all of our gains and advances. Here, refugees do not make their own way. They are helped with everything. They are given a life. It is not like America, where a hospital throws you out on the street when you cannot pay."

Maybe "racist" wasn't the right word. Maybe it was just the label I had. But he had just said talking was violence. I opened my mouth, trying to formulate what to say next. But Søren wasn't finished.

"When you come here as a refugee, you are given a place to live. Money, doctors, a whole life. Your children attend school for free. But the immigrants claim they are too traumatized from their little wars to ever work. High percentages take early retirement and never have to work. They can just live off the rest of us forever."

"Why do you care if a refugee retires early?"

"Because they live off my taxes, Roxana!"

Søren tried and failed to keep his voice level. "War is terrible. Horrible. The things that people do to each other are unspeakable. But I do not understand the entitlement. The rudeness. So they suffered. Do they get to be in a bad mood forever? I do not, no matter what happens to me. I do not just lie down in the gutter with all the other social class five people—"

Staring out the window, I said quietly, "I don't understand what you're talking about."

"Taxes here are calculated based on income. Social class five pays the lowest percentage. They are the poorest people, most simply working class, uneducated: factory laborers, construction workers, things like that. But of course this class also includes the most vulnerable people, and the ones who can't or don't work. Alcoholics, drug addicts, the mentally ill. Almost all immigrants and refugees are social class five, of course. The ones who pay taxes at all, anyway. I doubt Geden is actually social class five. The municipality probably pays him quite well. But he lives social class five. His little shit flat. Inside it is like Bosnia all over again. Dirty old rugs, everything stained yellow from cigarette smoke, some sort of illegal homemade distillery in the bathroom. He cooks all his food on a grill. Outside! Classic East Monkey. No interest in bettering himself."

Trying to understand him was trying to do what he would not do for anyone else, I realized suddenly. The knowledge tasted bitter. I scooted away from him, grateful for even three more inches between us. Inches, I thought with a perverse pride. I was from somewhere far away. I wasn't like him.

"These people," Søren continued, "think their problems are everybody else's fault. Never their own. Keep your own house clean, that is all I ask. I am not a hateful person, but I am not a fool, either. Do not dare—do not dare!—think it appropriate to tell me how to behave in my own country! Even with just a look. An attitude. Especially."

It was as though he was two men, or more than two, none of whom knew themselves at all.

He parked in a lot at the edge of a field. I was so grateful to leave the car. Outside, it felt like we could start over. I followed Søren through the iridescent grass to a sign:

VIKINGECENTER FYRKAT

Beyond stood wooden buildings with thatched roofs.

"More Viking stuff?"

Søren put his arm around me. "Yes, skat, but mainly just a nice place."

He was trying. I decided to try too. We walked into the field on a pebbled path, climbed a small hill, and came to stand on a massive raised circle of earth that enclosed an inner circle. Staircases were set into the rim.

"One thousand years ago, this was an important Viking fort," Søren said. "A ring castle to repel attack. The buildings are reconstructions of Viking houses. This is where the castle stood." We walked, squinting in the hot sunlight. "There is a museum."

The ugly things he had said echoed in my head. I tried to turn them down. To see the little white flowers in the grass, the filmy sky. *Choose your battles*, Mama had always said. I would try to talk to him about it when he was calmer.

"Do you want to see it?"

"Not really," I admitted.

"Me neither." Søren laughed. "Come, let's have our picnic." We headed for a stand of trees at the rim of the field.

He grinned and took my hand. He was a different person when he smiled. I had a soaring feeling. Everything could be okay. I could forget the car ride. The things he had said. It could be that easy. I didn't have to remember. Mama and Dad never seemed to be able to forget, to let anything go. I could choose to be different. Free.

When we were just a few paces from the woods, a little white butterfly flew in front of us. A little yellow butterfly joined it.

I squeezed Søren's hand. "What do you call them in Danish?"

"Sommerfugl."

"Summer fool," I tried.

"Close." He kissed me, his tongue moving in my mouth. When I opened my eyes we were surrounded by falling white and yellow flowers. I blinked and they became butterflies. A cloud of little butterflies. Søren held me against his chest.

"What's the word for this?"

"I do not know. What is the word in English?"

"I don't know!"

He took my face in both hands. His eyes were thin, watery. He was fragile. Just a person, made of water. I felt the passage of time and impassability of distance. Our ages, our nationalities, all the things we could not know about each other. All the pain

and bad feelings and loss. Couldn't it be helped, just a little bit?
I tried to remember when I hadn't known Søren, but the past
kept stepping back from me. So I had to go into him, closer, to
crush my body against his. If there was nothing left to go back
to, there was only him to go into.

We walked deeper into the woods and sat on a beach towel
Søren spread over the hard dirt.

"Roxana, I want to give you something." He opened his
palm, revealing a thick red cord, a coil of simple embroidery
floss, the kind that Sylvie and I had once knotted friendship
bracelets from. "For you to wear. If you want. I can tie it on. If
you like it."

There was a rushing in my ears. I thrust my left wrist at
him. "Yes."

He knotted it three times. I fingered the silky cord. "I love
it," I told him. "Thank you."

"I am happy that you are here with me. You make me a
better man."

He slipped his hand under my dress and into my underwear. Birds sang a strange high song above us. In the periphery,
butterflies rushed. I kissed him and palmed his rising cock.

Søren took off my underwear and pulled me onto his lap.
Over his shoulder I saw the Viking fort, the circle of raised
earth, the reconstructed buildings. I closed my eyes. Søren held
his face close to mine as he entered me. "My little Roxana,"
he breathed.

I hooked my chin over his shoulder, whispering his name
into his mouth and seeking the red cord. I stared at the ground,
at the insects moving in the grass. We fell into rocking back and
forth, his hand strong at the small of my back, and we came
quickly together, or nearly together, each of us giving the little

strangled cry, and lay back in the grass. Søren found my left hand and held it, stroking the cord with his thumb.

The day settled on my skin. We dozed in the grass and then ate our picnic. Carlsberg and leverpostej sandwiches. I put my head on Søren's stomach and looked at the sky. White, white-blue, silver-blue, silver, blue.

When we got home I went to Søren's computer and looked up the word for a group of butterflies. A flock? A herd? There was no agreed-upon term. Swarm, some people claimed. Or flight, the Internet said. Rabble. Kaleidoscope. Flutter.

"Søren!"

He had been in a good mood since Fyrkat. I wanted to show him the list. Extend it. There was no response. I said his name again, my voice bouncing around the silent apartment like a deflated ball. Had he fallen asleep?

He was not in the kitchen or the bathroom. I found him sitting up in bed, shirtless, covered by the duvet. His eyes were closed, and he didn't stir when the floorboards creaked under my feet. I sat on the bed and leaned into him. His purple eyelids were seamed with tiny blue veins. His hands lay loosely in his lap, palms up, the tips of his fingers intertwined. I had never seen him so prone. Even in sleep he seemed closed and strong, but in that moment he was open, vulnerable.

He smelled like the fabric of his backpack, the yellowy bar of soap we both used in the shower, and something else ineffably Søren, sharp and austere. I raised my arm. I only wanted to graze the soft skin of his neck. To see what would happen. Søren grabbed my wrist. His eyes opened with a jolt.

"Don't." His accent was heavy.

"Sorry." I tried to take my hand back but his grip was too strong. "Are you okay?"

He glared at me. I tried to withdraw my arm again, but he wouldn't let go.

"You're hurting me, Søren, please."

He released me, narrowing his eyes. "What do you call me?"

"I don't—"

"You don't know?"

"Søren. I call you Søren. That's your name."

"Get up."

I stared at him.

"Get up," he repeated.

I stood, covering the cord with my hand.

"Don't do that."

The duvet fell, revealing his cock. He was hard. I felt lost.

Søren stood, closing the space between us. He cupped my crotch, prying my fingers from my wrist, revealing the cord. He bent his head and licked a coiling path of X's back and forth across my throat, biting hard under my right ear. He held my wrist in front of my eyes.

"I gave this to you." He fingered the red cord. "Why?"

"Because you care for me."

"Yes." His efforts between my legs intensified. He gathered my skirt. "It marks you. Shows that you are mine."

Søren knelt beneath my skirt and took down my underwear with his teeth. Then his tongue was inside me. He burrowed, pinning me back against the wall with the force of his tongue. It felt like he was turning me inside out. The edges of the room pinked. Then he withdrew and sat on the bed stroking himself.

"Turn around. Bend over." I did as he said. "Lift your skirt."

I hiked up the long A-line, so tense I was almost laughing, and tucked the bundle of fabric under my right arm.

"Take off your underwear."

They were already half-gone, slung diagonally across my thighs. I flung them with my free hand.

"Bend over. Farther."

I thought about nature documentaries. The moment in the mating ritual when the female presented to the male.

"Touch yourself."

Thrilled, almost nauseated, floating in a ring of terrifying arousal, I reached for the edge of my body. The sensation was more haphazard than pleasurable. I managed to work one finger in. Two. This wasn't how I masturbated. It was a performance. For Søren to watch, not for me to feel. My embarrassment was part of the performance. What he wanted.

He licked me a few times, stopping just before my asshole, then including it, engulfing it. I pressed into his mouth, speaking words I forgot as soon as they left me. He stood and entered me. When I tried to prop against him, Søren pushed me away.

After a few minutes he withdrew and laid me on the bed, pressing my wrists to the mattress with his forearms, and thrust indiscriminately, not trying to give me pleasure.

"What do you call me?" Søren hissed, his accent heavy.

I said his name.

"No." Glaring at me, he lifted his right forearm from my wrist and pressed it against my throat.

"I don't know who you are," I gasped as his pelvis bored into my crotch. "I don't know who you are."

His eyes slitted. He was close. I wasn't. I closed my hand around the forearm still pinning my wrist and pulled it away, curled my calves around his thighs, pinning him to me, and flipped us so that I was on top.

Søren looked up at me incredulously, panting. We were flush, flat surface on flat surface.

"I don't know who you are." I ground against him. "I don't."

I put my forearm down against his throat. His mouth opened for my breasts but I took them out of his reach. I rocked back and forth, keeping him down, until it was almost over. Then I threw my head back and let my hips pivot while the vibrations ran through me, my bones pooling into hot fluid. Behind my closed eyes I saw a curved white rise, a pillar or a fin or a tooth. It went up and up into the ceiling. Through it. Even when I turned my blind head I couldn't see the top.

Below me, distantly, Søren began to orgasm. But I was high above, my head lost. I couldn't see him.

5

THE NEXT DAY I WOKE EARLY IN A DENSE, STICKY BLOT OF MY OWN BLOOD. My thighs and hands coated in a dry stain, as if they had rusted. Søren's white sheets and duvet covers bisected by wide brownish arcs dotted with viscous purple. I hoped the blood hadn't breached the dynes.

He did not wake as I crept out of bed and into the bathroom. I tucked a bundle of toilet paper into the crotch of a clean pair of underwear and returned to the bedroom armed with my toothbrush, the kitchen dish soap, and a small glass of water. I knelt beside the bed, dipped the toothbrush into the water, spread a drop of soap across its bristles, and with a circular motion worked it into the stains, as Mama had taught me. I managed to strip out the dark heart of the stain, transforming it into a pinkish shadow with a hard maroon edge. The sheets would need to be soaked in cold water and washed in a machine with stain remover, but I had gotten there in time. There would be no permanent marks.

I don't know how long Søren watched me spot-treat the sheets. He didn't speak until after I had changed the water in the small glass twice.

"You are quite thorough."

I jumped, splashing water on him. He swore in Danish, propping himself up on one elbow, shaking a hand like it was diseased.

"What did you get all over the sheets?"

"Blood."

He sat up. "What?"

"I got my period. While I was asleep. We just need to soak the sheets and wash them with stain remover." I leaned forward and kissed him.

He peeled the duvet from his body. "Well, you have made quite the mess. And we do not have any stain remover."

"If you take me to the store, I can find it."

"No." Søren pulled his gray sweater over his head. "I will get it." He left the room.

"Søren?"

His shiny head reappeared in the doorway. "What?"

"Can I come with you?"

Søren rolled his eyes. "I can retrieve the necessary soaps more quickly alone."

He disappeared again.

"Søren!"

This time he called to me from the hallway. "What?"

"I need a new toothbrush. I'd like to go with you. If it's not a problem." I hated how small my voice was.

His feet thumped back down the hallway. "Roxana," he said from the threshold, controlling his voice, "going out should be an adventure. A treat, like our trip to Fyrkat. This is boring. Let me plan our next outing."

Our trip had been a good time, had settled and rearranged things, I thought. I had a vision of the two of us standing

on the deck of a great ship, finely dressed, as a thick wake
stretched behind us. Stream upon stream of rich white foam.
Yes, I could wait.

"Can I have a kiss before you go?"

He entered the room, leaned over, pecked me dry on the
forehead, and left, slamming the front door. I went to the bathroom, filled the glass again, and peeled the sheets apart, removing
the cover from the dyne and the cover sheet from the mattress.
My blood had seeped into the comforter, the mattress cover,
even the mattress itself. I didn't feel like continuing to clean,
but Mama had taught me better.

One sticky August evening just before the start of eighth grade,
I went to pee and saw a dark slick in my underwear. I had become a woman.

Since I could remember, Mama had promised that when
I got my first period we would have a special day together, just
us two. She would take the afternoon off and drive me into the
city, to the hotel where she and Dad had stayed on their wedding
night. At our lunch there, I could order whatever I wanted. And
Mama would give me her rolling ring, the one that was three
intertwined gold rings, white, yellow, and rose.

How wonderful it would be to stand beside Mama as
she called in. "Can't make it today, Marnie. I need to spend
some time with my little girl. My"—she'd wink at me—"young
woman." Maybe we would go to breakfast first at the nice
diner that made Dutch baby pancakes and then fly downtown in her Volvo and look at all the magazines at the fancy
magazine rack in the hotel lobby, maybe even shop a little bit

in the gift store, which I believed to contain every treasure I had ever desired.

I wanted the magic to start in the moment I told her what had happened, wanted the whole experience to be elegant and open as a dream.

"Come into the bathroom with me now," she said.

Mama stood against the teal tile, watching me step out of my underwear. She turned them over in her hands, the pink fabric seeming to glow as she studied the crotch with her nurse's eyes.

"Well, here we go." She left and returned with clean underwear, a bottle of delicate fabric wash, and a green-wrapped parcel. "Wash your hands, Roxana."

"You have no idea how easy you have it." Mama unfolded a long white tongue from its crinkly green covering and pressed it against the crotch of the clean underwear. "When I started my period, you had to wear a kind of belt with hooks to hold your pad in place."

"Ew."

"Not ew. Menstruation is healthy and normal. A sign your body is doing the right things. But you have to keep your underwear clean."

I put on the new underwear and sat on the closed toilet to watch. She stoppered the sink and filled it with cold water, trailing a stream of opalescent delicate wash into the basin. Then she submerged my underwear. A reddish silt diffused.

Mama lifted my underwear from the water with one finger, draped the crotch across her palm, and rubbed the dark stain hard with a bar of white soap. Then she rubbed the fabric against itself until it foamed.

"Watch," she said. The foam pinked as the bloodstain began to lift. "Here, you try."

She showed me how to rub the cloth against itself by pushing my fingers against each other, moving the fabric like the paper fortune-tellers Sylvie was so good at making. When the foaming stopped, Mama submerged my underwear again and rinsed the soap out. We repeated the process until the stain disappeared.

"Always soak first," she told me. There was only one bathroom sink in my house, so after that, when I needed to wash my bloody underwear, I filled a bowl with water and did it in my room. Sometimes I forgot the bowls and they multiplied until I had three or four bowls of dirty underwear floating in cloudy water, like diaphanous fish waiting for their aquarium to be cleaned.

"Roxana," Mama said, trying not to smile when she saw the bowls. "You are a nurse's daughter. You cannot be unhygienic in your bedroom."

Mama was remote and severe, but the bowls made her laugh, and I liked that. The idea that my period was a little funny. Her thoughts often seemed far away and were, I imagined, always on her patients, those kids dying of diseases so rare they didn't have names. I was probably wrong—when my parents announced their divorce I figured I'd been wrong about pretty much everything—but whatever the reason, it was hard to reach her, harder still to split her moon-shaped face with a smile.

I thought there would be more laughter on our special day. But Mama didn't mention our plans. When I asked the next morning, she said she couldn't take the time off in an offhand way, as if she had forgotten, as if she couldn't imagine why I would even ask her. "It's a Thursday, Roxana. You know those are the worst."

*   *   *

Søren returned from the store with a small bottle of purple fluid. When he went to wash his hands, which was the first thing he did every time he returned home, he discovered I had put the sheets to soak in the kitchen sink.

"Roxana, this is very unsanitary. We wash food in the sink. Do you not plan to use the machine?"

"Can you show me how to wash the comforter?"

"What is a comforter?"

"Sorry. The dyne."

Søren put his hand over his eyes. "My dynes are stained, too?"

He stalked back to the bedroom without waiting for an answer. I didn't want to follow him, but when I did, I found him in the middle of the room, the duvets bunched in his arms.

"I must go buy new dynes and a new mattress cover. Please do your best to remove the blood from the mattress too. It is my uncle's bed. It does not belong to me."

"You don't need to buy new ones. Just show me how to wash the duvet and the cover."

"I cannot, Roxana."

"Why not?"

"I have no idea. I have never washed it. The covers have never been stained before."

I couldn't see how that could be true. "Will you show me how to use the washing machine before you go?"

"The store will close soon. Their hours are limited today. It is a holy day. You will figure it out, I'm sure."

A holy day? He left again, his kiss throbbing on my forehead. I couldn't decipher the settings on the washing machine, so I guessed, pouring the detergent and the purple fluid right on top of the sheets. After a full cycle he still wasn't back. The

stains were only lightened to a dull brown. When he finally
came home, he handed me a large packet of sanitary pads and a
new toothbrush. I thanked him, hiding them behind my body.

The next day my cramps were bad. I e-mailed back and forth
with Dad.

Hey Roxie! What's new in France? Love, Dad

Every time he wrote to me I was reminded anew of my
lie. Every time I remembered, I felt bad, but only for a second.

Dear Dad, Not much. Today we have free time but I
don't really know what to do. Just reading and resting
I guess. Sylvie met somebody who wanted to go to the
fashion museum with her, so I'm on my own.

I miss you,
Roxana

My e-mails were getting vaguer and vaguer. Søren had gotten
tired of helping me make up stories for my parents. "Just use
this," he had said one night, giving me the Parisian Experience
brochure Sylvie and I had spent so long studying once upon a
time. I could barely stand to look at it.
An hour later, Dad wrote back.

Why not get ice cream with some other new friends? Or
is it too cold up there? Love, Dad

I thought about inventing fake friends, a fake ice-cream parlor. But what if Dad asked me about them later?

> Dear Dad,
>
> I don't really know anyone here well enough to go get ice cream together. Other than Sylvie but she doesn't really like ice cream even. I don't know. I feel kind of lonely. I'm sure tomorrow will be better.
>
> I miss you,
> Roxana

Should I have told Mama and Dad the whole truth? There didn't seem to be any point, not anymore. I had gone this far, and they hadn't questioned any of it. They were wrapped up in their own world. They were probably glad I was gone.

I spent the day on the couch, sleeping and staring at the Internet. My lower back burned with a new pain, as if the inside of my body had graduated, too. I didn't bother cleaning up in the little ways I normally did, wiping down the counters and washing my coffee cups, and was still in my pajamas when Søren got home after seven. When he walked into the apartment, tall and elegant in his green pants and black shirt, I felt all my disarray at once. My oily face and hair. Every time I moved, the thick pad between my legs gushed.

"Hello!" Søren jauntily dropped his bag on the couch. Was he humming?

"I have had a phenomenal day. I discovered a work-around for a problem I've been having with the categorization of Ash's early novels. A breakthrough! Let us celebrate." Søren took a bottle of red wine out of his bag and went into the kitchen for the corkscrew.

I heard a drawer slam. "Roxana, are you ill? The kitchen looks as if someone died in here!" He laughed like he had said something funny and set to tidying up.

All through dinner I let him talk to me about his project, smiling at the right times, as he tossed incomprehensible jargon at me. After dinner we watched three half-hour episodes of a Danish sitcom that made Søren laugh so hard he neglected to translate. I sat with my knees curled into my chest, sipping my wine. If I held very still, I experienced the terrifying sensation that I did not exist.

When he nodded off I put my hand on his crotch and stroked him urgently. Only now did it seem safe to do what I wanted.

Søren's eyes fluttered open. "What are you doing?"

"Nothing," I muttered, resisting the urge to skitter my hand away like a spider.

He exhaled heavily. "Please do not touch me when I am sleeping. And please, when I am sleeping, do not stare at me."

What can I do, then? I wanted to ask. "Well, do you want to . . . ?" I tapped his fading erection.

He sat up. "Please do not be vulgar. I do not feel like it tonight."

For the first time since the foxwoman's, I slept in my pajamas.

My period lasted a full week, longer than ever before. Every day I approached Søren for sex, and every day I was rejected. One night he was tired, another he was too keyed up from working, a third he had a stomachache. His habit of falling asleep next to me on the couch began to seem willed. I had always wanted to know what it was like to have sex on my period. But we did not.

My body did not draw his eyes. I kept bleeding, unpenetrated, and wondered.

Alone in the apartment, I reveled in my unwashed body. Blood dried in thick stripes on the inside of my thighs and between my legs. Every membranous violet smear on the gritty toilet paper was proof to me that I existed. When it was time to change my pad, I rolled the old one up in the new one's flimsy wrapper and pushed the little package down to the very bottom of the trash can. All day I flitted from bodily need to bodily need, until the sky took on the purple tinge that meant we were passing into the second, dimmed brightness. When I realized Søren would soon be home, I arranged my hair and carefully washed my hands, working out the crusts of dried blood from my cuticles.

The day after my period ended I wanted to start fresh with Søren, to be perfect for him. I took a very long shower, scrubbed the crack of my ass and the backs of my thighs with a soaked washcloth. I shaved my legs and armpits, trimmed my pubic hair. I massaged oil into the ends of my dry hair and braided it tightly. For perfume, I rubbed a cut lemon under my ears. I set my eyes in my face like lockets. In the mirror I was an icon, middle part and sharp lines. Who could resist me?

When I heard his key in the lock, I stretched out on the couch naked. I wanted to look like the odalisque paintings Sylvie and I had been obsessed with one summer. Slave—that was what odalisque meant.

Søren came in absorbed by the tiny tasks he completed every day upon returning home. His keys went exactly on the corner of the table near the door, his wallet beside them, his bag on one of the chairs at the long table. Without seeing me, he turned to wash his hands in the kitchen sink. I listened to his ablutions, still spread on the couch. He would have to notice me at some point.

He dried his hands by grabbing the entire roll of paper towels and turning it over with his wet palms and fingers, a habit I hated, and strolled back into the living room, whistling.

"I had a good day, if you can believe it!" He still didn't see me. "I figured out—" He saw me. He did not smile. "What's going on? Are you okay?"

I kept my face pretty. "I was just waiting for you."

Søren blinked, turned around, and walked down the hallway to the bedroom. He returned with a dyne and covered me. "You could catch a cold."

"What?"

"If you sit around naked like that, you can catch a cold."

What? I wanted to ask again, but I did not. I pushed the duvet down to reveal my breasts.

Søren looked away. He sat down beside me and patted my thigh through the duvet. "Where's the control?"

Another night I waited until we were stoned, leaned over, and kissed him as deeply as I could. Took off my shirt and pants, tried to sit in his lap.

"Roxana, please!" Søren scooted out from under me. "I can't see the TV!"

One morning in bed I touched myself in front of him, spread-eagled on top of the duvet, imagining that my hands were his hands. Søren shifted. I held my breath.

"What are you doing?"

I opened my eyes to his horrified face. He began to laugh, awkwardly, awfully.

By eleven on the day I finally sneaked out, the sun had emerged in full, heat coagulating around me in the apartment. The atmosphere inside had changed. What had been calming, dulcet, like being suspended in clouds, was now claustrophobic and stuffy. But I still had no key and I couldn't figure out when to ask. Søren had no safe mood. Once he had brought the key up himself, as evidence of his worthlessness, moaning that he had forgotten once again to have it cut. He pulled a throw pillow over his face and screamed into it.

The apartment, once a place of abundant possibility, now seemed crowded with emptiness, haunted. Søren never came home before five o'clock. Farsø was the deadest place I'd ever been. I could slip out and back in without him ever knowing.

Take myself out.

It was so easy. I tied my purple sneakers. Wedged Sylvie's heart-shaped rock between the door and its frame. Went out, down the stairs. Outside.

For a moment the light was so bright all I could do was stand, stunned. Time was a blinding elevator and I was in it, going up and down.

The main road took me to a distant stand of trees. Across the way stood a row of long low buildings Søren had told me housed sick people. I passed three young women in summer outfits, linen tunics and straw hats. An old lady in a little garden raised her trowel in a gentle wave. Two middle-aged men in gray scrubs played chess. It was good to have left, I thought. I could get some fresh air and return home rejuvenated, able to begin the project of figuring Søren out again. I had thought of the apartment as "home," I realized, and this made me happy.

I arrived at a large pond. A grove of trees had grown together into a canopy above the water, blotting out the sun, shrouding everything in soft green. Moss grew on the surface of the water like a reflection of the trees. A little red shack stood at the pond's far edge. I circled the water, admiring the flowers that dripped from tree branches and flowed up from the ground, bright paint smudges on the bushes and dirt. Even the close-buzzing bee that would have sent me into a panic back in Creek Grove did not lessen my pleasure.

Three teenagers arrived at the park. Two girls with sipping-straw legs, skinny all the way down. A blonde and a dyed redhead. Half of the blonde's hair was up in an ornate bun, and the rest fell past her shoulders in loose ringlets she had made with a curling iron. The redhead's was shellacked into a stiff chignon. Both wore short shorts, white on the blonde, dark blue on the redhead. Polite breasts rose beneath their spaghetti-strap tops. The boy was good-looking, with a swoop of honey-colored hair, big eyes surrounded by dense black lashes, a long lean torso under his gray T-shirt. He reminded me of Hunter.

Their conversation fluted across the pond to me. I had made the goal of having brief Danish conversations with Søren over breakfast, but he never showed much enthusiasm for teaching me. "Just find some videos on the Internet," he suggested, but it made me too sad, lying in bed, watching people enunciate Danish words on a tiny computer screen while outside real Danish people spoke real Danish.

I stood behind a bush so the teenagers wouldn't see me. How old were they? The girls' makeup and push-up bras made it hard to tell. The boy, lanky and beardless, could have been fourteen or eighteen. They continually swapped their cans of soda. They made faces and laughed, touching each other often, contact disguised as necessity or accident. The boy leaned over too far and dropped his head into the redhead's lap. The redhead tried to fix the blonde's hair and ended up stroking her shoulders instead. The blonde played a game in which the boy had to lay his hands atop hers, palms up, and wait. He won if he pulled away before she slapped him. She won if her slap landed, and she won again and again.

I had played these games. Not the hand-slapping game but the real game. Playing at wanting each other. I looked hard at the teenagers. Which one did I want? The blonde had better legs, the redhead better breasts. The boy would be awkward and shy. I imagined kissing each of them, somewhere else. In a bar, where I would discover they were underage and have no choice but to take them safely home.

The teenagers played on, oblivious. The girls began to casually hold hands for the boy's benefit. Then he took their hands, too, and the three of them sat there like it was a prayer circle. It wouldn't be long now. Soon they would stroke each other's arms or ankles, unleashing what had been waiting all along. A kiss, eyes closed, for the third to watch.

Watching was making me too sad. I left the park and headed toward the home for invalids. Watched my purple sneakers walk in zigzags, lifting my arms into wings. Where would I go, if I could? Back?

I closed my eyes and tried to conjure Sylvie's face, her smell. My left foot fell and I tripped into the street, my eyes opening too slowly, my hands flying automatically out in front of me. A sharp pain jolted my chin. I was bleeding.

A pair of black steel-toed boots appeared. A man, his face blacked out by the sun, spoke to me in Danish.

"I'm sorry." I held my hand to my chin. "I don't—"

"Are you all right?" The accent was different from Søren's. I still couldn't see his face. He dangled his hand like bait on a fishing line and I took it. It was hot and dry. I tried to stand with one hand still on my chin, but couldn't. I started to apologize. The man shook his head, grabbed my wrists, and pulled me to my feet.

He took my head in his hands and turned it. "A scratch."

From between his wrists I saw him properly. He was tall, with curly black hair that grew down into a short beard. The lowered front zipper of his coveralls revealed more hair bubbling above an undershirt. His eyes were steely and still as he let me go. Geden. The Goat. Did he recognize me?

"Thank you for helping me. I'm Roxana." I extended my hand.

He ignored it. "You must be careful when you're walking."

"My eyes were closed."

He cocked his head. "Why?"

"Excuse me?"

"Why were you walking with your eyes closed?" He reached for my hand, lifting it. More an embrace than a handshake. "No matter. They call me Geden, but it is not my name. Be careful when you walk, Roxana."

He looked as if he would say something else, but instead he turned, climbed into his truck, and started the engine, winking as he pulled away. I sat back down on the pavement, dazzled. He had touched my hand, looked in my eyes. He had lifted me. More importantly, I had stood.

You can choose, I repeated to myself until the words held no meaning. You can choose you can choose you can choose you can choose . . .

6

AFTER THAT I WALKED TO THE POND EVERY AFTERNOON, HOPING I MIGHT SEE GEDEN. Fall in front of him again. I daydreamed of sustaining a worse injury. Requiring his care.

I perimetered the park, entered it. I looked for him and didn't find him, and I kept looking. I sent my desire out into the day hot as a knife passed over a flame. My power grew threefold as I walked farther and farther, into the declining violet light, not caring who saw me, not minding the looks I got when I ordered ice cream or bought bread in plain American English, my want for Geden emanating from me like a directional fever. You don't know who you're dealing with, I thought, hissing air out my nose at the Danes.

It surprised me to discover I was angry at them. So precious with their tax money. The young people in Farsø all looked sickly to me, pale and snot nosed, clad in ensembles of tracksuits and cheap T-shirts sporting poorly translated English phrases. PARTYING IS LIFE WITH THE BULL SHIT CUT OUT read one meek little girl's black tee, beneath a photo of a woman on her knees.

*   *   *

Then one meltingly hot day I finally saw Geden again. I was about to go back to the apartment when I spotted him walking toward the stand of trees on the other side of the pond. I froze and crouched behind a bush, sure that if I made a careless noise the sound would travel the distance and drive him deeper into the woods.

Geden walked like no one I had ever seen, his feet meticulous, each step plotted and yet utterly natural, something long and shiny in his left hand. When he reached the edge of the woods, I almost called out, but instead I ran for him, putting the scream into my breath. Be with me, I thought. Want me. He turned his head for just a moment and I lost my nerve at the sight of that sharp profile, those questing eyes. I ducked behind a tree. When I looked again he was gone in the green.

My socks and shirt were soaked with sweat, my head full of buzzing. The hair on the back of my neck and arms stood as if drawn by a current. Bring him to me. His head on a plate, I thought before I could stop myself. And then I felt guilty, and then I felt good. I rustled the leaves, hoping he'd return.

When he did not, I walked to the mall in Farsø and bought the biggest ice cream the hot dog stand sold, pointing at the picture of a vaffel is, twelve balls of ice cream stuffed into a waffle cone, topped with a flødebolle, meringue cream on a wafer covered in dark chocolate, and a scoop of the strange pink froth called guf. I ate it like I hadn't tasted food in weeks.

That was the first night I didn't try to seduce Søren. It was such a relief.

What had gone wrong between us? Was it something I had done, or had his newness worn off in a month? His fine slim body and pale eyes, that way he had of drawing me close with one quick swoop of his long arm. That was the only touch he had for me now, other than a dutiful peck in the morning and before bed.

Thoughts of sex swarmed me. I'd be out on one of my walks, staring into the storefronts on the street that served as Farsø's downtown, and the want would come on all at once, overwhelming.

I wanted and wanted and wanted. I masturbated three and four times a day, bringing myself off so hard that my legs shook and cramped and my ankles ached and I struggled to keep from crying. Five times. Six. I slept and lived in the same pair of leggings and underwear for days at a time, coming in my underwear so frequently that the combination of my clothes and my body began to produce a completely new smell, a rich pre-rot. A dare for Søren, a lure for Geden. Come smell me, I thought. Come to my smell.

I luxuriated in my unwashed body. Once I had planned every outfit for every day of the sixty we were to spend in Paris. Sometimes two, day and evening both. Now, when I took down my underwear to pee, I had to peel the sticky fabric away from my skin. When I smelled myself I thought of Mama doing laundry. Sylvie walking through a museum in a brand-new dress. I lay supine and spread, waiting to be given a reason to move.

I needed more information. At dinner I took a deep breath and pitched my voice as casual as I could. "Søren?"

"Mm."

"Do you remember that day we went to Fyrkat?"

He rolled his eyes, expecting sentimentality. "Of course."

"You remember how on the way there we saw that man? The one you said was called Goat?"

"Geden." He didn't even bother to make eye contact.

I made my voice light. "How do you know him?"

He took a bite, chewed. Frikadeller again. "I know him as everyone in Farsø knows him. He has been in this miserable little place a long while."

"And he's not nice?"

Søren sighed and put his fork down. "The man cannot be bothered with anyone other than himself. The things I hear about him have served to bolster this impression."

I cut my meatball in half, halved the halves, halved the halved halves. How long could I keep going? Could I cut until the frikadeller simply disappeared?

"What kind of things?"

"Stories. Apparently as a teenager he reported his neighbor's dog. A pit bull. It is against the law to own one. Their jaws can lock, and if they attack a child, not a pretty picture. But Geden's neighbor's dog was sweet, not very large. Little children lived in the house with it and it never did them any harm. He did it out of sheer spite. To hurt them." Søren gulped his beer. "The other things are only rumors, I suppose, but rumors of this sort tend to be true. He has some minor underworld involvement, works off the books. Dodges his tax liability, which is infuriating. Bosnians are lucky in Denmark. They look European. Until they speak, no one knows they are different. They take advantage of that."

"What do you mean, take advantage?"

He threw his fork down and considered me sternly. "I am not going to have an argument with you about your American superiority complex. That is a lie. You know that, right? Look at your prisons. At your schools, at the health services in your country. Pay or out into the street you go. Or into the prison, depending."

"Søren."

"You are not Danish, Roxana. You do not understand. The system we have built functions only if everyone follows the rules. There can be no exceptions. Even cutting in line can unsettle everything."

A haze descended, obscuring everything. There was no arguing with him. He went on.

"You are suffering the result of years of bad behavior from people like Geden. He has some tragic tale, as they all do, and that is of course very sad. The problem starts with the idea that it is our job to respect the backward customs and Stone Age lifestyle of these people and their religion. Religion! There is nothing worse in the world than religion."

Søren downed the rest of his beer. "I see your expression. You damn me. I am not intolerant, Roxana! Why should the workday be divided into many parts so they can get down on all fours every so often to pray on their little magic rugs? Why is that my problem? If you claim you can speak to a man in the clouds, why does your insanity need to be recognized and accommodated with special dispensation? What does any of that have to do with the promise between the state and the citizen?"

Søren's voice inflated, monotone. I already knew what he would say if I tried to respond: that he was concerned about preserving the culture of Denmark, that Americans were the real racists, that I didn't understand what I was talking about. I felt more and more invisible beside him. How could he care so much about abstract categories and so little for concrete details?

Something inside me started humming. I tuned him out, tuned it in. Saw Geden slowly turn his head, walk into the trees.

Nothing seemed to give Søren pleasure anymore. He grew sullen. I had to be the one to take the hash from its place in the cupboard, to pack it into the little glass pipe. He smoked as morosely as he drank. The closest he came to being happy was after three or four beers and several pipes' worth, when I found an old American comedy on the television. He brayed at every joke and fell asleep as soon as it ended.

Old movies had always depressed me. When Sylvie went through her New Wave phase, I watched the films begrudgingly, one eye on the magazine or coffee table book on my lap. Colorized films were even worse than black-and-white, that fuzzy grain, the familiar-but-not clothes and hair, the hopeful looks on the young faces of actors I knew only as wizened and creased. But I grew adept at feigning interest in Søren's films, second- and third-tier comedies and made-for-TV dramas set in nameless soundstages. I had to. Absent entertainment, Søren buried himself in bad news on his computer, bathed in its blue light, his eyes boring into the screen. When I said his name, he jumped.

But all this was preferable to Søren in full fury. The attacks of rage and sadness could come at any time, could be set off by anything, his anger generalized and inescapable, a way of being. It filled every space in the apartment, made the front windows rheumy and opaque. We couldn't see through it and no one could look in. If I parted my lips Søren's anger flooded my mouth and choked me.

I wished he would do something violent and plainly crazy—break a chair, punch a hole in a wall, throw the TV out

the window—just to break the spell of his melancholy. Sometimes I saw my original Søren, romantic and delicate, trapped
inside the suffering gray shell perched on the other end of the
couch, watching, hoping that he might be released.

No two of his moods were alike. Each carried a million
new tiny shades of self-loathing. "I'm a moron, I'm a drone, I
don't know what I'm doing, why did I think I could do this?"
he raged. "God, I'm such a fucking loser," he would say, until
the words no longer meant anything. I heard only the sound of
his unhappiness and my powerlessness against it.

When he was like this, everything stopped. All of me
clenched terribly, even my thoughts. And he never wanted me,
not anymore.

One day I bought a bottle of lotion at the grocery store just
to have something that was my own. I put it on the floor next
to my side of the bed. It was one of my clocks. My little birth
control pills were the other. Every night I popped one from its
blister pack and swallowed it without water. Then I pumped my
hand full of lotion and spread it over my legs to heighten the
sensation of climbing between the sheets. In the dim twilight
and searing daylight I hung upside down off the edge of the
mattress and watched the line inside the bottle sink past the
word emblazoned across its beige plastic hips, LUKSUS, which
Søren said meant "luxury."

What if Søren just didn't know what I wanted? Perhaps I had
been doing that thing women's magazines talked about so much.
Thinking he could read my mind.

We were on the couch, already stoned. His hand was on the remote, ready to start up the evening's entertainment. I touched him, smiling as gently as I could.

"Can we talk?"

He didn't put the remote down. "Right now?" He kept his attention on the black screen, his finger twitching on the button.

I made myself be direct. I couldn't look at him. "I just really like it when we're making out and I feel you get hard through your pants. I like to feel it under my hand. Before we even take off our clothes. It's exciting. I like it when you lie on top of me and I feel you."

I tried to keep my voice level as I looked at him. "You know?"

He raised his eyebrows. I kept my smile steady.

"Maybe it sounds silly. I just wanted you to know."

He nodded.

"Are you okay?"

He stretched his fingers out in front of him, as if expelling a toxin. "Yes, thank you!" He stood and left the room.

I had to wait until I stopped shaking before I could follow him down the hallway. Søren was lying on the bed in the dark in all his clothes, facing away from me. I stretched out on my side of the bed. He did not move. I put my hand on his back.

"Roxana," he warned.

I withdrew my hand, then folded my arm against my torso and rolled over it onto my stomach. If I could have erased my arm from my body, I would have.

"Are you okay?" The words felt old in my mouth.

"Yes! I'm fine! I don't know how to respond when you say things like that to me! What the hell am I supposed to say?"

In that moment, I didn't know what he was talking about. I searched my mind for an accidental slight.

"I don't know what I'm supposed to say when you talk about things like this. Erections through my pants? You want me to get hard but I can't do that on command! I'm sorry!"

I want to have sex, I thought. I want your sex. I want you to put all that violent energy into a kiss. Remember the night I was in my flowered pajamas and you called me onto your lap and held me there, feeling me through my clothes, and we talked lightly, lightly about how I was twelve, about how no one else could know about what happened between us? And remember how after you took me to the bed and fucked me and stopped halfway through to put your mouth on me, and you ate and ate until I was just my lower face salivating and beating like a heart in your mouth?

"I'm sorry."

He didn't answer.

"I didn't mean to make you feel bad."

I felt alone in the room.

"I was trying to be nice."

Was he even breathing?

"I'm sorry."

Silence upon silence. I waited in its long breath.

Finally Søren exhaled. "I am sorry, Roxana, that you are stuck with someone as fucked up as me. I do not doubt that you are very much looking forward to going home."

He rolled away from me. I lay in the cold room until I was sure he was asleep. Then I made a pilgrimage to the bathroom, where I took off all my clothes and prostrated myself on the floor and cried until I was out of tears and my body was just a problem on the tile.

7

INDEPENDENCE DAY HAD COME AND GONE UNNOTICED SAVE FOR AN E-CARD FROM MAMA AND DAD, AN ANIMATION OF RACING AMERICAN FLAGS THAT MADE ME FEEL FIRST LIKE CRYING AND THEN AS IF I WAS LOSING MY MIND. The Fourth of July had been the midway point of every summer of my life, the reminder that it was passing. In Farsø it was just another day in an endless stream. Life would get more and more like this as I went on, it seemed, meaning leaching out along with everything that had once made sense. I went out into the white-hot day.

I wasn't hungry for a hot dog or an ice cream, nor did I need any of the wares displayed in front of the stores I passed, final markdowns and last sales. My right hand skimmed the plastic and the not plastic, the spaces in between, until I reached a corner and turned left, into the scaffolding's shadow.

All day I had been having a silent argument with myself about writing to Sylvie. Would she understand about Søren, or would she see the situation to its sad bones: a depressed older man who had secreted a young woman to a remote location. She would ask if I was Søren's girlfriend, and I would tell her about the time we had talked about that, kind of, and she would withdraw into a reflective silence.

"Well," she'd say after a while. "You have your answer."

It was ridiculous to think about, I told myself to loosen the ringing in my head. I was in a place where no one knew me. The summer air carried Jutland to me like a hallucination, the bright sun and grassy smell muted, gauzy. One breath, and everything would disappear.

My eyes landed on a distant figure. I blinked and he sharpened. Familiar and tall in his khaki coveralls. Geden. I made my face still and kept my pace.

I had walked all over Farsø looking for him. I had come to recognize perhaps a dozen strangers. The tired young brunette mother struggling with her triplets. The old man out for his daily constitutional. The legging-clad teenager with Asian eyes and blonde hair, jogging. But I had not seen Geden since the day he walked away from me.

Then we were beside each other and my hand was in his.

It happened so quickly I thought I imagined it. Geden's hand was at his side, mine at mine. We came toward each other and at the moment of passing he took my small sweaty fingers in his large dry ones. I was still moving when my arm registered the connection. Caught. Recoiled, sending me back to him. We stood at a diagonal, eyes downcast, as if we were about to dance.

"Roxana." Geden's voice was unsurprised. "Hello."

"Hi." I willed my hands to stop sweating.

"What are you doing?"

"Walking."

"Walking where?"

"Nowhere. Just a walk."

He smiled, revealing perfect teeth next to his luridly soft lip. "Keep your eyes open."

"Yes." I smiled back, cursing myself. Don't be unfair, I thought. To Søren. The tops of my thighs were already wet.

"Where is Søren?"

"Excuse me?" I shivered. How did he know?

"This is a small town. People see each other. Søren is also having a walk?"

I looked away from him, across the street, where two women openly watched us. Geden did not turn. I caught the eyes of one of the women, a dyed redhead. Was she the teenager from the park? No—and I dropped my gaze, let her float away from me like refuse.

Geden's mouth was pink and soft in his beard. I had a feeling of déjà vu.

He let out a painful little sigh. A wince. "Are you lonely, Roxana?"

My heart careened around in my chest, drunk. What would Mama say? "Excuse me?" I said again.

"Are you lonely?" He looked very serious, as if much rode on my answer.

"No." I lied. "I don't know anyone here, that's all,"

Geden nodded, his hand still in mine. I remembered the International Abroad Experiences mission statement, the one Sylvie and I had memorized in the hours we spent over the Parisian Experience brochure.

The purpose of International Abroad Experiences is to connect people. When you make friends in another country, you become a citizen of the world. We believe strongly that this experience is one all young people should have. It enriches lives and deepens character.

I know you will make lots of friends, Dad had written.

"Don't let anybody think they know more than you," Mama said on the day I left. "Except for when they do and you need their help."

"It's difficult to meet people," I said to Geden. It felt like a concession. "I don't speak Danish."

"Danish is not my first language, either."

"I know," I said, before I could stop myself.

He gave me a tiny smile. "It is not fair that I know nothing about you and you know so much know about me. An imbalance we must even. Have you been to eat in Farsø?"

"In a restaurant? No." All Farsø's three restaurants stood together among the conglomeration of barren storefronts on the main street. When I asked Søren which was his favorite, the answer was a stream of derisive laughter.

"In another town, then? Aars? Randers?" Geden asked.

"No."

He squinted at me. "How do you fill all those lonely hours in Søren's uncle's apartment?"

A chill ran down my spine. "You just said you know nothing about me, but you know how I spend my days?"

"A guess," Geden said. "Which you have confirmed. Tell me you have something to do in that flat other than tidy the same rooms over and over."

I raised my eyes and then dropped them, ashamed.

"And he has not even taken you to a restaurant. I'm sorry." And he did look sorry. Anguished even. What was going on?

"It's fine."

"No." His hand moved. I thought he would drop the clutch. Instead he lifted his other hand and pressed them together around mine. My palms flamed. "I have an obligation, one foreigner to another. I will take you to eat. And in this way I will learn about you."

"What do you want to know?" I found it hard to breathe.

"Oh, anything." For a burning moment his palm was on my cheek and I raised my hand to hold it there and we looked at each other and then it was over.

"Meet me here at this time next week. Yes?"

"Yes."

He let go of my hands. I closed my eyes. When I opened them, he was gone.

Was the street I took back to the apartment the same one I had walked to get there? Were the stairs the same? I almost expected a new apartment behind the heavy door, vibrant colors and loud music and billowing fabric in the place of Søren's uncle's tepid minimalism.

But inside, the same low blue sofa still sat across from the pressboard coffee table. The same coffee-stained dishtowels still hung from the oven door in the kitchen. I opened the cabinets and cupboards, peered into their same dark corners. How could they be unchanged? It didn't feel the same inside, to stand under the poor water pressure and wash my hair with athletic determination. Something was different. Finally I saw the change in the steam-fogged mirror. My face had shifted, become subtly other. It was me. I was what had changed.

I tore the bedroom apart. Emptied the closet and drawers into a great heap and wiped the surfaces down. Hustled dust bunnies out from under the bed, crushed them under my feet, swept them into the trash. When everything was empty and clean, I sat panting beside my pile. The cheap closet door bobbed on its hinges, excited too, showing me the locked metal box. I hadn't thought about it since the day we moved in.

It was cold to the touch and heavy as I remembered, so heavy I couldn't lift it, only pull it out onto the floor, where it landed so loudly I worried I had cracked a floorboard. The intricate combination lock was printed with rudimentary little slashes, characters I didn't recognize. I pushed it around, trying to pry it up by its corners, but the box's lid stood firm.

I fell backward onto the clothes mounded on the bed. I closed my eyes and held Geden's hand under the scaffold again. I couldn't invent anything better than what had happened. The way we had come toward each other and touched.

That night was no different. Søren, despondent about his thesis, defrosted tiny cold shrimp in the sink and served them to me on toast spread with mayonnaise, a wet meal my stomach morosely accepted. It would sit there a long time. I was constipated from all the processed flour and meat. Or maybe I was just knotted up with thoughts of Geden.

After dinner Søren suggested we watch a movie. A famous old film that every Dane knew and loved was on television that night, even running with English subtitles! His excitement fatigued me.

The movie was about a pair of vagabonds who come to a farm and befriend the family that owns it. Much dull fun is had until evil businessmen show up to buy the farm out from under the family and the vagabonds jump into action to repel the opportunistic capitalists, uniting everyone in bucolic joy. This was apparently one of the most beloved films in the history of Danish cinema.

The actor who played the younger vagabond, Søren explained, had been so iconic in the role that for the rest of his career he had been typecast. As long as he could pass for young, the actor played honorable boys on the verge of manhood who swept into the lives of farm girls and impoverished noblewomen and shy Copenhagen schoolteachers and showered them with morally upright kindness and love and respect. He made honest women of them and was a true husband. There was a Danish word for the actor's special character type: førsteelsker, "first lover."

"First lover." I passed the words through my mouth. "Who is the second lover, then? Who comes next?"

"Roxana." Søren shook his head and put his arm around me. It was the first time he had touched me in days. I stiffened, afraid he would take his arm back. He looked deep into my eyes and for a moment I was sure he would kiss me. His tongue would slip into my mouth, a word I had forgotten. I would speak it again and time would restart.

He stroked my face. "Silly Roxana, there is no second lover. The førsteelsker is also the girl's last. Once he wins her heart she can never win it back."

Something happened in the movie and Søren yanked away. His impenetrable laughter fell on me like snow.

Every day in the week before I was to meet Geden for lunch, I made a silent promise. If Søren showed me one ounce of interest, I wouldn't go. It was an illogical pledge. Why shouldn't I? Lunch was not infidelity. And the strangeness of Søren's dislike for Geden made it easy to lie. Besides, he didn't even know that I had been leaving the apartment.

One of those nights we were at dinner, pushing wilted lettuce across our plates, and I heard Sylvie's voice. She always knew who and what I wanted before I did. "Do you want to fuck Geden?" The question turned me so red that Søren opened the window in concern, saying, "You wanted a salad," as if I had complained.

I left the table, went to the bathroom, closed the door, and took off my pants. My feral smell rose to greet me. I conjured Geden's eyes. Licked from the tip of my pinkie to the knobby bone in my wrist, brought myself off with that.

The next morning we went to the grocery store to buy ingredients for an American dinner I was supposed to cook, Søren's idea.

"I've cooked every night you've been here. You've had enough Danish food. Do I get an American abroad experience?"

"Ha," I said. "An American broad experience, maybe."

He didn't get it. We paced the aisles with one of the tiny grocery carts that passed for useful here. What was I supposed to cook? Sylvie and I had made obscure French things together: hachis parmentier, tartiflette, magret de canard. Outside of these experiments, I didn't have much experience in the kitchen. I could produce toast, a grilled cheese sandwich, cereal with milk. Søren wanted baked potatoes, a steak, a hamburger. Tacos.

We trailed through the meats. Ground pork, pork chops thick and thin, the sausage medisterpølse, other, paler sausages. Chicken, steaks. A package of oblong pigs' hearts. I reached to tap their cellophane wrapper with my fingers and jumped at Søren's sharp intake of breath behind me. He dropped his hands heavily onto my shoulders, swearing in Danish.

"For helvede, Roxana! I'm starving."

He let go and walked away. A pack of boneless, skinless chicken breasts stared up at me from the refrigerated case.

Suddenly Søren was beside me again, whispering in my ear. "Pick something, pick something please, please, please, pick something. I'm starving."

His needs were always so insistent and my own were nothing.

I turned to face him. "I haven't figured out what I'm cooking yet! Give me a second!"

Søren somehow shrank and became more erect at the same time, as if both embarrassed and smugly confirmed by my behavior. "Please keep your voice down."

"Who cares?" I made my voice louder. "Honest to God, who cares? No one is listening!"

As if to prove me wrong, an old lady in a sweatshirt slowly shook her head as she made her promenade around the meat cases.

"Why does everyone here act like that?" I asked Søren.

He covered his eyes with his hand. "You are making a scene."

"Oh, I'm sorry!" I said. "Please excuse me!"

I couldn't breathe. I would cry. I couldn't cry. I wouldn't.

Søren grabbed my shoulder and pulled me close. "What? What are you apologizing for? Everything's fine." He said "fine" exactly as Dad did when he was mad. A nothing word, a cold little shrug.

"I just don't know what I want to buy! I'm not a very accomplished cook! Give me some time!"

Søren took the cart. "Fine, we'll have chicken tartlets again. Please grab those chicken breasts." He turned away.

"I didn't say I wouldn't cook. Søren? Søren! Talk to me! Søren!"

He whipped around and took my elbow. "We are leaving."

"But I still want to cook dinner."

"Be quiet." He sighed heavily. "You make everything so complicated. I just want to get in and out of here before the entire day is gone."

Why was he always in such a rush? What else did he have to do? It had been his idea that I cook in the first place. My face was immediately all wet, as if I'd dunked my head in a bucket.

"I need a second to calm down," I whimpered. "Then I'll figure it out."

"Stop it," Søren whispered, furious, as if this was the worst thing I'd said yet. He began pulling me to the exit.

"No! No!" I cried. "I don't want to go with you! I don't!"

The teenage boy sweeping the floor twisted his neck unnaturally just to keep from seeing me. Søren stopped, put his arm around me, drew me close.

"I'm sorry, Roxana." he said in a low voice, almost kind. "Come on, let's get out of here."

I looked up into his face. "What are you sorry for?"

"Shut up, shut up, shut up," he hissed. "I cannot bear to be here any longer. This is exhausting. Please leave the store before you embarrass yourself further."

You were supposed to run away from alligators in a zigzag, I remembered, so I zigzagged out of the store. Back out into the day and the cave-like car. I collapsed in the seat, slit my eyes. Søren drew my seat belt over me, clicked it shut.

"What did I do?" I whimpered, suddenly wanting to be small, a child who had misbehaved and could be forgiven.

He set his mouth and looked straight ahead, turned the key in the ignition. "Be quiet. Please just be quiet."

By the time we got home I felt as flat and blank as a sheet of paper. Søren brushed his lips against my forehead and said he hoped I was feeling better. For dinner, we had chicken tartlets.

The next night Søren brought home a movie he thought I would like, about a poor young girl growing up in a housing project in England. One morning the girl goes downstairs and puts a saucepan of water on the stove. She is dancing alone when a man's voice surprises her. A shirtless stranger has entered the room. Lithe, muscled, rough. My eyes traced his golden triangle of shoulders, waist, crotch. The Swiss actor from the science fiction movie. The android. She is in her underwear and a purple T-shirt, and he is in jeans only, which sit low on his hips, revealing the incipient curve of his ass. The ridges of muscle in his torso, his flickering arms as they make breakfast. The camera her eye.

Beside me Søren fell asleep, slackening, his breath slowing, his soft lips pressing. His elegant hands unclasped, released.

At a party, the girl steals a bottle of vodka from a couple engaged in the early stages of intercourse in her kitchen. She drinks herself to sleep on her mother's bed, waking to her mother and her mother's new friend the lovely man talking beside her. The mother wants to tell her to leave, but the man shushes her, scoops up the girl in his arms, and carries her to her bedroom.

The girl is awake but the man thinks she is asleep.

They pass through the hallway in lush layers of darkness, gray-on-black.

The man's arms around her, the dark passage of the hallway, her secret wakefulness.

He lays her in her bed. Takes off her sneakers. Rolls down
her socks. Gently, gently.

Her body asleep but not, that reverent state in which the
form, independent of the mind, seeks to be perceived as uncon-
scious. If he learns she is awake the spell will break. He takes off
her pants, revealing modest white underwear. He folds the pants,
covers her with a blanket, turns off the light, leaves. That's all.
He's a good guy, at least for tonight.

The girl opens her eyes in the dark.

Søren's breath caught in his throat, made a kind of sucking sound.

Sometimes when I watched movies stoned I couldn't focus.
Sometimes I fell asleep and woke, slept and woke, deeper and
deeper, until waking up was like dragging myself out of a pit.
This annoyed Søren. "Wake up, skat. We are spending time
together."

I wanted what I saw when I let my eyes unfocus and the
shapes on the screen went blurry. The contours of his body and
the beats of the scenes already inside me, ready for replaying.

I turned off the movie when Søren was safely asleep. I was
tempted to rewatch the scene where the man carries the girl
to her bedroom. But instead I rose from the couch as quietly
as possible and went into the bathroom, the only room in the
apartment with a lock. Not even a lock, really, just the little latch
bolted to the door frame. It would do.

I had learned to avoid the mirror when entering the bathroom, to hold my head so I wouldn't see my unholstered breasts
loose hanging above my tummy in Søren's shirt. Seeing my body
would compromise my ability to dream the man. The fantasy
was coming together in dissonant, embarrassing points. I had
to not think about it too much.

The girl in the movie was thin, with skinny arms, knobby breasts. Even smaller in person, I was sure. But all she did with it was wear those hideous giant sweat suits.

I lay down on the floor and pressed the first and second fingers of my right hand up into my crotch. The bath mat was damp under my head, smelling of mold. I pressed the rise of my pubis, a sustained pat, the way I firmly pressed Mushi's head, over and over, until his eyes closed. Here. I am here, I thought with each press. I am inside here. Where I live.

I want to go somewhere, I thought.

I had to be careful not to cry.

I pushed again, harder, releasing a flash of wonderful feeling, vibrant and fast. A horse I could ride. I knew where I wanted to go.

During my senior year I had become preoccupied with a different actor. I saw him on an award show and had that same sinking feeling. He was the one for me. Not in real life. In my fantasy life. He had a jagged, angular face and a spare tall body. He was awkward and funny in interviews. His mother, I learned, was a renowned painter with a significant body of work, which made me like him most of all. Son of a strong woman, learner of her worth.

I cut pictures of him from magazines and pasted them in a photo album with a soft blue cover. I took the train into the city with Sylvie to see a movie that would never make it to Creek Grove in which he played a petty criminal, a con man in love with a pretty girl. It wasn't good, but I didn't care. All I wanted were the lovemaking scenes.

The whole time I was hung up on that actor I thought: This is the last time. I am in my last year of high school. I am eighteen years old. I will leave school and go to another school in a city, by myself. This is the last time I will clip pictures of a handsome stranger from magazines.

Maybe there was never a last time, only a concerted gap between nexts. I curved the fingers of my right hand between my legs and pulled up, unleashing an arc of pleasure that settled against the flash in a kind of firework. A little one. A starter.

When I was younger it was harder to assemble a world. Fantasizing felt silly, put on. I just pushed and pulled at the approximate location, blank, until I couldn't breathe anymore and bright flowers blossomed and I blinked around the room, incredulous, and the purple smoke came.

It wasn't like that anymore, after Hunter. After Søren. I learned that when someone touched me I changed. Every time.

There was a truth here. Søren would not give himself to me as I wanted.

In the bathroom I was safe. Søren could not find me. I wasn't with him here. I was leaving. I was going somewhere else.

I closed my eyes.

A fancy hotel room. Fluffy towels, marble surfaces, windows full of sparkling sea behind lowered pearl shades.

Behind me, the actor from the movie.

I made the rules. The actor looked at me with cold eyes.

I ran one and two fingers against my clit, and thought what would happen.

He would come to me and take off his jacket, loosen his tie.

He loved the taste of my sweat. The way it collected sour in the crevices of my body.

First he would kiss me. His tongue would paint mine. Our teeth in each other's way.

He cupped and groped my breasts. His hands diligent, trained, knowing. He would rub his palm up and down the central line of my body, reaching between my legs.

No questions. No conversation.

Him behind, biting the back of my neck. Him on top, hitting me across the face with an open palm over and over again. Solidifying the diffuse pain I swam in, making it solid and real. It felt so good to be seen.

Where were we, back there in the hotel room? On the cold marble floor or in the sheets?

He told me to spread my legs.

To spread them wider. I opened my mouth and was bidden to put my tongue on every part of him. To lick the bottoms of his feet.

When the purple feeling began to smoke inside me—blooms and combustions and exploding bulbs tornadoing up, fierce and terrifying—I sat up and threw my crotch back and forth against the heel of my hand, hard. The purple smoked and I tensed and released and tensed and it smoked and I released. Every lean brought another gust, another wash. Each tensing was complete, crystalline, the fantasy coming together now, complete and determined.

I sat on the actor, breasts aloft, hair wild. He was naked and mine. I rocked back and forth. He looked up at me, helpless, lost, begging to be shown the way.

I leaned and cut a little nick in the shallow, thin skin above his clavicle with something sharp. My fingernail? A knife? It didn't matter. I opened him with the sharp and blood puddled at the wound. He threw his head back. This was what he wanted, the thing he couldn't speak. To be opened.

I pressed my mouth to the wound. Tongued the edges of the cut. He climaxed, convulsing like a death rattle. The feeling of him beginning to fill me took me there too.

In the hotel room I coughed, moaned, screamed like I was dying.

In the bathroom I panted and whispered.

He would be gone soon, but it wasn't over, I was still caught in it, an anemone in a thunderhead. There was one last image before he left. His expression of horrified gratitude.

I threw myself against the tile, slapping my face, frantic to stay high as I fell back down to the bathroom, to the apartment, to Farsø. My life filtering in, my self, the lights coming up after the film.

I spoke the words out loud. "Oh God, oh Jesus, yes, please, hurt me, hurt me. Hurt me."

When the vision had left me I leaned against the wall, satisfied and sad. I sobbed fiercely for a moment, curling my body in on itself, feeling the vacuum of want inside, the blowsy, ugly place where Søren had left me alone.

"No," I said, standing on shaking legs, the blood that had rushed to my face at the slaps already leaving me. I could never do it hard enough to leave a mark.

Avoiding my face in the mirror, I washed my hands and went back out into the apartment.

8

THE MORNING OF MY LUNCH WITH GEDEN I PULLED MY
LILAC DRESS OVER MY HEAD AND EXAMINED MYSELF IN
THE MIRROR. The color still complemented my complexion
and the fit hadn't changed, but the dress was wrong. I couldn't
see or feel it without seeing the faces in its history. Sylvie's,
on the day we had bought it together, and Søren's, sometime
later, taking me from behind in the bedroom with the skirt
bundled at my waist.

I stripped the dress off and dropped it on the floor, barely
restraining the urge to stomp on it. What would I wear? The
rush of practical anxiety was comforting. It had been weeks
since I cared.

I dumped my drawer out on the bed and picked through
it, vetoing everything with a memory. Not the T-shirt from
the Michigan City Corn Roast. Not the maroon skirt with the
elastic waistband that Mama brought back from Boston. Not
the hard-won jeans I had found after hours of searching. I was
left with black pants, a black T-shirt, a black sweater. It wasn't
the prettiest outfit, but it was more important to be free.

The sky was a seasick green. Trees crashed together in the wind. I rounded the bend. Geden stood beside his little beige truck. He saw me, smiled, and waved. I ducked my head, scared that Søren would appear. The pulled-down top of Geden's coveralls hung at his hips like a skirt. Beneath he wore a close-fitting black pullover. When I came close he said my name, bending the *r* in his strange way.

"Hi," I said.

"Hi," he aped, as if he had never heard the word before.

We stared at each other. This is a bad idea, I thought.

Geden opened the passenger door. "Please."

For a moment I was sure I would leave, just turn and go. How could I know this was safe? Then I was in the car. I clicked my seat belt closed, keeping my hand on the buckle like it was a gun. Geden shut my door and walked around back, drumming his fingers on the body of the truck.

A bald man appeared at the margin of the park. My breath caught in my throat. Søren, with his bag and his dark green pants. I closed my eyes and counted, bracing myself. Geden climbed into the driver side, bringing with him his own smell. Woods, sweat, smoke. He had taken off the coveralls and undershirt and now wore only what looked like a pair of black leggings. I gripped my door handle.

"We will go to Viborg," Geden said. "A medieval capital. A Viking capital."

"Okay," I said quickly, trying to take deep breaths. I thought I could see Søren's facial expression. First, total incomprehension—eyebrows slightly lifted, little mouth forming a question—segueing quickly into baffled anger lit by a victorious sense of offense. My mind spun out, seeking plausible explanations for what I might be doing here in the park at Geden's truck. There were none. Søren would perceive everything.

Crazily I hoped he would hit me. I wanted some physical proof of his cruelty to show Geden. To show, to explain it.

Geden started the truck and pulled away from the curb. I expected Søren to rush the car, to put himself in its path, bang on the hood. But he did nothing. When I turned to look, he had already passed. Now all I could see was his back. His gait was off, his shoes a garish yellow, his pants gray. It wasn't him.

The truck careened through a roundabout, barreling out the last exit. Buildings pulled away from the road and we were out in farm country, alongside wide fields. I let myself look at him. A dense black fur covered the center of his slender chest, his shoulders rising over his jutting clavicle. His neck ran up to his face in careful hollows.

I put words in my mouth to fill it. "Do you have a restaurant picked out?"

Geden snorted. I couldn't tell if it was a form of laughter or an actual snort. "Yes, I have one 'picked out.' " He set the words apart with delight.

"Are you making fun of the way I talk?"

"I do not make fun."

"Then why say my words like that?"

Geden turned and I saw with surprise that he was hurt. "It is unusual for me to meet native English-speakers, especially Americans. Forgive me for finding the way that you speak novel." He took one hand from the wheel and extended it toward me. "I will not insult you. Will you treat me with the same respect?"

I took his hand. "Of course."

"You say it as if it is automatic, but it is not," Geden said, still holding my hand with his right as he curved the wheel with his left. "I respect you."

"I respect you."

"Thank you." Geden dropped my hand as easily as he had taken it.

We drove through shopping areas interpolated by stretches of farmland specked with horses and cows and a few sheep. Long low houses with thatched roofs. Exurban Denmark, a new landscape. Big-box stores or what I assumed were big-box stores, massive rectangles of black glass and smooth white cement at the center of vast parking lots. People hauled uncooperative children out of cars.

The silence in the truck hung heavy.

"I don't know anything about you," I said to make it real. What we were doing. "But you know so much about me."

Geden laughed. "I have only observed. I am used to learning about people, about strangers, by watching. The habit of a friendless man." He smiled, bare, reticent, concerned.

"And what have you observed?"

"You are a young woman in the care of one older man and currently in the vehicle of another. Both men are foreign to you. Recent acquaintances."

I crossed my arms at the elbow and let my hands flop in my lap. "So?"

He spoke softly. "You are a young girl, and you live with a grown man who speaks a language you do not. You live with him in his country."

"I am not a young girl," I said. "I am a woman."

"Fair enough." He leaned back into his seat. "What do you wish to know about me?"

I straightened, trying to catch my breath. "What do you do for a living?" He looked at me oddly. "I mean, what is your job?"

"I am a skovrider. The word translates to 'forest rider.' A bit like Oliver Mellors, you might say, although I care for the trees rather than for game." He gave a naughty little grin.

"I don't know who that is."

"He's an imaginary man from a long-ago book." Geden wiped the space between us. "I am employed by the municipality. I keep track of the forest. I monitor the growth of plants as well as the populations of deer, birds, and other animals."

"Are you from Farsø?"

He shook his head. "I've lived here a long while."

"How long?"

"Since I came from Bosnia when I was thirteen years old."

I turned to examine him more closely. "Why did you move?"

"My family lived in Sarajevo until the city was torn apart by war. We feared we would die and fled our country as refugees. We were held in a camp here in Jutland until I was nearly eighteen."

"A camp. Like a concentration camp?"

The corners of his mouth twitched a brief, flickering smile. "Our camp was humanitarian. In intention, anyway. Limbo. My parents were not authorized to work until we were granted asylum. By that time, any idea that my grandparents would find new lives here was completely lost."

"Your grandparents came with you, too?"

"Yes."

I looked at my hands, my chewed-up cuticles and unlined palms. "Are you a Muslim?"

He laughed. "You sound very grave."

"I'm sorry, it doesn't matter. I'm being rude."

"You are not being rude, Roxana," Geden said. "You are being direct. I admire that. Yes, I am Muslim. Not particularly observant, for my own reasons. Although not practicing makes me better in the eyes of everyone here."

"Is that why Søren hates you so much?" I asked before I could stop myself.

"Because I am an ambivalent believer in the Koran? I do not think so," he said. "I always had the sense Søren disliked me on sight."

I studied his face for a long time, long enough that I expected him to turn away, but he did not.

Eventually we came to what looked like the outskirts of a city, with dense buildings clustered on the horizon among a handful of spires and towers. Geden wove the little truck into the winding streets, past brick and stone buildings, countless iterations of ceramics showrooms. An austere old church, white and dignified on a hill. In a small lot he parked and leaped from the car. I watched him climb back into his coveralls in the rearview mirror, pulling his black shirt over his head.

He opened my door. "You must think I'm a beast, driving shirtless like that. Forgive me. My work makes me very hot."

He licked his lips. I looked away. "Where are we going?"

"An American restaurant."

It was tucked inside a white building with a red tile roof, one in a curving line of white buildings with red tile roofs on a square, a Place—the Danish word was "Plads." But I thought of a square as somewhere people would want to linger, with cafés, a fountain. This was just a parking lot. From the outside, it looked like any other Danish restaurant, a dim storefront whose exterior no one had given much thought to. Geden opened the door, shaking the shiny red buckle of silver sleigh bells attached to the hinge. Mama put a set like this on our mantel every December, beside the giant pinecones she kept in a big Tupperware box in the attic the rest of the year. But it wasn't Christmas. It was August.

We stepped inside. The lower half of a submarine marked with the words DEEP DIVER protruded from a green-painted oval surrounded by track lighting in the center of the ceiling. Every surface was covered in a label or sign or poster or other bit of American ephemera. NEW YORK SANDWICHES! CHICAGO DANCING—NEW ORLEANS PIZZA—CALIFORNIA STEW!

The wall above the table was decorated with a pair of ice skates, a framed black-and-white photograph of old-timey football players in leather helmets, and a giant neon sign offering BUICK SERVICE in hot-orange cursive. The place was called Bones or Bone's, both spellings plastered interchangeably all over the dining room.

A listless blonde waitress appeared, wearing a black polo shirt with BONE's embroidered over her slouchy left boob and led us to a blond wood table identical to the one on which Søren and I ate dinner every night in the apartment. The chair spindles were cut into the shape of bones. The waitress thrust two laminated menus at us.

"Thank you," Geden said in an exaggerated American accent. "We are so excited to have some real food from home!"

I stared at him incredulously.

She slurred uncomfortable English. "Would you like beers?"

"Two beers," Geden said, still playing American, hissing the *s*. "Please."

The waitress disappeared. Geden made a neat stack of the menus at the edge of the table.

"I didn't get a chance to look yet," I protested. "And why are you talking like that?"

He resumed his normal voice. "You will have a cheeseburger."

"Don't tell me what I'm going to order."

Geden laughed. "Cheeseburgers are the only edible item here." He handed me a menu. "You do not want to eat the ribs. The less said of the barbecue, the better. Trust me."

I looked into his eyes, rimmed with black lashes. His eyebrows were so evenly shaped I wondered if he waxed them. The hollows under his cheekbones were violet. His hair was blue where the light caught it. What did he see when he looked at me?

"I do," I said softly.

He grinned at me. "We are getting married?"

"I trust you." My face was hot.

The waitress reappeared with two pints of golden beer.

"Thank you very much," Geden said, American again. "We would like two cheeseburgers, please."

The waitress reluctantly opened her pink mouth. "Pomfritter?"

Geden gazed at her uncomprehendingly.

The waitress sighed and tucked a hank of yellow hair behind her ear. "Do you want fries?" she fairly spat.

Geden smiled like he had won the lottery. "Oh! Yes, please. And salad on the burgers."

"Go to the salad bar," she said. We watched her black work pants slump away.

"Why are you pretending to be American?" I whispered.

He opened his hands. "Look around the room. What do you see?"

The other customers were families with children. Nearly every table had red balloons tied to its chairs. Towheaded little kids toddled aimlessly, politer and quieter than any American children I had ever seen.

I looked back at Geden. "Balloons?"

"This is a place people bring their children. Popular for birthdays. What could be more lovely than feeding your little child some Dane's idea of American food in a windowless restaurant in Preislers Plads?"

"You didn't answer my question."

"I pretended to be American because I wanted the waitress to treat us well, Roxana. We are not Danes to her."

"What do you mean?"

He leaned across the table, speaking quickly. "Danish families come here. People who work in factories and as pedagogues and in shops. Who knows what they might do if they discovered two suspicious foreigners in their midst? You are a bit swarthy, as am I. We could be Arab." His eyes twinkled. "We could be Bosnian."

A little boy in a red shirt ran by, bleating, "Nej, nej, nej, nej!"

"What do you think would happen?"

"Let me show you something." Geden unzipped his coveralls and withdrew a folded newspaper and handed it to me. The entire front page was a mess of red and pink, like an abstract painting. My eyes refocused and I saw that it was a photograph of a blonde woman's badly beaten face, blown up so big there was room for hardly anything else on the page, only the name of the paper and a headline I couldn't decipher.

SIGRID, 19 ÅR: "JAG SÅG ALDRIG HANS ANSIKTE"

Dark rivers of blood split the woman's face under her light hair. One of her eyes was completely swollen shut.

I pushed the newspaper back across the table. "I can't read Danish."

Geden did not touch the newspaper. "This is a Swedish newspaper from a few weeks back. It says, 'Sigrid, nineteen years old,' and then a quotation: 'I never saw his face.'"

"The face of the man who attacked her?"

"Yes."

"That's terrible." I refolded the newspaper so all I could see was her pink neck and the stained collar of her white blouse. A little girl from a nearby table darted in our direction. I slid my hand over the image. "Can you put it away?"

Geden looked at me as if I were small. "Not yet," he said. "Do you believe it?"

"What do you mean?"

"Look at the picture. In the article it says that Sigrid was beaten until she lost consciousness. Does she look as if this happened to her?"

I pulled the newspaper squarely in front of me. "She's bleeding."

"Yes, but what else happens when you are beaten?"

When I was ten, one of Mama's patients had taken a swing at her as she worked on his PICC line. She came home with a deep blue bruise glowing to the right of her left eye. Dad and I had watched her press a bag of frozen spinach to her face. "It was an involuntary muscle reaction," she told us.

"You get a black eye," I said to Geden. "Bruises."

"Look closer."

I reluctantly returned to the image. Sigrid had no visible bruises, only streaks of blood that striped evenly down her neck. Her eye wasn't swollen. It was closed and red, not purple or black.

"There are ways to beat people up that don't leave bruises," I said.

Geden pushed the newspaper closer so that when I looked down all I saw was Sigrid's bloody face. "Do you think that's what happened here?"

Now I couldn't unsee his doubt.

Geden waited. I sucked in breath. Stared at the picture again.

"She doesn't have a black eye. The cuts on her face could be makeup. Maybe. Is that what you're saying?"

"Smart woman."

I was thrilled, but I tried to keep it off my face. "So what then? The newspaper is fake?"

"It's a real newspaper." Geden tapped the image. "Some Swedish gentlemen got together and hired a young lady to sit in a makeup artist's chair for some hours before walking into a police station and claiming she had been assaulted. By men whose faces she never saw, but who, she was certain, were Somali, Turkish, or Palestinian. Immigrants or immigrants' children. Even better, perhaps, refugees. Syrians, men named Khaled or Abdul. Dark skin, curly hair. Men who beat her because they were driven to unimaginable rage by her very existence. Certainly it is not impossible. There is no end to the horror men do to women. A Muslim or an immigrant or even a refugee could have attacked Sigrid. Her story could be true."

I watched his alert eyes, asking me a question. "But you don't think that it is."

Geden shook his head. DEEP DIVER hung above us, a moon, lighting our faces with underwater glare.

"Believing that Sigrid was attacked by this specific type of unwanted person also serves a purpose," Geden said. "A purpose that suits many people with the power to make it a reality."

"You think it's some kind of conspiracy? That the government did this?"

He brought his face so close I thought he would kiss me.

"No, I do not think the government planned the crisis any more than they planned for unemployed young men in public housing to come under the sway of radical ideas. But they didn't see fit to give those young men jobs, either, or think twice about passing laws that allow them to repossess all the worldly belongings of the poor damned who can even make it here. Scandinavians do not like the idea that anyone would have reservations about their country, even the passing thought that it might not be the best place in the world. They require absolute conformity and obedience. They have fetishized the art of tolerance, but only as an accessory. Something to put in the front window of their design stores."

As he spoke the moles on his face sharpened into black diamonds.

"Why were you reading a Swedish paper?"

"I sought out a copy once I learned about this. I keep it as proof."

"Didn't the newspaper find out the story was fake?"

"Of course. They printed a correction in small font on the thirty-eighth page of the Tuesday edition."

A white plate bearing an anemic cheeseburger descended over the front page. I covered the edges of the image with my palms, but the waitress was beyond caring.

"Do you think things in America are better?" I asked.

Beside us, a family burst into song. Geden laughed as the children's high voices revved. At the singing, maybe, but mainly at my question.

That day was a split screen. On the right, Geden's eyes, the newspaper, our conversation, dried-out cheeseburgers, and Danish children. On the left, my gauzy fantasy—the Goat and me in some blue-velvet dark together, stacked like elegant cutlery, turning and tuning. His bare chest in the close heat of the truck's cab, his neat hipbones peaking over the hem of his leggings like noses. I had to blink and blink to square the halves.

We did not speak Søren's name again until the ride back to Farsø, until we were almost back to the place where I had found Geden, or Geden had found me.

"So," I said, when the park came into view. I already had a stomachache at the idea of going back to the apartment. Could he sense it? Would he touch me?

"Are you unhappy?" Geden asked gently.

"Excuse me?"

Geden pulled back into the spot where his truck was always parked, took the keys from the ignition, slipped them into the pocket of his coveralls, settled back into his seat, and looked at me. "Are you?"

I took his hand. Held it against my roaring gut. His fingers tensed, monitoring, and then relaxed. I couldn't look at him. A bead of sweat traveled from behind Geden's left ear down across his throat, into his collar. He dropped his other hand on his thigh. His palm glared at me like an eye. If only he would move his hand lower.

"This was a very pleasant lunch," he said. "Thank you for joining me."

He had paid the bill while I was in the bathroom at Bones. I didn't want to owe him. I already owed Søren too much. The day before I had gone to an ATM for the first time in Denmark and withdrawn a thick roll of money, brightly colored and the wrong size. I took my wallet from my pocket, counted out a hundred kroner, about twenty dollars, and pressed it into Geden's open hand, trying not to linger against his skin. "For my burger and the beers."

"Thank you." He folded the bills and pushed them into the pocket that held his keys. Why was I disappointed?

The lip of the pond was just visible in the far right of the windshield, unreal, as if it could be peeled away. Geden exhaled. I couldn't go back to the apartment as if nothing had happened.

He looked at me. "I am here in the park every day at one o'clock."

No, you aren't, I almost said. I looked for you so many times and never found you.

"Every day I am here."

It was time for me to go. I looked out my window.

"Roxana." All the humor had left Geden's face. I leaned into him, wanting his whole smell, and he pressed his open hand right between my breasts, stopping me. The tiny red bow at the center of my bra met the heart line in his palm, separated only by the thin black fabric of my shirt. It soared up, shocking me: my cathedral feeling. I was in the presence of some great order, witnessing its acts.

When he spoke his voice was silken. "If you like, you can come visit me. I will take you to my house in the woods."

I didn't dare look at his face. "I'm afraid."

"Mmm," Geden purred, a sound that made my thighs clench. "It is frightening to be free. To trust."

I nodded, frantic. I couldn't think.

We stared at each other, my heart thundering under his palm, and then Geden took his hand away and used it to open my door.

"Good-bye, Roxana. Thank you for a nice afternoon."

My walk back was an act. I was a woman walking back to her apartment. I may have been out for a pleasure stroll, or I may have been out running errands, but I certainly wasn't driving to another town to have lunch with a man I barely knew. If the occasional passing Danes—two women wearing identical high blonde ponytails and gray fleece pullovers, the invalids outside their care home, an elderly bicyclist in head-to-toe spandex— noticed or appreciated my performance, I couldn't say. It was for my own benefit that I walked with such measured, ordinary steps, for my edification that I swung my arms as if nothing could alter my trajectory. I needed to summon as much normalcy as I could. I had never stayed out so long before. Søren might be waiting for me in the apartment, sitting very still and upright at the dinner table, his elbows neat right angles on its surface, waiting for me to explain. What would I say?

But it was the same apartment I had left that morning, clean and spare and empty. I wandered through its rooms, a ghost, until there was no part of it I had not visited or checked, and then I went into the bedroom and slept until I heard the key in the lock.

The next day, I wrote to my parents.

> Dear Mama and Dad,
>
> Today we saw some museums and then afterward went
> to eat. Sylvie had a headache and stayed home. I hope
> she's okay. I had onion soup.

That day, Dad responded immediately. What if he suggested we talk on the phone? Wouldn't he be able to tell from
the area code that I wasn't in France? The prospect scared me,
but I also kind of wanted it to happen. To come clean, for
someone to know.

> Hey now, Roxie, that doesn't sound so bad. Send some
> pictures!

I hadn't taken any pictures, not one. What was there to
photograph? The apartment? The pond in the park? I wrote back
quickly, ignoring his request.

> They took us to a super old library where we saw some
> medieval books. Kind of boring but cool I guess.

Mama wrote back to that one. When I saw her e-mail address, I
expected a missive about appreciating my unusual opportunity.
But she didn't chastise me.

> Are you homesick? Try to enjoy the time you have left. Not too
> much longer now.

I checked my return ticket. I had ten days left in Denmark. What had seemed a comfortably interminable span of time now felt abrupt and sudden. My whole world had slowed, become an orb of Juttish amber, the earwax-colored stuff all the design stores on Farsø's main street pushed. Every conversation with Søren now held the same metamorphosing silence. We ate dinner at the table in front of the television now.

How could I go home in ten days? What story would I tell?

9

THE DAY OF THE FIGHT BEGAN LIKE ANY OTHER. I woke to
the sound of Søren making coffee in the kitchen, got out of
bed, and found him wiping the grounds into the sink.

"Hi." I yawned.

Søren frowned. "Put on some clothes, Roxana. You'll catch
cold."

Even a week earlier I might have pointed out that it was
quite hot outside, that we were inside, that the blinds were
drawn. But that day I just silently returned to the bedroom
and stepped into my pajamas. He didn't want to see my body.

When I came back to the kitchen, he was packing his bag.
By the time I poured my coffee, he was out the door.

"Have a nice day," I told his back.

I took my coffee to bed and undressed.

Before Søren, porn had held an illicit glamour, a peek behind the curtain, an insight into the fate I still awaited to befall
me. Even the idea of watching it brushed up close to the place
next to Mama's bedroom vampire, just this side of exciting. But
increasingly now I needed it in order to feel anything at all when
I masturbated. To dream myself desired.

I opened Søren's computer and pulled up *College Teen Girls
Fuck a Hard Cock*. They were rail thin, with tiny swelling breasts.

I wished I had picked a video with women whose bodies were more like mine. But the search terms alone were depressing: Chubby, MILF, thick, BBW, mom.

I didn't want to watch porn. I wanted to watch a movie of my fantasies. A man's hand moving across a woman's stomach, a woman's toes curling against a man's furred thighs, two women's faces pressed together, two men fused in closed-eye ecstasy. That diffuse, floating wanting. To be able to imagine being wanted back.

I pressed Play. The bedroom was white and spare. The guy wasn't that bad, youngish, gentle enough to start. The college teen girls pressed their faces together and licked each other and the man too and eventually fucked the hard cock, and I came with my hand wedged between my thighs, shrouded in a horrible boredom. The video played on, outlasting, as they often did, my excitement. I put my hand on the trackpad to close out the window, an act that always felt encouragingly virtuous, like sweeping up after myself. Then one of the college teens looked directly at the camera with bright green eyes, her long blue-black hair thick and straight as uncooked spaghetti, her eyebrows sharp as lines drawn in permanent marker. I paused the video, disbelieving, almost happy.

Sylvie?

Once I had woken to the sound of Sylvie weeping.

She had kicked off all the covers and stripped off her nightgown in the night. I admired the shape of her body, her flat torso, her small breasts and tiny dark areolae, the wide jutting V of her hipbones. Her long smooth thighs. I pressed the pad of my thumb to her tears. Brought it to my mouth, licked them away.

Asleep, it seemed she suffered a grief locked away from me. In the window clouds moved, setting the moonlight full on us.

I turned my back to her, pressed my hands between my thighs in prayer position, aroused. All night I dreamed of pressing my face into her pubis, so intensely that when I woke I feared I had actually done it. But she was up, already dressed, and had cut a mango for breakfast.

Of course it wasn't Sylvie. This girl had a thicker jaw, a pointier chin, acne under the pancake makeup on her neck where I knew Sylvie's skin to be pure and clear as mountain water. I was drawn back into their saga of sucking and fucking, those two brunettes and their lucky blond paramour. I read through the tags on the video, looking for the actress's name. Estrellyta Jackson she was called, like a villain in a cut-rate western. I found other clips of her and came until I lost count, until my legs ached and a dull pain throbbed the base of my neck. I pressed past the pain and came, a little mouth opening and closing in my mind. Black space, white space. I felt nauseated. Her pink darting tongue. The skin between her breasts. Beneath her eyes. Sadness bore down on me, dark and full.

I opened another window and began.

Dear Sylvie,

I miss you so much. I'm sorry I haven't written to you this whole time.

I have a lot to tell you and I don't know if you will want to hear it but here goes. When I got to Copenhagen,

I met a guy named Søren who works for International
Abroad Experiences. We hit it off pretty well and—

The front door slammed.

"Roxana?" Søren's voice echoed down the hallway. "Little
Roxana, where are you?"

I thought about leaping out of bed, pulling on my pajamas,
closing the computer. First I had to clear the browsing history.
But I didn't want to put on my pajamas and get out of bed and
pretend I had been doing something productive and useful. I
wanted to finish writing to Sylvie. I wanted to tell her everything.
About Søren and Geden.

So I let him find me like that, in bed with his computer.
One of the browser windows still full of Estrellyta's charms. In
the other, I continued my e-mail.

—and basically I know this is crazy but I kind of ran
away with him. To Farsø, a town in Jutland, a part of
northern Denmark. It's been interesting but mainly—

Søren came into the bedroom. I didn't look up.

"What are you doing?"

"Writing an e-mail."

He pulled away the crumpled duvet. "Are you ill? Why are
you in bed? Why are you naked?"

I rolled my eyes. "Because I didn't want to wear clothes."

"But what's going on here?" Søren's voice rose. "Why are
you lying around like this in the middle of the day?"

He had no idea what I did with my days, I realized. I could
be here, naked in bed, at lunch with Geden, on a plane back

to America for all he cared. I looked at his face, so warped by disappointment. "Was there something you wanted me to do?"

He shook his head. "No, Roxana, your time is your own, of course, but I guess I do expect you to do something with it! Does that make me a bad person?"

I returned to my e-mail. Søren stood over me, watching.

It's been interesting but mainly kind of good. I sure have had a lot of experiences that I would never have imagined—

It was starting to sound like an application essay. I chewed my index finger, trying to figure out how to fix it.

It's been interesting. I have had a lot of experiences that I would never have imagined—

Søren lifted the computer away from me.

"Hey!"

"What are you doing?" He balanced the machine on one palm, clicking through the browser windows. "Watching pornography?"

He pronounced "pornography" in a prim, offended voice. I couldn't help it. I laughed.

"Why is this funny?" Søren closed all my windows, including the e-mail.

I fell backward and sprawled across the bed so he had no choice but to see me. I thrust my chest out, folded my arms behind my head. Spread my aching legs. Smiled up at him wincing.

"You're funny."

"Put on some clothes. For fanden"—Søren averted his eyes—"you'll—"

"I won't. I won't catch a cold. It's summer."

He let out a disgusted sigh. "Roxana." He walked out of the room.

I followed him down the hallway and into the living room, shouting at his back. "Why do you always look away from me? Do you hate having me here so much?"

He raised his eyes to me, and for a moment I thought it would be more of the same—a dodge paired with recrimination, a handspring out of the conversation, a shrug at what I was trying to say to him. Instead he looked enraged. His voice crescendoed.

"You have no idea what it is like to live with you," he said. "All day and all night, all I hear, all I think about, all I dream is how much I am disappointing you. Because of something I am supposed to automatically do without thinking. Because I am a man and it is my duty. But I cannot and I am worthless because of it. I feel your disappointment all the time. I am never not thinking about it. It makes me sick to think of it now. Sex. I feel fucking sick when I think about sex. You have made it that way for me." His voice an inferno. "Do you want me to take one of your country's pills to make me have an erection? Do you want me to pretend to feel something I do not? Do you not ever think of anything else? I have never been made to feel as vile, as much like a failure as you make me feel. God, I hate the way you have made me feel! I hate sex!"

Søren was wailing now, braced in a wide-legged pose, his arms raised to the ceiling. I crawled backward from him, curled into a corner. Did he really want me to feel sorry for him? I felt faint. My heart raced. There's nothing to be afraid of, I told myself, but it was a lie.

A sound was starting in my chest.

"But you brought me here," I said, already sobbing so hard I couldn't breathe. "I met you and we had sex and I loved it. I loved being with you. I loved the way your hands felt and you looked at me. I had never experienced anything like that before. You brought me here—"

"That," Søren said, "was a mistake."

My nausea pitched. "Fuck you," I managed and launched myself at him. He raised his hands. For a moment I thought he would strike me, but instead he caught me and sat on the floor.

I settled heavily on his lap. The bleats rose around us, chiming bells. *Hwuh hwuh hwuh.* I couldn't move. Søren stroked my back rhythmically, the way one might an overtired child. The bleat settled like a rock in my stomach. *Hwuh hwuh. Hwuh hwuh hwuh hwuh.*

His hand was a tide, washing me away.

Do you have a sex drive? Do you know what it's like to be wanted and not wanted? Do you know the difference? Do you care? Maybe these are obvious questions, but now I want to ask them of everyone I meet.

Do you know what it's like not to be wanted? Do you think it is always the man who does the wanting? That women are the always-wanted gatekeepers of sex?

Or maybe you are a woman, too. What about you? What do you think?

You have felt the slick seam between your legs, dividing you into halves. The place you go in and see. You know. Where the answers live.

I held my position in Søren's lap for a long time, shifting and turning. A deep quiet drifted in and the room receded, leaving me gray.

I pressed my face into his jean-covered thigh and inhaled. Then I turned my head so my entire face was buried in Søren's crotch. His faintly soapy scent seemed to reach me from a great distance. A good memory.

Ever so slightly, Søren recoiled.

I sat up and hardened my naked body into an imitation of his rigid posture. How long did we sit there, staring at the black television, our reflections frozen on its slick surface?

Eventually Søren roused himself and went into the kitchen. I stared dully at the wall above the television with unfocused eyes, hearing the sounds from the other room as a series of disconnected cues. The light switched on. The cabinet opened, the glasses clinked, the cabinet closed. The sink turned on, the sink turned off. The light switched off.

Dark. We were in darkness, even amid all that northern light.

He brought me a glass of water I took carefully as medicine and stood drinking his own in tiny sips until it was gone. Then he took both glasses back into the kitchen and sat beside me.

"Let's get high," Søren said, not looking at me.

He rolled a joint with medical intensity. I held it to my mouth as he lit it, seeking his eyes, but I couldn't catch them.

After the joint, we smoked the bowl out, and when it was done Søren repacked it and when that was done he repacked it again. Then he went into the kitchen and poured us each a little sharp one. It was ice cold and burned on the way down. Time loosened and thinned.

I handed him the glass. "Another."

We drank schnapps until the bottle was almost empty, and then we smoked more hash to cut the burn. I liked to hold the smoke in my lungs, liked the idea of them convulsing, those little translucent white bags beating like wings. Washed them down with more schnapps for their effort.

Søren watched me cough.

"Do you want some water?"

I shook my head. "I'll get it myself."

When I stood my vision swam with black. I felt so dizzy. And I couldn't see. I took a few steps forward, expecting it to clear. It didn't.

"I can't see," I whispered. Søren didn't hear or didn't care.

My eyes were sparks swabbed with dark. I turned and turned but only saw the edges of things. Never a whole thing. I put my hand on the counter for balance but it wasn't there. I took a step forward, into a corner.

"I can't see!" I shouted.

"Calm down," Søren said from the couch.

"I can't! I can't!" I rushed back in the direction of his voice, tripped, and fell face-first onto the wood floor. A yellow rose of pain grew on my left shoulder. I wanted to cry but I was too high. Sounds came through the floor, movement below. I pulled

my hands up to my face and stroked it, like a lover. Pretty girl,
I thought. Good girl, pretty girl.

Søren was laughing at me, I realized. A tiny titter like falling rain.

"Come on, little Roxana." The floorboards creaked under
his feet, his body was a system of movement in the dark. "I think
it's time for bed."

Geden came toward me and we touched face and hands, friendly,
as two souls, and then deeper, coming into each other, and I
thought, How odd, we hardly know each other, even as I began
to melt around him, even as he was hard against me.

I woke and blinked my dry eyes, still stoned and drunk. The
sun had finally gone down, leaving looming lavender shapes in
the windows. I cursed myself for waking, wanting to return to
the dream. And then I realized that a man was still hard against
me. In his sleep Søren was moving against me softly, groping
my breasts, pressing his erection into my hip. He raised his un-
conscious face to me, moved in for a kiss. My eyes filled with
tears. I rose and walked into the living room and undressed in
the deep shadow in front of the couch. Naked, I stretched out
on the floor, my pointed toes reaching for the orangey rectangle
of light from the big front window. I extended my arms over
my head, tried to make my round soft body long and hard as
a sword, wishing Geden to me. He had come once before. He
would again. I got to my feet and went to the glass.

Outside was the street as it had ever been, a place that
did not matter and would have remained forever unremarkable to me if not for the fact that Geden had once stood on it.

I thought of that moment, and then I felt sad that the street was not charged with Søren's presence, that we had not shared more happy moments. I had a sudden flash of him emerging up the street through falling snow, carrying a tower of brightly wrapped presents—a joyful holiday moment we'd never share. Had I failed? Even then the possibility of happiness with Søren felt near and distant both, a room I could enter if only I could find the door.

I shook my head and stepped back into the shadow. Found the pipe and relit it, sank deeper into the dark. The room boomeranged around me, up and down, purple angles, creaking light. Every sound was a terror and every shift the emergence of Søren's face. I kept seeing them, these men I'd given myself over to.

I sat on the couch. I'd get up in just a few minutes and get dressed and go out and find Geden. I'd go to the park in the night and track the treads of his truck in the gravel. I'd follow and trace and know and see him. I'd go and go with the moonlight to guide me until the road took me to his door. I'd knock and he'd open and it would begin. I would end this painful thing and begin something else. One last trip and I'd be out. The humid night air in my lungs. I found my way there. Geden opened the door and opened his mouth. We fell and did not come up for air.

In the morning I awoke stunned, lazy with grief, alone in bed. Had my pilgrimage to the front room been a dream? The light moved across the wall, unyielding. I forgot and then remembered that it was possible to see Geden, that he was not just a dream.

When I looked at the clock, it was almost twelve thirty. If I wanted him, I would have to be quick. There was no time for a real shower. I walked to the bathroom, climbed up onto the sink, propping my ass on the lip, which creaked under me. I was both afraid and hopeful that it would break, permanent damage to Søren's uncle's flat: proof that I had been here, proof that I had existed.

But the sink held my weight. I spread my knees and washed between my legs with Søren's big yellow bar of soap. Another old trick from Mama. She called it rinsing out your undercarriage. My smell formed a kind of mist, stronger than the hot water and soap. It was all around me. I scrubbed hard, trying not to cry.

I did my hair in twin braids, put on my black clothes. Left.

The day was bright and hot. I had walked to the park in a rush, and now I was sweaty and panting in front of Geden, not the vision I had hoped. He sat eating a sandwich on the lowered back of his truck: bare chested, his coveralls puddled down around his waist.

"Roxana." He said my name completely differently from Søren. A precise and shallow *x*, like a sigh.

"Hi."

"How nice to see you."

"Yeah." I looked over his head at the back of the truck cab.

"Or perhaps not." Geden ate the last bite of his sandwich. Drank long from a chrome thermos and offered it to me.

I shook my head and he put the thermos down.

"It is." I reached for the hand that had held the thermos, curled it around my hip.

He gave a pleased little grumble. "Would you like to sit down?"

"No thanks." I felt so twitchy.

He considered me. "Would you like to come sit in my truck?"

I tried and failed to exhale.

Geden put his hand on my arm. "Breathe," he said. "Take a breath."

I shook my head, staring at the trees, trying not to feel.

"Breathe."

I opened my mouth and filled my lungs.

"What's wrong?"

I looked down. "Søren is very unhappy, I think."

"I do not know if he has ever been another way."

I laughed shakily. "I wish I had known." Tears came and I twisted my head away.

"Roxana, it is not my business, but you are so upset. Has he hurt you? Hit you?"

"No. No. Of course not."

Geden took his hand away, leaving a damp spot on my arm. I missed it already. "Then why are you here, crying?"

I wiped under my eyes. "I want to go to your house."

"What do you want to do there?" It was like a question on a test. I summoned the courage to meet his eyes.

"Take off your clothes."

Geden put his hand to my face, his thumb under my jaw. He smelled of earth and plants, high summer, grassy and clean. I closed my eyes. He held his hand against my forehead, as if I had a fever. "You want to take off my clothes."

I held his gaze. "Yes."

"And to get away. From Søren, from Farsø. To forget."

"No."

"Then why?" He looked genuinely curious.

"I think about you," I said. "I don't even know your real name, but I think about you all the time. I have since the first time I saw you. Do you remember when we first saw each other?"

Geden looked at me evenly, his lips slightly parted. In his mouth waited his white, white teeth. In the dark.

"When you fell."

I pressed my fingertips to his mouth. "No."

His eyes slid back. "The window."

"The window." I nodded, hoisting myself onto the back of the truck.

His hands were at my waist. I intertwined our fingers, pulled him closer. I leaned forward, limned his ear with the tip of my tongue for just a moment. Felt him squirm under me, his breath catching.

"My home is just another place," he said, almost whispering, apologetic.

"I leave Denmark on Saturday," I said, pressing my hand into his mouth.

He pursed his lips against my fingers, stricken. "You will come now?"

I took my hand away. What would it mean to really leave, to disappear like that? I needed a little more time. One more night. "Tomorrow."

He nodded. My body filled with a thick energy.

I lifted myself out of his lap with the same move I used to love at the pool, both hands on the deck. A simple push up and I was out. On the ground, a shining black lizard scampered into the sun and held itself there.

Søren was waiting for me, a straight-backed zombie on the couch. He wore his black knit cap like the Søren I had met in Copenhagen. I felt a pang. Then I felt nothing.

"Hello," I said. He didn't respond.

I walked down the hallway to the bedroom thinking I would pack, but of course I wouldn't. I'd have to come back, but I could figure that out later.

Søren's gray lockbox was open on the bed, its contents strewn everywhere, a sight so at odds with his careful sense of order that for a moment I worried that the apartment had been broken into. But only the box was open. Nothing else had been disturbed.

There were no weapons or drugs, no banded stacks of bills. Just photographs, a small pile for such a large box, in a variety of shapes and styles that traced a backward progression of cameras. The first were washed out, color but sepia in mood, round edged. There was a run of oddities, ovals, squares, black-and-white snapshots that looked as if they had been cut out by hand. Then a dense stack of Polaroids, their white edges still crisp, and finally a collection of the slick, oversize prints I remembered from my own childhood.

The first was of a little blond boy standing in a field in front of a wire fence. Brown ground littered with patches of snow. The boy was not smiling. He wore a stiff khaki jacket, green corduroy pants, an oversize no-color knit hat over long hair. Was it Søren? I held the picture close to my eyes until the boy's face, smaller than my thumbnail, dissolved.

In the next photograph—round at the edges—a tall woman and a short man stood stiffly beside each other in ugly, handmade-looking clothes, a mustard-colored vest and high-waisted trousers on the man, a dun sack dress on the woman. It had been taken in a banquet hall with cheap wood paneling along the lower half of the walls and sparse decorations strung halfheartedly across the barren stucco of the upper. A card table stood behind them. An unflattering halo of thick, curly hair around the woman's head, a pale fall on the man's shoulders. Their hands hung at their sides, so close it seemed they were touching. But when I looked again I saw that they were not.

The rest of the round-edged photographs continued the story. The blond boy appeared with the man and woman or more often just one of them. They stood in a forest, holding walking sticks. They waited in line at a restaurant, the boy dressed in a green jumper. Usually it was only the boy and the woman. Her clothes got uglier as the years went on.

In the Polaroids the boy was an adolescent, nearly always alone. He had clearly taken them himself. In one he wore a stiff white shirt open over a pink tank top, a black chain around his neck, his face concerned, devout. In another he was in a bright red soccer uniform. In the next he wore a plaid flannel open over a white T-shirt. He had let his hair grow. Like the man's it was lank and blond. He looked into the camera with an expression of rage and expectation, his brows like wings over his dark gray eyes. By the last of the Polaroids, his long hair was already thinning on top, bits of scalp showing through fine, scanty strands.

I took a ragged breath and went on. A stack of school portraits, Søren with a series of unfortunate haircuts. In the standard-size photos he appeared with a girl who wore a high yellow bun and dressed in ill-fitting outfits like the ones his mother had worn in his childhood. They were together in a run of ten images, standing in front of gloomy buildings, holding hands across a small table strewn with empty glasses, hugging, a tower rising behind them. Then she disappeared. Søren alone atop a frozen makeshift throne of snow, laughing, his hair completely gone.

A statuesque woman with short bleached hair appeared. Mette, the girlfriend who had decamped for a nursing career in Norway. The pictures of them together outnumbered all the others combined. I flipped through them like playing cards, unwilling to let my gaze settle.

When I looked up, Søren stood watching me, his body a line in the doorway. For a moment I could see inside him, under his clothes and under his skin, into his organs, to the place where he was only component parts.

I let the photos fall out of my hand. Stacked them back inside the box.

"Roxana, can I ask you a favor?"

As if he didn't see what I was doing. "Yes."

"Will you read the opening of my thesis? I have translated a new version today."

The way he avoided my eyes; it was like he knew. I followed him out of the room to the table, where his laptop awaited. I wanted to tell him again that I didn't know anything about what he was writing about. I didn't want to read his thesis. It wasn't my job. I couldn't fix it for him. A mistake couldn't give good critical feedback, could she?

But I would do this thing for him, I decided. Not because it was owed but because it was something I could give. I sat down and opened the computer.

The file was open, titled, but there was nothing typed. I scrolled through empty pages, my pulse quickening. Had I somehow deleted it? Panic moldered, held me.

"Where is it?" I asked.

I felt rather than heard his reply. "I have deleted it all."

I turned to face him. "Why would you do that?"

It seemed his face could not form an expression. "I hate who I've become," he said. "A whiny lonely mess. I did not use to be like this."

How could he be so lonely when I had been there suffering with him?

"I have nothing," he said, almost philosophically. "I live in a place that has no use for me among people I don't understand. And being with you, Roxana—"

He raised his light eyes. Once he had given me that light, his newness, the idea that there was another way to be. That I was that way.

"I'm always reminded how little I have in my life, being with you. Because I am alone even in your presence. The older I get, the harder that is to deal with." He grimaced. "But hey I made this bed of mine I guess. That is a phrase, yes? In America."

There was no end unless I chose one.

"Good." I closed the laptop and pushed it away from me. "Good job."

ARDEN

1

THE LITTLE TRUCK WAS IN ITS USUAL PLACE ON THE ROAD
BEHIND THE PARK. I tapped the window.

He turned, smiling, and opened the door. "Hello," he said.

Geden, the Goat, I thought, trying and failing to hear the
soft *d* in my head. It didn't matter that I couldn't pronounce
the word.

He pulled away as soon as I shut the door, not waiting for
me to buckle my seat belt, and for long moments I struggled
to secure it. Then it finally clicked shut and I released a sigh of
relief so loud I almost apologized.

I shut my mouth. I was done apologizing.

We left town, heading straight into the fields. The sound
of road under tires filled the truck.

"How are you?" Geden spoke without turning his head.

"Better than yesterday."

We fell silent again as he drove deeper into the countryside.
I considered the bump in Geden's grand nose. His thick eyebrows
grew up toward the mass of black curls on his head. It looked
made to twine my fingers in.

Geden's eyes were the troubling color of the sky before a
tornado. How had they ever reminded me of Sylvie's?

We passed a field. "Oh, ponies," I said, before I could stop myself.

"Not ponies. Little horses," Geden corrected me. "You call them—miniature."

Their golden shapes receded into figment.

"The small horses like to eat the wildflowers beneath the fencing," Geden said. "We can go back tomorrow. The farmer knows me."

We headed into the forest, up a hill, to a thicket of tall trees, their tops so lush I felt like crying. Life, waving at me in the wind.

Hello, hello, good-bye, the trees said. We love you.

I love you too, I thought.

The road turned to dirt and we came into the shade under the trees, the light thickening as we bumped curves, gaining speed. A ravine appeared, dropping steeply to moss and rocks. Geden accelerated. We hurtled for the edge.

At the last possible minute he braked and parked. I tried to catch my breath. Geden turned my face with his palm, brushing his fingers across my mouth. I dipped them against my tongue and took the longest one down my throat. Plunged the shallow webs between his fingers with the membrane under my tongue, a trick I repeated until he puckered his lips and took in air as if in pain and then I knew I'd won.

He got out, opened my door, and gave me his arm for balance. The house stood at the top of the hill, hidden from the road by a dense stand of trees. A tall triangle set with a great red-paned window that ran the entire length of its front side. On its thatched roof, a short chimney; beneath, portholed white stucco. I followed him up the neatly landscaped front path past wildflowers as high as my waist to the door, a shining expanse of varnished red wood.

The abode I had expected shamed me—the East Monkey bachelor pad Søren had described, its yard thick with noisy, perpetually unemployed neighbors in tracksuits, a bucket overflowing with cigarette butts. Inside, cheap plastic-coated tablecloths in fake brocade print, chipped mismatched china, grimy sausages hanging from the stained kitchen ceiling. A bedroom like Dracula's, all velvet and wrought iron, smoke and disarray. For lack of other knowledge I had bought Søren's fundamental idea of Geden even after I came to know him, believed he was an odd hermit who smoked meat and made moonshine between illegal weekend jobs, that he burned hot dogs on a blackened grill for dinner every night.

Geden led me into the house. In the first room a long wood table stood in front of the tall window hung with gauzy white curtains, a pale green ceramic bowl of strawberries at the table's center. The kitchen was gray and blue tile with a gas six-burner stove, a deep stainless steel two-basined sink, and a wood-paneled refrigerator that matched the butcher's block in the middle of the room.

Geden did not offer a tour. He sat at the table, unlaced his muddy rubber-bottom work boots, rolled down his thick oatmeal wool socks, balled them, held the ball under the faucet, and used it to clean his boots, rubbing the black rubber and gray leather until it shone clean. The cool breeze from the door smelled of spruce trees. The sight of his pale feet was a cramp in my chest.

He unzipped his coveralls and stepped out of them. Beneath he wore two pieces of waffle-cotton long underwear: leggings and a shirt. He shook the coveralls three times and closed the door, hanging them on a hook.

In his skivvies the shape of his body was plain. My eyes drifted to his crotch. Geden bore my gaze without joking or turning from me. He stretched, pulling his head against one shoulder, his lips moving in a silent count. Then he reversed the movement, offering me his furred neck. I longed to taste his sweat, the intoxicating scent that enveloped me when we first met. We would be honest with each other now.

I felt the tiny weight of the red cord Søren had tied around my wrist at Fyrkat. The beach towel under the trees. I found Søren's sweetness and lost it again, a sharp pain behind my eyes. I covered the cord behind my back with my other hand.

"What do you want?" I asked Geden.

"I was about to ask you." He waved his arm at the kitchen's many amenities. "Water, beer?"

"No."

He opened his arms wide. "You are sure?"

I nodded.

"Come with me."

I followed him down a blond wood corridor through purple and silver dark. The falls of his feet on the floor seemed to come from inside my chest. Just the thought of his soles quickened me.

Geden led me into a third room, bigger than the others put together. An entire wall of windows faced the green depths of the forest. Against the far wall, a huge bed with an intricately carved headboard and a thick spiked sentry topping each post made with gray sheets, a pearly comforter. Over the bed hung a giant framed black-and-white photographic print, a grid of images of a city at night. Bridges, sky, domes. Light transformed the city into a mouth of fire. I walked closer and saw that the photographs were metallic exposures, slightly askew on paper thick as cloth. I put my hand on the headboard to steady myself against its grooves and ridges. Old as a ship.

Geden watched me from the doorway. He crossed the room and opened an invisible door in a wall I had taken to be an unbroken expanse of wood, revealing a gleaming white bathroom in which he vigorously washed his face.

Had he brought me home to witness his ablutions? I did not want to talk to another pajama-clad man about his feelings. I wanted to drink the sweat from the backs of his knees.

Geden returned, taking off his shirt as casually as his first undressing in the threshold. He stood still, showing himself to me. A long scar bisected his chest, crossing his left nipple. The cramp in my heart pulsed. I wanted to kiss his scar, punish the thing that had hurt him.

He dropped the shirt into a drawer he pulled from the same wall of wonders. He hooked his thumbs into the waistband of his leggings, pushed them down, and stepped out, pulling his feet through like an elegant animal. I saw his legs, furred as a real goat's. His bare slim hips. The rise of his buttocks. His crotch was the locus of the soft black hair that covered Geden under his many layers of clothing. His sex was half-tumescent, circumcised, mostly concealed by his thick hair. Oh. His naked genitals, flesh of blood, lobes and curls of skin hanging with the vulnerable loveliness of a baby animal, a thing that has not yet learned evil, and I thought: This is a performance, and because it is performed, it is more real.

I looked for only a moment, determined to be calm. It could end at any time. He could cease, withdraw, close the door on the golden sliver of light. I would have to do this without flinching.

Remember this, I told myself. Remember.

I walked to Geden and pressed my mouth on his, steadying him with a hand at his nape. My tongue painted his, lighting him up before I even got to the roof of his mouth. I felt him rise against me. His plant smoke smell and a third flavor I could recognize. Chocolate. I took his hand in mine, interlacing our fingers, squeezed. We went on like that, falling together and apart, until there was no air left and we had to separate to breathe. How sweet, I thought, dizzy, and I grabbed his cock as hard as I could.

Purple spots flashed in my eyes. Geden cupped the back of my head. I leaned into his arm. His green eyes filled with emotion. Fear? I did not want him to fear me.

His pink lips moved in their black cloud as I lost consciousness.

When I woke it was evening. The leaves on the trees in the long windows had turned cobalt, amethyst, evergreen. I lay beneath a wonderful blanket, a real, full-size duvet layered under a beautiful blue quilt embroidered with yellow stars. Four pillows were arranged around my head, exactly as Mama always did.

Mama. Her face.

Where was I?

I reached behind the pillows, felt a carved wooden headboard. I couldn't remember where I was, but I wasn't frightened.

I looked down. I was in my clothes, my shirt buttoned up to the top, my pants pressing the impression of my fly into my stomach. My feet in the black socks with the hole over the left toe. Søren came to me in a clear diving bell, ash eyebrows, straight back. My wrist still bore his red cord. I untied it and slid it into my pocket.

My boots were missing. There was no armoire or dresser that might conceal them, only the windows, two white walls, and one of smooth blond wood. I sat up, releasing another gust of dizziness, and swung my legs over the side of the bed. My heart rate accelerated. Black. Black and purple.

A man appeared in the far corner of the room, carrying a wooden tray, and it swam back in. Geden. The pond in the park. His truck. His house in the woods.

"I would not get up so quick, if I were you." He walked to the bedside and balanced the tray in one hand, shooing me with the other. He was dressed in a gray sweater and black jeans. I remembered his lovely naked body, the kiss, and blushed, immediately wet.

"How long has it been since you have eaten?"

A few sips of coffee that morning. The night before there had been no dinner. For breakfast the day before, more coffee. Not since the evening of the fight.

The soup smelled wonderful.

"Roxana? I am concerned for you."

He put the tray down on my lap, unfolding its four short legs. A steaming red bowl held a gleaming yellow soup. Beside it there was a tall glass of water and a bottle of beer labeled Sarajevsko Pivo.

Geden handed me a spoon. "Eat. Do not drink the beer until after the soup is done. It will balance you."

"Please don't tell me what to do," I said, still mad at Søren, wanting everything to be different. Then I was so embarrassed. "I'm sorry. I don't feel well. Thank you."

"Yes," he said evenly and stepped away from the bed. I hoped he wasn't angry. The soup was lemony and rich, containing in addition to the carrots and parsley chicken with crispy skin surrendering its crunch to the broth, melting onions, and tiny chunks of celery. After a few bites I found another vegetable, okra, my favorite when I was a little girl. Energy ran into my stomach like gasoline. I wanted to go out. I wanted one person who lived here to show me a good time.

"Take me dancing," I said. "Please?"

He did not laugh. "Finish your soup first. And drink the beer in small sips."

"Promise we'll go dancing," I said and gulped the beer. "Can I have another one?"

"One beer for madam," he said, considering me. "Dancing. All right. You have my word."

I bolted the rest of the soup, feeling it warm a path through my body, alternating spoonfuls with swigs of freezing beer, urging the food into my system and feeling myself light up, glow more incandescent with every dose. When the bowl and bottle were empty I raised my eyes to him.

"Thanks for the soup. Now. We had a deal."

He sighed. "I'll keep my promise."

I stood on new legs. "Where are we going?" I wondered if he had something I could borrow. Saw myself tying one of his work shirts over my belly.

"There are no dance clubs worth our time in Arden or the surrounding area, I am afraid," Geden said. "Nowhere for us to go." He laced his fingers behind his head. "Unless we drive to Arhus, our best bet is a grim place like Crazy Daisy." He yawned.

"Take me to Crazy Daisy, then."

He laughed.

Søren had laughed at me. Why was everyone laughing at me? I felt like crying, which itself felt crazy and made me want to cry even more. "It's not funny to break a promise." I pouted.

"I am not going to break my promise. I'm explaining. If you want Crazy Daisy, we will go to Crazy Daisy."

I felt more than a little unhinged, desperate to follow the bright thread of inadvisable behavior that I knew held my freedom. I tried to do differently than I had before. I didn't want to be rude, but I couldn't be perfectly pliant anymore either. "Do you have any clothes I can borrow?"

"Roxana, listen. Crazy Daisy is a vile nightclub, a grim scene. People competing to see who can drink themselves into the deepest stupor. Surely not the place you are wanting." He scrutinized me, the corners of his mouth tugging upward.

"Surely it is," I said, already digging through his drawers. "Let's leave in ten minutes."

Out we went into the evening. I'd swept my hair under a green bandanna Geden dug from the bottom of a tiny drawer. He tied an ornamental knot at the base of my skull and then produced a kohl pencil from a slot seemingly made for the purpose. I watched him rim his eyes and then I let him rim mine and in the mirror we were weird twins, everything and nothing alike.

He parked on some Plads and led me by the hand to a back door in an alley off the main street. A man stood at the door nodding as we passed over the threshold into a room so hot and loud I almost for a half second regretted my demand.

Terrible music thundered, happy-go-lucky anthems programmed on computers somewhere in Florida or the Eastern Bloc. When my eyes adjusted, I saw we were in a space that looked for all the world like my high school's black box theater. In every direction people fight-danced, crouching grimaced, their fisted arms stabbing the air in layered swoops. Everyone blond, with skin an indeterminate shade of sunburn or fake tan. Thick white eye shadow and skintight dresses on the women, pressed jerseys and muscle shirts on the men. Geden turned to the bar and turned back to me with a glass of pure vodka. "You will need it," he said into my ear, stealing a kiss on the lobe.

I downed it as quickly as I could, turning myself in half circles. I wanted to be dizzy. I wanted to be drunk. Geden leaned on the bar, watching me, and then once his drink was gone he came to me. We embraced and then he led into the center of the room. A song different from all the others started just then, tremolo, a woman's echoing voice, and we swayed into each other like waving palms. With my eyes closed I was on a beach, in sand, turning him into my arms. I took him wide by the right hand and then crept up under his chin and licked and kissed my way down to the collar of his shirt and back up until he coiled me away from him, a release, and the guitarist rolled her solo and the drums came down heavy, thudding again, again. His eyes in the dark like birds.

Back at his house I went into the bedroom and began to unbutton my shirt before he could say anything. By the time the shirt was completely undone he had come into the room and stood close to me. I unbuttoned my pants and pulled them down, my underwear catching, revealing the crack of my ass, so I took it off too in one movement. The familiar smell of my body floated up to me, friendly, reassuring. Only my bra remained. I pinched the closure. Let it fall. Saw my body in my periphery. Watched him see me. I wanted him to touch me, but it wasn't time yet.

We returned to the bed. Geden drew back the sheets and I got in. He walked to the other side and I saw the difference between the way he had undressed for me and the way he undressed now, rhythmlessly yanking down his jeans, slipping one arm and then the other out of his sweater, and for a moment I felt such a loss at the notion of time passing in this never-dark, at the very problem of yesterday and today—yesterday, when he had performed for me, today when he did not. I reminded myself to catch my breath. At least to try.

He climbed in. I tucked my face into the groove between his neck and shoulder and closed my eyes. Geden wrapped his arms around me so that our bodies touched all the way down. His cock awoke at my skin, settled again.

"What is your name?" I asked.

"You no longer wish to call me Goat?"

"I never called you that. I can't even pronounce the word."

"It's all right, Roxana. It is my name in Farsø. How else could you think of me? However." Geden cleared his throat. The words he spoke next might have been the wind moving in the trees outside. "Moje ime je Zlatan Zlatar."

"Zlatan." I tried it out. "Is that right?"

"No one has called me that since my mother's death."

My face in his forest of chest hair. "When did she die?"

"Five years ago. She was not old. She had cancer of the pancreas."

Hot tears spilled down my cheeks, surprising me. All at once I was weeping. I had always been so afraid of losing Mama. Of losing both of them. But they still existed, I thought. We weren't done with each other yet.

"I don't know what's wrong with me," I said. "She was your mother. I shouldn't cry."

"In the broken world, crying is resistance." He drew me closer. "I envy you. I have not cried since I came to Denmark."

"Really?"

His face moved in the dark. "Since the day we left Sarajevo I have wept for nothing."

I waited for him to say more. When he did not, I asked, "How old are you?"

He wheezed. "Old."

Was he? I recalled his face. It had lines, and his hands, though clean, had been used for heavy work. But I could not imagine his age. I felt strange, unmoored, captivated. "You don't have to tell me."

"I was born in nineteen seventy-nine," he whispered, his tongue catching my ear.

"Thirty-one. That's not old."

"You are eighteen. I am old."

"You do seem older than Søren. In a good way."

"He will have to learn to be kind to himself in the way that you have been kind to him, after you are gone."

Gone. Soon I would be gone.

I listened to his heartbeat, feeling easily empty. Taut. Sealed like the chamber inside a drum.

I awoke in another new body. Zlatan sat beside me, nude, reading.

"Good morning." He closed his book and gave me a long openmouthed kiss. Mint on my fetid tongue. "A coffee?"

I nodded, shy. He rose and left the room, returning with a tall white mug. The coffee, laced with thick whole milk, was the best I'd had since arriving in Denmark.

"Do you have a computer?" I asked.

He handed me a white terry cloth robe. "I will show you," he said and led me back into the hall.

I hadn't seen this room before. Three walls of windows and shelves that held hundreds of books. I trailed my fingers along the spines, reading the authors' names. Nedžad Ibrišimović, Jakob Ejersbo, Clarice Lispector. The world was full of things for me to read, I realized, and for the first time I felt excited about college.

Zlatan's library surprised me, just as his perfect English and beautiful house had. Why had I still expected the sleazy Slav so reviled by Søren? Or even a simple man of the earth in a barren shack, living in symbiosis with nature? But Geden and Zlatan were inseparable. One had drawn me, revealing the other.

Dear Mama and Dad,

Hi guys! It's been a while since we've written. I just wanted to let you know that I am really looking for-ward to being home in a few days! Sylvie is going to stay a little longer, so it'll just be me on the flight. I miss you both a lot.

I love you,
Roxana

When I returned to the bedroom he was dozing, still naked, on top of the sheets, arms folded behind his head. I put my hand on his concave stomach and he opened his eyes.

2

ZLATAN DRESSED IN THE BLACK LONG UNDERWEAR HE HAD WORN THE DAY BEFORE, OR MAYBE IT WAS A NEW SET. I pulled my pants from yesterday back on, wishing I had brought a change of clothes. He said we were going to the most beautiful part of the forest.

"Wait." He raised his hand. "It may be muddy, and I think you should not wear your nice clothes." He opened another of the innumerable drawers hidden in the blond wood wall and withdrew a set of long underwear like his but gray. From another drawer he produced a pair of coveralls, smaller, made from a fatigue-green fabric instead of khaki and much washed. A patch was stitched near the right shoulder: ZLATAR.

"When we first came to Denmark, years before my father received employment authorization, he would take long walks in the forest every day to pass the time. There he befriended the skovrider, Ole, a kind man. At Christmas that first year, he surprised me with my own coveralls, like the ones he wore but embroidered with my name," Zlatan said, handing them to me. "He knew that in the camp my mother struggled with laundry. Now I was free to get as dirty as I liked, and I loved the coveralls so much that I never took them off, not even to go to school. The other children were thrilled; how easily I gave them something else to mock. But I felt that the outfit made me invincible, that in it I could go anywhere, even back home, which I wanted quite badly at that time."

He shook his head. "All my poor mother wanted was for me to have a respectable career, to be a doctor. A scientist, a teacher. In Sarajevo, she always reminded me, she and my father were what she proudly called professionals. She managed a laboratory at the Workers' University, and my father was the editor of a magazine he had started himself when he was nineteen years old. But for the first five years in Denmark they could not work. It took that long for the Danes to realize that we were not going back, could not go back, and then they finally let us leave the reception center—a refugee camp, do not be confused by the polite title—and move into a horrid flat not far from here, in Aars."

Zlatan handed me a pair of his oatmeal wool socks. "For you."

I rolled the socks up my calves and pulled on the leggings, the top, trying to think of something to say. Everything was snug. My breasts required a significant portion of the material, leaving a three-inch gap of flesh between. But that didn't matter. Zipped up, the coverall covered all.

"I'm sorry," I said to Zlatan.

"Perhaps if I did not immigrate I would have died," he said, looking past me. He shrugged. "Or perhaps I would be fine, better than I am today. It is impossible to know."

"I probably wouldn't have met you, if you hadn't left."

He smiled. "Something to be grateful for, then."

I walked into the bathroom to see myself in the mirror. New acne had sprouted in the crevice below my lower lip. I wore neither bra nor underpants, and I had not brushed my teeth or washed my face in over twenty-four hours. But I saw fresh beauty, newly hatched.

Zlatan wrapped his hands around my waist. "Come with me."

We laced our boots up over our coveralls at chairs pulled from the great table in the front room. He lifted a backpack, and out we went into the woods around his house, a district of green light and mossy trunks.

"This is Rold Skov, the second-largest forest in Denmark," Zlatan said. "There are no mountains, nor much forest in this country, and I am lucky that we were settled near here. When I came here with my father for the first time, I vowed that I would live here one day. Perhaps that is the greatest success of my ridiculous life."

"How long have you lived in your house?"

"Six years. Before that I lived in a tiny apartment in a misfit building full of suffering people on the edge of Farsø. Addicts, abused women, squalid children. No one worked. I did not have a kitchen, so I cooked most of my meals outside, on a grill. Inside I had just a few things, a bed, an old rug. Herbs hung to dry from the ceiling fan. Probably what you expected, no?"

Shame filled my face. How did he know?

Zlatan laughed. "Do not look so guilty. I know what people in Farsø think of me. My neighbors at the flat hated me because I called the police on their drunken parties and screaming arguments. I am an immigrant, and even worse, an asylum holder, so in their view I should have been grateful for every broken beer bottle in my front yard and every black-eyed woman sobbing on my front porch. There are all sorts of rumors about me. Because

I keep to myself no one has ever bothered to learn the truth. Or perhaps I have purposely kept the truth from them."

The muffled crunching of the forest floor beneath our feet. "You lie to them?"

He held my gaze. "I suppose I do."

"Why?"

"There is a certain safety in being thought a dangerous international criminal. If Danish women believe that I traffic Bosniak girls through Farsø to be sold as prostitutes, then they will leave me alone at the bar, instead of drunkenly demanding I teach them how to say 'fuck me' in Croatian so they can get laid on their next trip to Dubrovnik. If men like Søren believe I am some savage squatting in a cave, then I avoid their token interest and university-funded oral history projects. If I speak to no one, I do not have to bear comments about how articulate I am, how I have changed their minds about Muslims because I drink beer and do not give a fuck about whether or not I eat their pork."

He took my hand as we walked.

"I have known Søren since we were young, you see," he went on. "He has always visited his uncle in the summers. He is not a mystery to me. He is a lonely man, angry at the world because he is angry with himself. Danes are a tender people who are ashamed of their tenderness and bury every pain. During the Second World War, Nazis occupied this country. Everyone you meet is the descendant of either a collaborator or a resistance fighter. Most people, both."

"But they helped so many Jewish people," I said, remembering one of Søren's history lessons.

"They helped them because they were Danes in peril, because they hated the Nazis, not because they approved of their Jewishness. That is their way. They can never truly accept difference. If they lose the myth about the great ancient kingdom, they will recognize each other for what they are, a nation of lonely people who disapprove of each other's loneliness."

I realized that Søren had never mentioned speaking to another person in all his days out of the apartment, save for the Madsen brothers who sold him hash. I saw him alone in the library, squinting at his screen. Transactional interactions seemed to be all he could stand. One night he had explained that the newscasters were discussing a newly released statistic, which held that one-third of all Danes were estranged from at least one member of their family.

Zlatan fell silent. We came to the foot of the hill, got into the truck, and drove. The streets rolled past, a mandala coiling and uncoiling with us at its center.

Gold sun painted golden ponies yet golder. Zlatan rooted in the back of the truck as I approached the fence. Four miniature horses stood at some distance, considering us warily. There was another animal, a little bigger with a different face. As all five began to approach I saw that it was a donkey, its fur a silvery down. Soon the donkey and horses were at the fence. The donkey was the friendliest, grinning and peeking at me from the corner of his eyes. I looked at my feet and saw little yellow and white flowers growing there among weeds, or what I thought were weeds, anyway. I wanted to pick a flower and feed it to the sweet donkey, see him close his eyes in pleasure as he ate the bloom. But maybe that wasn't allowed.

Geden came up behind me. Not Geden, I corrected myself. Zlatan. But what was in those names or any name that made him who he was? He was bigger and deeper than language.

There was the sound of a hinge opening and then a crunching. I turned to see him slice a green apple in half with a bone-handled pocketknife. He handed one of the pieces to me.

"Thanks, but I'm not hungry," I said.

"For the horses. Or the donkey, if you like."

I took the apple and let him show me how to hold it out to their mouths with my palm flat. The friendly little donkey came and sniffed it and held his mouth in a half-open grin, as if he couldn't believe his good luck. In the donkey's dark eyes was an animal wisdom, deep, stalwart. I took a shaky breath. Then one of the horses bounded over and ate the apple half in one bite. I cracked up.

"A moment of poetry with the donkey, interrupted?" Geden said.

"I guess," I said, trying to catch my breath. I held out my hand and stroked the donkey's soft ears. "How long do these little donkeys live?"

"Ten years, fifteen." He reached and scratched the donkey's head, turning the soft taco ears over in his rough hands. "Maybe this one will last a little longer as he has a nice life. Even if he is blind."

"He's blind?" I peered at the donkey's eyes. "That's sad."

Zlatan gave me the other half of the apple, took another apple from his pocket, and halved it, too. "Perhaps. But I think there is no reason to be sad for him," he said and fed the donkey both halves. "Look at how much pleasure he finds."

The donkey gave me a demure smile, almost hopeful: *You have something else for me, don't you?* And I did. He took the last apple half from my hand as gently as a kiss.

We drove to the far end of Rold Skov and walked to the deepest
part of the woods. Zlatan unzipped his backpack and spread
a quilt on the ground, laying out a large clay jug, a big metal
thermos, and two foil packets. He sat down and unwrapped the
packets, revealing a loaf of bread and small grilled sausages on
a bed of chopped onions. From the thermos he poured a thick
pink soup of braised purple meat, islands of white sour cream,
and a dusting of dill. The sausages were crisp on the outside,
juicy on the inside, the bread like pita but fuller, richer, and the
borscht cold and sweet. I drank almost all my broth before I
remembered the jug.

"What's that?"

"Herzegovinian wine. Tart." He handed it to me.

"No cups?"

He laughed. "We must drink from the jug, in the way of
true East Monkeys."

I hoisted the heavy jug. "I hope you know I don't think
you're an East Monkey."

He sighed. "I know I am harsh about the Danes. Whatever
their failings, they are the people who took my family in, who
gave us homes and the opportunity at a new life. I am putting
on a show for you, a little bit. I eat rye bread and smørrebrød like
everyone else. It is not always a festival of Bosniak cuisine at my
house. I brought these foods because I thought you might have
tired of Danish cooking. And because I wanted to explain myself.
Why we are doing this at all." He looked at me until my face grew
hot. "Am I not right? That is why we are together right now."

"So that you can explain yourself?"

Zlatan drank from the jug for a long time before speaking.

"You see, I once had a story. A tale that I liked to tell, which
explained who I was and from where I came, that gave meaning

to all of my wandering and shyness and inability to tolerate small conversation. My friendlessness and my resistance to even the smallest attempt to know me. It was a grandiose tale that began in Bosnia and ended here, in these very woods, where I fell on my knees and wept for the first time since we were driven, my family and I, from our home in Sarajevo. There were great peaks and deep nadirs to my story. A lovely sister named Renata with hair like flames, or pennies—I could never decide which, and pennies were so exotic, from America, like you—who was valiant and braver than us all and fell for her bravery. A great gray cat, Mače, which means 'kitty,' a banal name no Balkan child would ever give an animal, who died at the hands of the Serbs, a psychic symbol of the violence that was visited on us all. Whenever I told this story, I cried." He closed his eyes.

My throat was suddenly dry. I swigged more wine. "I thought you said you hadn't cried since you left Bosnia."

He opened his eyes. "That is true. The tears, like the story, were a lie. I lied to everyone, every Dane who tried to grow close to me, to help me, to lift me from what they saw as my benighted state. I should tell you that I did this because I had yet to process my grief or because I was trying to gain friends by making my past seem more dramatic than it was, but none of that is true, no matter how hard I try to have compassion for my younger self. And really, by the time I stopped telling the lie I was not so young. Twenty-one, a man already."

Still older than I am now, I thought.

"The truth, if there is a truth, is that I lied because I hated Denmark. I was livid at the Danes simply for existing, and then on top of existing they did all these tiny awful things without even realizing or thinking about them, all from their enormous sense of centerness. I saw how they looked at me when I spoke, with my rapidly disappearing accent, and even as I erased my accent miserably, desperately, I also wished to never know their tongue, nor to be able to decode the tiny network of slurs and ignorances that led them to treat my parents and grandparents and all the lost souls in the camp so badly. I told such a good story, Roxana, with wailing and Koranic Arabic and the third-act reveal that it was I who killed dear Mače, not the soldiers." He looked at me hard, squinting as if it hurt to be seen.

I looked back at him, tracing the dark places under his eyes with my gaze. "Did you really kill a cat?"

He nodded grimly. "I have in my life been required to put three poor cats out of their misery. One I ran over while learning to drive. Two my bastard neighbor Daniel fed to his pit bull. I did it with a shovel as quickly as possible."

I shuddered, thinking about Mushi. "That sounds awful."

He shrugged. "You see an animal suffering like that, you get over yourself pretty quick. But no, I never killed a cat in the way I told it in the story, with my bare hands, to heroically free my family from war-torn Bosnia."

We sat in the woods, food smells souring around us, my stomach upset, my vision smeared. His story weighed heavy in my mind. I worried that his magic was leaching out, creating a distance between us. I was leaving in three days now, nothing would happen, and maybe that was best. Who did I think I was to bandy myself about on so many waves, to feel so many things, to never be still, never be satisfied?

He spoke again, his voice soft, his eyes far away. "I will tell you what I remember: From the kitchen window in the home where I lived until my thirteenth year I could see the river Miljacka flowing wide and brown under the ancient bridges. Everything we needed was on our street. The butcher, the grocer,

the kafana where the adults spent every afternoon. Each day,
after I returned from school, I ate the snack my father left for
me in our narrow kitchen and then ran down the concrete staircase to play with my friend Sandar and romance his twin sister,
Milena, who lived on the first floor. My grandparents had a flat
a few streets over but they were in our home almost every day,
my grandmother yelling at my father. He was the family cook,
which she thought was an aberration of natural law. And my
grandfather would play dominoes with my mother at the tiled
table in front of the big window."

I sat very still, watching him as he spoke, not wanting to
give him any reason to stop. Here it was, what I had wanted
most of all: his story. He spoke steadily, in a hushed tone, as if
telling a holy parable.

"For a year before the war began the city was strange. Everyone was on edge. We knew trouble was coming, but everyone
kept making excuses for the tension. It was the strange wind off
the mountains, they'd say, or a funny cast to the air from industrial pollution. I was only a child. I did not follow the news or
the arguments that my parents and grandparents began to have
after dinner. Now their voices were low and tight. My father
insisted that safety was most important and wanted us to leave
immediately. My mother sided with her parents. She said that
the reports were overblown, that the rhetoric would soon calm
down and everyone would stop talking, crazily, of violence. I
didn't understand, Roxana. In my life there were no divisions
between me and Sandar and Milena, who were Serbs, or between
me and my friend Vladek, a Croat. Of course I understood that
I was a Bosniak, a Muslim. But like many people we knew, we
were Muslims in name only. My parents drank beer and my
grandparents took rakia after dinner."

He hoisted the jug, took another long drink of wine, and went on.

"In that strange year there were parties all the time. At my friends' parents' houses, the adults got drunk and danced. My parents had parties, too, elaborate ones with ten trays of sarma and ćevapi, like these"—he raised a little sausage—"and popara, bread soaked in boiling milk. Wonderful food, but I was not happy. No one was. Everyone just waited to be drunk. At a certain point in the evening, my parents screwed a red lightbulb into the ceiling fixture and turned off all the other lights so that the guests could dance. Even when the parties were adults only, I always came out of my bedroom when the red light was turned on. No one paid attention to me.

"At the last party, Milena appeared. I hadn't even known she was at the party, and then she stood before me, the girl I loved, and asked me to dance. We were the same height. In the red light her eyes looked violet. I thought she was the most beautiful girl I had ever seen. The song swelled, the singer weeping with all of us now, the violins screaming and climbing the walls.

"'Close your eyes,' Milena said, and when I did, she kissed me."

He paused, and I realized I was holding my breath, there with him in the red-lit apartment, in the arms of the most beautiful girl. It did not feel so far from where we sat in the Danish woods.

"I tried to put my arms around her but she had disappeared, like a ghost. So I went into the bathroom, locked the door, and turned on all the lights. I put my fingers in my ears to drown out the music, louder now because some of the guests were singing, sob-singing, the most terrible sound. It rose around me like a second room. I fell on my knees and vomited into the toilet until there was nothing left in my stomach.

"The next day, or the next week, or the next month—I do not know when exactly, those days were so distended and unhappy—the war began. Everything made sense now: the crying, the drinking, the sick. Snipers shot at our apartment building, shattering the windows in Milena and Sandar's apartment. This was before Srebrenica, before the war became famous. But it was already happening to us."

He fell silent. Seeing him there in his apartment, the party crumbling all around him, I wanted to give him something. I crawled behind him and enclosed his body in my arms. I held my palms over his heart and forehead, trying to only touch, not think. Eventually his pulse slowed to sleep and I lay back with him on top of me. When we woke the light in the forest had shifted. We were well into the afternoon, heading toward evening, our hours together dwindling.

Zlatan's green eyes opened and closed slowly. I turned him onto his back and kissed him. At first he didn't respond. But then he sent his tongue into my mouth and we lay kissing under the canopy of birdsong and drifting high clouds, occasionally breaking to breathe before diving under again. He probed my mouth with his tongue, our torsos flush, fused at the navel. My hair full of hot wind and dust. I buzzed all over, sore in a way I hadn't felt since the early days with Søren. So it was possible to be broken into all over again, to be made anew. So all my life I would open and close, and open and close again, and open again.

By the time we returned to the house, the light had turned blue, signaling the beginning of the long hours of falling sun and rising moon before real dark. In Søren's uncle's flat, the indomitability of this time of day had overwhelmed me. I knew only the changing shades of his temper, the movement of shadows across the wood floor. Outside was nothing to me.

Zlatan dug in the refrigerator, shooing me toward the bedroom. "Rest. I will prepare dinner."

"Let me cook for you," I said, peering over his shoulder into the fridge. I wanted to feed him. To give him something, he who had given me so much. A piece of my body, my heart, that would enter his and become a part of him forever. "You can tell me the rest of your story."

"It was a long time ago, Roxana." He reached over my head, took two beers from the refrigerator, and opened them with his teeth, kissing the lip of mine before he passed it to me.

I held the cold bottle against my chest, awed by this trick. "Do you not want to tell me?"

"Have I not always done as you ask?" He gave me a naughty look.

I blushed. "You have."

"What do you wish to cook?"

"Tacos," I said automatically.

He laughed. "Well. We do not have those breads, the thin soft ones. But beyond that you are welcome to do as you will with the contents of my refrigerator."

I went to it, took out a block of cheese, ground beef, lettuce. There were pitas, or something like them, like the ones we had had for lunch. In the bin beneath the sink, onions and garlic, and on the counter, tomatoes.

"You have picked all of the American items. I was going to make you a cheeseburger," Zlatan said.

"Thank you," I told him. "But today I want something different."

He spoke as I rendered the ingredients, bent them to my will.

"We left in October, but I don't remember the flight to Copenhagen, or the hours that followed. We were detained in customs for a long time, of course. Everything in the airport was gray, white, and silver. Cold. I was afraid to touch anything, afraid I would soil the gleaming surfaces. It had been several days since I had had a shower; in the madness of leaving, no one had remembered to make me bathe. In Sarajevo, it was a silly game I played with my parents, trying to dodge a bath. But in Denmark such childishness was out of the question. I desperately wanted one. I worked myself into quite a state, imagining that my dirtiness would get my family ejected from this freezing, safe place.

"The first Danes we saw must have been customs agents or policemen or humanitarian aid workers. I'm not sure. They all looked the same to me, tall and handsome, with pale hair and clear blue eyes. Of course there are short Danes, dark Danes, clumsy Danes. But on that first day, they all carried themselves so stiffly, with such great discipline. Their feet hardly seemed to touch the ground.

"My parents acted like scared children, my grandparents like senile fools. They muttered in low voices, refusing eye contact. Only my mother could communicate with them in English. No one spoke our language. I was so scared that I started singing under my breath. I didn't even realize I was doing it until my grandfather slapped me.

" 'You've been singing for hours,' he hissed. 'Be quiet.'

"He had never laid a hand on me before. I burst into tears and couldn't stop shaking. The Danes noticed, but they didn't say anything. They never say anything. My parents pleaded with me to calm down. Finally my mother pulled me into her arms. Still I did not stop crying for hours. I sobbed until I couldn't breathe."

He was speaking to the middle distance, to the empty air. I stopped my busy hands and looked at him. Zlatan raised an eyebrow.

"Please continue," he said. "It is easier for me to talk to you if you are not arrayed in front of me like a committee I must convince. I have had a great deal of that, in my life."

I bowed my head, ashamed of my interest. "You don't have to tell me anything."

"Yes. But I want to," Zlatan said, looking down. "It—heals something."

"Thank you," I said.

"Please keep cooking," he urged, and I returned my attention to the ground meat, releasing it from its container into a glass bowl.

"At some point we were put on another bus. I slept and slept, so much that when we finally arrived the doctor at the camp told my parents that I must be kept awake for at least twelve hours every day. He was concerned I would enter a fugue state."

The flame beneath the flattop on the stove lit blue, flashing into red.

"A fugue state," I repeated.

"You lose all memory of your identity and behave strangely. People in fugue—fuguing, doctors say—flee their families and disappear. Sometimes they are found years later, living entirely different lives. A married businessman in Zurich may fugue into a cattle farmer in Spain. Most are never found. Many, I imagine, die."

I put the beef in a frying pan, added chopped onions, turned the burner on high. I crushed a clove of garlic, two. Tossed them into the pan. "How did you stay awake?"

"They did it by playing Danish talk radio day and night. They never turned it off."

His eyes saw past me, above and beyond my body. "The camp was a big institutional place. Rows of long low buildings. Everything white linoleum or cheap wood. We were given a tiny antiseptic apartment where everything had been scrubbed bare. We prepared and ate our food in giant communal kitchens. We were allowed to play where we liked, within the fence. But adults could not work, nor were they given language classes, which is now standard for new arrivals. It was as if we had moved to the strangest, saddest apartment complex in Yugoslavia."

I took the head of romaine and chopped it crosswise. Found a stick of butter, rubbed it on the pitas. "Your apartment in Sarajevo sounded beautiful," I said.

He laughed, one note. "Yes," he said, shaking his head. "Yes. The camp was not a place any of us could make our own. The Danes decided that the best way to prevent Balkan violence from carrying over was to indiscriminately mix the displaced people together. Serbs and Croats lived there, too. The camp was tightly controlled, so there were few fights, but the tension was almost unbearable. The war had come on so quickly that none of us had gotten used to hating each other. I kicked a deflated soccer ball around a parking lot with other faceless boys, and it would be fine, unremarkable. Then, as if a switch was flipped, I would notice the small differences—their accents, the little pendant icons of the Virgin Maryam some of them wore, the soccer teams they followed—and be filled with a terrific fear, a fear so strong I thought that I would wet myself.

"Other times, instead of fear, I felt anger. Violence. Whatever I felt, when the switch was flipped, I simply fled without a word. Ran back to our apartment and closed myself inside a closet. Waited for my breath to return in the dark, for my heartbeat to calm. This was how my reputation began, you see; even among the refugees, I was odd, a misfit. And in that closet is where my story began. My lovely imaginary sister, my tragic murdered cat. Heroics on all sides, a cunning escape by bus rather than the hired car that took us to the airport well before it was closed."

I shivered, turning to look at him. His eyes were on the table, wide, as if he were reliving those hours, his child's body in the closet.

"What did your parents do in the camp?" I asked, wanting to pull him out, to save him the little bit that I could. "Did they know what a hard time you were having?"

Zlatan shrugged. "They were suffering too. If they noticed that I often ran into the apartment and hid myself in the closet, they said nothing. But I think they didn't notice. My grandfather took to drinking rakia all day long with some old Bosniaks who brewed it in their apartments, although this was against the rules. He had never been much of a drinker. He hadn't tasted beer until he was in his forties. But in the camp, everything changed. My grandmother, a cosmopolitan lady in Sarajevo, became in the camp a nattering old woman, one of a clutch of hens that camped out in the communal kitchen, chain-smoking all day as they gossiped about which women were sluts, which men wife beaters. For the first time in her life, she began to wear the hidzab. She said she had been called to greater religiosity, but I think she merely wanted to fit in with her new friends, harpies with closed faces without a nice word for anyone."

"Zlatan, what's a hidzab? A hijab?"

The meat was done. I turned on the oven, put the pitas inside. I found a grater, made it rain cheese. Put the meat in a bowl, arranged the lettuce on a plate. Chopped the tomatoes.

"Yes. The head covering. May I help you?"

"It's okay." I took the pitas from the oven. "Everything's done."

"I'll do the dishes, after, then," he said, departing for the next room. "I suspect you have had your fill of housework."

His words invoked that just-past me, a stung spirit haunting the pale hallway between the kitchen and the room where Søren and I had slept. I could see her sweeping and wiping. Slinking back to bed to touch herself and cry.

I followed Zlatan into the other room. We sat across from each other at one corner of the table. He arranged silverware and blue cloth napkins, pouring glasses of water from a tall glass carafe.

He watched me assemble a makeshift taco and then raised his beer. "To you."

"To you," I repeated, lifting my bottle. We smiled at each other.

My food tasted real, immediate, part of the known world. Not a thing given to the past but made from the present. With deep satisfaction, I watched him eat.

When the first resounding pang of fullness hit, I asked, "Did you start school immediately?"

"No," he said. "It took some weeks, maybe months, I am not sure. Initially the Danes thought, as we did, that our situation was short-term. Everyone believed we would be back in Sarajevo by New Year's Eve, then by the first day of spring, then by the summer solstice. We were becoming indigent in the camp. Older boys were forming groups that without intervention would have become gangs. The seclusion was so different from our lives in Yugoslavia. There, we had the world; in Jutland, we had only the camp. School was necessary but I was not prepared for how difficult the transition would be.

"We were given special tutors, but the policy was for refugee children to attend regular classes with Danish students in their age group. So I was thrust into classrooms where I couldn't understand anything. In Sarajevo we had learned about the history of our city and country; in Denmark, children learn about the history of this country, its glorious past as an imperial power, its dominance of millions of people. The successful conquest of Greenland, where the natives dissolved into alcoholic despair at the first sight of Dannebrog." He trilled the flag's name. "The language came to me in pieces over the course of an excruciating year. Now I recognize how quickly I learned, but at the time I felt I was barely keeping my head above water.

"Most of the other children ignored me, but a few took special joy in tormenting me. Every day that boy Daniel followed me on my route back to the camp with his pit bull, a wretched beast that snapped at me on his command—"

"The scar on your chest," I said, seeing it through his shirt.

"Yes." Zlatan looked up now. "Who can account for the cruelty of children? It comes from a deep place, but it does not exist in a vacuum. Later I became aware that Daniel's parents had their own problems. His father was a petty thief, his mother a terrible drinker. His elder sister had cerebral palsy. The dog had been bought to protect her from her own bullies, who were crueler to her than he was to me. But this knowledge did not protect me. I did not feel better when, three years later, I went on to university while Daniel ended his education completely."

"You went to university?" I wondered why I had not known this, and then I wondered why, how, I possibly could have.

"Yes. I have two degrees in forestry."

"I don't mean to be surprised. I don't know why I'm surprised."

"We have only just met," Zlatan rubbed his hair.

This unavoidable fact. It kept being true, no matter how much we told each other. "Keep going."

He folded his hands on the table and smiled, squinting at me. "I am not sure how much more there is to tell. Eventually, after some years, we were moved from the camp into a small flat in Aars. My father began his work for the skovrider before that, so he continued in that job. My mother never returned to work."

"Is forest rider really what your job is called?"

"That is the official title. My official title."

"It sounds medieval."

"It is a medieval term I think. Maybe 'woods magistrate' is a more accurate description." Zlatan laughed. "My father enjoyed the work, as I do. It sustained him through his divorce from my mother. Through my grandparents' deaths. They died just a month apart. They knew they would never return to Sarajevo. As did my mother." He shook his head. "My father is still alive, which is more than any of us could hope for. He lives in Vejle now, with his second wife, a Dane. She has her own money, so he no longer works. They like to go to estate sales. In the summer they take package vacations to Majorca. It's funny, there is a place in Bosnia just a letter different from Vejle, Velje. Like a mirror image."

He stopped talking. We sat with our empty plates.

"Thank you," I said awkwardly. "Let me do the dishes."

Zlatan shook his head again. "Allow me, Roxana. Go and run the bath."

3

ENTERING THE IMMACULATE BATHROOM FELT PROFANE. The bath's faucet, a sleek chrome stripe, was flanked by knobs cast in the shape of the negative space inside a human fist. I plugged the tub and twisted the left knob, releasing a heavy stream of clear water. I held my fingers under it until it warmed, pricking my ears for Zlatan, but I could hear nothing above the rush of water. I closed my eyes and dropped my hand into the tub, imagining his movements around the kitchen. Rinsing the plates and setting them in the wooden drying rack beside the sink. Wetting a towel and wiping the table clean, knocking the crumbs to the floor, where they would stay overnight before he vacuumed and destroyed the last evidence of my time in his house.

My mind went back. All my scrubbing of Søren's uncle's apartment had failed to impose the order that held easily here. In trying to show him what was inside me, I had instead offered an amnesiac surface, reflective enough for Søren to see his own hated face. The tub had filled almost to the rim with boiling water. A delayed burn shot up my arm. I cried out.

"Roxana?" Zlatan stood naked in the doorway. "Stand up," he said indulgently and undressed me like I was a tree he was tending. I stared at him, trembling as he unzipped my coveralls and pulled them down and over my feet. He bent and kissed me on the top of my head hard, like a punch, before sinking into the tub.

I put one foot in the water. "It's so hot! How can you stand it?"

He smiled. "When you have been very cold, hot water is always lovely."

I climbed in, willing myself not to wince, and sat between Zlatan's legs, pressing my back into his chest. His member sleepily poked my coccyx as he closed his arms around my shoulders. For long minutes we sat silently cooking, my skin flushing mauve. I watched my toes and fingers wrinkle. My back slid against Zlatan's body, petted by his damp chest hair. I slept, or something like it, as the bath slowly cooled.

When I came back to myself, the water had turned Zlatan hot pink. He let me see him. Then he turned my body in his hands and brought his face close to mine. He pressed his left hand against his chest and his right hand between my breasts and kissed me, a mash of color behind my closed eyes.

Zlatan washed me with a great yellow sea sponge soaked in mint soap, cleaning the easy parts first, the slouch of my tummy, my swollen breasts, my smooth thick thighs, my back. He lifted my arms and sponged beneath them. He made me stand and washed between my legs, holding my labia apart, careful not to push soap inside my body. He turned me around and washed my ass until it tingled.

When it was my turn, I was not so gentle. I scrubbed his body industriously. I separated his toes, which made him giggle, frothed suds in his armpits, shaped his chest hair into a sodden heart. I rubbed his feet and hands until they squeaked. Then I stood him up and sponged his thicket of pubic hair, washed his penis, remembering the lost motion of pulling back Søren's foreskin. I pulled Zlatan back down into the bath and threw my arms around him, pressing my chin into the hollow above his collarbone.

I love you, I said in my mind. I love you I love you.

Eventually the water grew cold. Zlatan loosed himself from me and undid the plug. We stayed until the tub was empty, clutching each other as the drain took its shuddering last breaths, our own breath shading in and out, the white ceramic shining all around us.

We walked into the bedroom still wet from the bath, holding hands, and we lay down on the bed. I stared at the ceiling, bracing myself. Zlatan put his hand on my waist and I pushed my thumb into a light bruise on his throat. Had I done that? Whatever we were moving through was also moving through us.

Desire lit in my chest. I gripped the cleft of his buttocks and threw my leg over his hip, kissing him deeply. For a while it was simple, a salve on my body's aches. No frenzy, only a contentment one shade away from sadness. Then he broke our kiss and held my face in his hands. I saw his pores, my own tragicomic expressions of pleasure reflected in his clouded eyes. Our clutching embrace, our struggle for dominance, the payment for silent passage to a space of prophecy where we were observed by the expectant faces of the dead.

Words bubbled in my throat. I had to tell Zlatan that I loved him, to promise. If I failed, we would tilt and keel, moorless. I would lose him and be alone. An opaque pearl grew inside me, whiting out the room, the bed, his face, my face, my voice. We were only bodies.

"Don't move," Zlatan whispered, with an edge I hadn't heard before. I opened my mouth to speak, releasing a kind of rattle. "Don't speak."

He tightened his arm around my torso and moved his other hand behind me. His cock presented itself, pressing the cleft. With his two longest fingers he roughly sought me, parting my pubic hair and stroking my bared labia until it became slick and pliant. His breath wet against my neck. I tried to turn my head to see his face and he shook his head against my nape. He's going to take me from behind, I thought, liking and not liking it, but I was wrong again. He brushed his lips against the back of my neck and kissed the space between my shoulders, moving down my spine and crisscrossing my back with his wet mouth until I moaned into the pillows.

Those diagrams I had pored over for hours came back, the exotic names of my parts ringing through my head as he worked on me. The tender boundary of the perineal raphe, the frenulum of labia. Names like orders of nuns. Vestibular fossa, vestibular gland, I do not know what you do but you live inside me, on me, you demark the regions of the happiness of my body. Labia majora, labia minora, now gently parted by his tongue. An entire architecture of pink depth. Above, the Skene glands, the urethral opening, and now the clitoris itself, turned over and over in purple shapes against his face. I sat up. The fantastic beauty of shape and form went on and on, until he pulled away and rested his cheek on the rise of my sex, nuzzling the hair with the moist lower half of his face. He turned me over, flipped my body between his hands, and kissed me between the legs from behind. I slid my fingers into his hair and made a fist.

His hands held me open so he could slide in. With an almost involuntary movement I began to push back against him, seeking the hard rebuke of his body. He pried me apart and with one thrust entered. Rode me hard, his arm tight around my chest, a harness. I let my body go limp and tried to concentrate on the feeling of him inside me, the harshness of it, of being full and then not. His tempo quickened. He brought his hand to my front, cupped my pubis. Pulled up.

I waited for the purple and gold to come, but all I saw was the light beginning out the big windows. The shadows of leaves, of trees. Zlatan began to speak his language, louder and louder in the dark room, until finally he was shouting. As if we were fighting and he was winning. The feeling came. Pleasure diffuse as loss. My smoke surprised me, sneaking in, at first almost an afterthought. Then I was nothing in its grip.

Zlatan's eyes were slits. Burning danced up and down my back and arms and legs. I rolled us over so that I was on top. He tried to sit up, but I held him down.

"Roxana," he said. "Roxana."

I wanted to say his name, too, but my words had not come back to me.

The scene became darkly familiar: the beautiful room, the lovely man who wanted me to open him and take his blood. I bent and bit Zlatan on the neck as hard as I could. He did not resist.

I leaned back. He pressed his hands on my distended stomach. I saw his face. He needed me.

The razor blade he had used to shave lay on his bedside table, inches from my thigh. I closed my hand around it. He watched me, his eyes narrowing and widening.

I curved over and pressed my mouth to his in another kiss, and then in one darting motion, as if I was lancing a boil, I pressed the thin skin above his clavicle with the razor's tiny

edge until a bead of blood appeared. A stain. When the red
bloomed, I dropped the razor. His eyes opened wide, but he
did not pull away.

I pressed my mouth to the wound.

Purple smoked all around us.

He held my hips so that there was no space between us.

Everything metallic, the edges peeled back.

Blood in my mouth like flight.

He cried out.

I saw stars.

We drifted back like falling snow.

I put my hand on Zlatan's neck, covering the wound. "I
hurt you." I started to cry.

Zlatan lifted his arm, wincing. "Come here." I scooted to
his sweat-slicked body, lay against his chest. The cut's angry eye
flashed in my periphery. "Why are you crying?"

"I have to tell you—" I almost said it then, the sound
already on my tongue.

Zlatan drew me closer. "Don't."

"Why?"

"What you want to say doesn't mean what you think it
means."

"I know what I feel."

He shook his head sadly. For the first time he looked older
than me. "The love you feel is for yourself, Roxana. It is your
freedom speaking its joy to you."

It seemed too easy and too hard, too much and not enough
all at the same time. What I wanted was to attach, to give myself

to him. But he was right. That wasn't it, not exactly. I couldn't keep the tears from my voice.

"Will I ever see you again?"

He smiled. "Who knows? Maybe not in my house in Denmark. But we live inside each other here now."

Everyone cloud icons, the floating notes of a surah in the sky. I resisted the beauty. Even as calm descended, I insisted to myself that I loved him, that this was a reason for the sadness I felt. I pressed my face into his chest.

"Sweet heart," he said. Two words. "You feel love, Roxana, a terrible openness, so open that it injures you. The pain that tells us that we live, that we have not yet gone into the earth."

Time, plastic, compressed and decompressed. The lights were put out. Zlatan and I burrowed into each other, searching sleep. I tried to relax, to stretch each of my toes, to unlock my hard-held fists and move my eyes behind their closed lids to the four cardinal directions and then finally cross them, tricks Mama had taught me to summon rest, but it would not come. I drifted on a warm pink sea, almost reaching slumber, but each time I neared its shore I remembered the cut. Zlatan's eyes opened wide, his blood in my mouth.

Hours passed. I fell into a dream of the white slats of a fence, only to rouse to my pulse beating my temples. By the middle of the night I was irrefutably awake. Zlatan's embrace became sticky and hot, impossible to stand. I was afraid to break his clasped hands, his fingers interlaced against my chest, just beneath my breasts. I tried to creep from under his arms and roll onto the cooler sheets. When I was almost out, my forehead just behind Zlatan's wrists, he resettled me in his arms, erasing my progress. A wave of despair washed over me. I jerked my head away from his and sighed loudly. I wanted to dream, but I didn't. Not at all.

When I woke the light was lavender and strange.

Zlatan came in, bearing coffee. "Good morning."

"Hi." I wrapped the duvet around my body, suddenly shy, and took the coffee. When our fingers touched I felt nothing, or almost nothing, a sensation so muted it was painful. Zlatan watched me drink. I wanted him to hold me, but we didn't seem to know what to do with each other anymore.

He wore a white T-shirt tucked into black jeans. My clothes were crumpled in the far corner like a dead body. I would have to put them back on, turn the underwear inside out. Shake out the wrinkled shirt, the gnarled pants.

He put his hand to my face and a hint of the old feeling rose. We sat like that, his hand on my cheek, both of us staring at the comforter, for a long while.

When he spoke again, Zlatan's voice was dry. "There is no point in me telling you not to be sad. But do not be sad."

I stared at the ceiling. "I know it's dumb. Especially after what you've been through."

Zlatan shook his head. "There is no sadness Olympics, Roxana."

I laughed, surrendering entirely to tears now.

He took my hand. "You will have my address. I will not be lost to you."

My mind swelled crazily with hope. I forced it back down to normal size. Zlatan was not going to visit me, would not be my pen pal, my long-distance boyfriend. We were not going to get married in some beautiful place. Why did I always think of weddings?

"I'll give you my address, too."

"Of course." Zlatan let me cry against his chest a while. I drenched his T-shirt, sucked at my own salt like an animal.

The rooms of Zlatan's house passed through me as I passed through them. Walking felt unnatural after so many hours in bed. When we came upon each other in a hallway or a corner of a room we embraced fiercely. Every time, my tears came back, running into his hair when we kissed.

The beer I drank with lunch exhausted me. For a long time I sat at the table, watching the skylight move leaf shapes across the wood. We had agreed to leave at six, but I wouldn't look at a clock. I gauged the passage of time by Zlatan's cleaning rituals, which became more frantic over the course of the afternoon. He swept the floor, did the dishes. Swept again. Eventually he called me into the bedroom.

We sat facing each other, the ornate headboard curling and jutting behind us.

"Kiss me," Zlatan said, and I did. "Again." When I leaned into him he held me off with an open hand and pulled down the collar of his shirt, exposing the wound from last night. A closed eye, a burgundy shadow. "Here."

I leaned and pressed my mouth to the opening I had made. Grew bolder, licked it. Bolder still I sucked and it opened in my mouth, offering a tiny gel of blood. He closed his arms around me.

I loosed my mouth. "Zlatan."

"Roxana." His green eyes floated above me and he gave me a little smile. "We know each other."

"We know each other," I repeated.

He pressed his lips to my forehead. One more kiss. Courage was inevitable now. Required. He handed me a slip of paper. His name written in blue ink, *Zlatan Zlatar*. Gold of gold. Beneath, his address.

He brought his mouth close to my ear and spoke softly. "Put me close to your heart and keep me there." He pressed his palm against my right breast. I slipped the card deep into my bra.

"Are you ready?" Zlatan asked.

"No," I said. "Yes."

"Yes?"

"No."

He waited.

"No. Yes. Okay."

He took me back, out of the woods, on the winding road back into the green fields, his truck like the inside of a snow globe, places safe from the world where nothing happened.

Farsø appeared, low-slung buildings clustered together like scared people, and then we were in front of the apartment.

"Well." Zlatan opened his arms and held me. Memorize this.

Outside, summer, the hum of tree bugs. We kissed, a kiss as lovely as each that had come before, different only because it was the last one. He held me tightly.

"Now you will go inside," he said. "And you won't be sad."

"How is that possible?"

"How is anything possible?" Zlatan asked.

I put my hand to my breast and felt the card.

"Good-bye, Roxana," he said. "Travel safely."

He waited as I entered the building and climbed the stairs. On the landing, the door to apartment Ø was propped slightly open. When I went to the window in the living room, he was gone.

Søren was in the bedroom. Without thinking I lay down beside him, not even wondering why he was asleep at such an early hour. Normal, I thought vaguely. Maybe these last hours will be normal. His pale face glowed in the artificial dark of the pulled shades. I closed my eyes.

Søren rolled on top of me and buried his nose in my neck, sniffing furiously. My hair, which bore Zlatan's semen. My neck, bruised by Zlatan's mouth. He investigated my torso, the waistband of my pants. Thrust his nose into my crotch like a dog, where he finally found what he was seeking and turned away, giving me his back.

Did I dream?

When I woke I was on the couch, as if I had never gone into the bedroom at all.

Later there was singing from the invisible neighbors downstairs. A man and a woman together, loud, voices braiding in a happy duet. A love song, I could tell.

The path to the train station lit in my mind. Søren did not wake. I rose in the dark and began to pack.

4

I FLEW BACKWARD THROUGH TIME, CHASING THE SUN, ITS HOT GLEAM AT EVERY WINDOW EDGE. I did not sleep, not for one moment.

My customs agent's metal nametag said LUIS F. A young man with shining blue-black hair and a neat mustache. Our fingertips touched briefly as he took my passport.

"The purpose of your trip, business or pleasure?"

"Pleasure."

He flipped the pages, squinting. "You don't look anything like this. Old picture, huh?"

Sylvie and I had taken them together in April, not four months earlier.

"A long time ago," I said.

Luis F. marked a blank page with his metal stamp. The little door swung wide.

"Welcome home," he said.

In the baggage claim an old woman and a young man crept toward the exit, clutching matching rigid orange plastic suitcases. Two girls, maybe fourteen, held hands, anticipating with rapt intensity a bulbous white sack they hoisted off the belt and bore out. A little boy with sweeping black eyebrows stood alone, wearing a crimson blazer and a gray plastic lanyard shaped like a cat.

One by one, they left, until I was alone with the flickering fluorescent tubes and the conveyer belt. Finally out my duffel came, toddling askew, and I took it down.

Through figments of men I passed down empty corridors to the double glass doors squared in my vision like gates. I saw myself reflected there.

ACKNOWLEDGMENTS

This novel began in longhand in a blue notebook in the humid dream of summer in the Vesthimmerland region of Jutland in July 2010 and ends on my computer in October in Middletown, Connecticut, over seven years later. I am deeply grateful to everyone who helped this journey reach its end.

Thank you to my lodestars, my agent Marya Spence and my editor Katie Raissian, for their extraordinary efforts and unstinting belief in this book and its author.

Grateful acknowledgment is made to *The Nervous Breakdown* and *Your Impossible Voice* for publishing excerpts of this book in slightly different form.

To my colleagues and students at New York University; the University of Southern California; Mount Saint Mary's University; Colorado College; the University of California, Los Angeles; and Wesleyan University for giving me work and space in which to do it.

To the PhD program in Creative Writing and Literature at the University of Southern California, Prairie Center of the Arts,

Virginia Center for the Creative Arts, Djerassi Resident Artists Program, Tin House Summer Workshop, the Mendocino Coast Writers' Conference, Maureen and Tony Eppstein, and Diana Sallinen, for granting me space, quiet, beauty, and friendship.

To my teachers T. C. Boyle, William Handley, Dana Johnson, Mat Johnson, Dinaw Mengestu, Viet Thanh Nguyen, and most especially the radiant Aimee Bender for the time you spent with this novel and with me, for your patience, wisdom, and interest. I am honored to be the product of your teaching.

To the friends who read full or partial drafts, offered helpful ideas, multifarious support and diverse succor, who convinced me to keep going: Shea Abba-Herlihy, Katya Apekina, Diana Arterian, Kendra Atkin, Janalynn Bliss, Val Britton, Jackson Burgess, Susan Buss and Max Buss-Young, Samantha Carrick and Caitlin Eubanks, Katie Davis-Young, Denise Domergue, J. T. Farrell, Cristina Fernández Recasens, Christine Fadden, Kate Folk, Emily Fridlund, Annelyse Gelman, Farah Ghniem, Julian Goard, Lalena Goard, Maricel Goard, Erin Graves, Bryan Hurt, Katy Jarzebowski, Sami Kelso, Daniel Kibblesmith, Alexis Landau, Winona Leon, Karen Lewis, Ruth Madievsky, T. M. McNally, Lewis Meineke, Ceilidh Morgan, Leon Neyfakh, Robert S. Pesich, Jaume Pujadas, Rob Rabiee and Melissa Scott-Rabiee, Zane Ranney, Mariel and Robert Reeves, Narcis Serra, Conxita Boldú and Marina Serra Boldú, Diana Siegel, Ben Weber, Axel Wilhite, Robert Wilhite, Jennifer Wright, Alex Young, and Michelle Young. I beg forgiveness and give thanks to anyone I've neglected to name here.

To the Danes who welcomed me lovingly and without reservation: Elna Duelund Jensen, Bente Duelund Jensen and Erling

Hess-Nielsen, Torben Duelund Jensen and Ann Hyllested, Nicolai Duelund Jensen and Dorthe Lykke Jacobsen, Mads Peder Lau Pedersen, Lise Steen Nielsen, Andreas Graae and Heidi Jønch-Clausen, Mikael and Heidi Randrup Byrialsen, Sisse Foged Hyllested, Jacob Hyllested-Winge, and Jens Bjering. Thank you for showing me your country and inviting me into your lives.

To my Mendocino clan for keeping me honest and wild: Linda Ruffing, Chuck Henderson, Elias Henderson, Richard Shoemaker, Cassie Henderson, Griffin Hodgkinson, and Stacey Loré.

In memory of my beloved grandparents Adeline and Lawrence Locascio Sr., Charles William Goldfinch, Elizabeth McCaw Goldfinch, and Christina John.

To my family, whose love made this book possible: John, Margaret, Jonathan, and Chloe Stuckey; Nydia Salazar; Dan, Carol, and Daniel McWhirter. Most of all to my mother, Anne; my father, Lawrence; and my sister, Julia.

To Jasper Nighthawk Henderson.

To Theis Duelund Jensen, without whom this book would not exist.